Breaking the Mold

Adelaide Vaughn

Published by Adelaide Vaughn, 2024.

This is a work of fiction. Similarities to real people, places, or events are entirely coincidental.

BREAKING THE MOLD

First edition. October 7, 2024.

Copyright © 2024 Adelaide Vaughn.

ISBN: 979-8227717535

Written by Adelaide Vaughn.

Chapter 1: Broken Pieces

The clattering of pots and pans filled the air as the other cooks rushed around me, oblivious to the shattered glass that still lay like a crystalline constellation at my feet. Connor moved with a grace that belied his rugged appearance, his hands deftly chopping vegetables, each slice punctuating the noise of the kitchen. I couldn't help but admire how he commanded the space, orchestrating chaos with a calm that eluded me entirely.

"Everything okay?" he asked, glancing my way, his brow furrowing slightly as he caught sight of the debris on the floor. The softness of his voice was disarming, almost like a gentle hand reaching through my turmoil, and for a moment, I considered confessing my worries, my fears. Instead, I forced a smile that felt as thin as the glass shards themselves.

"Just a little mishap," I replied, trying to sound nonchalant, as I bent down to start cleaning up. But the shards felt like more than just broken glass; they symbolized everything I was trying to escape—the expectations of my family, the pressure of the culinary world, the nagging self-doubt that whispered I wasn't cut out for this. As I picked up a piece, its jagged edge caught the light, glinting like a cruel reminder of my shortcomings.

"Here, let me help," Connor said, kneeling beside me, his fingers brushing against mine as he reached for the same shard. The contact sent a jolt through me, and I momentarily lost my grip on reality. It was unexpected and warm, a small flicker of connection in a world where I often felt isolated. "You know, I think this glass was just trying to escape your culinary genius," he quipped, a smirk dancing at the corners of his mouth.

I chuckled softly, the sound surprising me. "If it was, it was doing a terrible job of it," I replied, my mood shifting slightly as the tension in my chest eased. There was something refreshing about his wit, a contrast to the heavy silence I had become accustomed to in the kitchen.

As we finished cleaning, I noticed the way his eyes sparkled when he smiled, and I felt a flutter of something unfamiliar in my stomach—was it hope? I quickly pushed the thought aside. Hope was a dangerous thing, especially for someone like me, whose dreams felt like a fragile balloon at the mercy of the sharpest pin.

"Ready for the dinner rush?" Connor asked, standing and dusting off his knees, his gaze steady and sincere.

I nodded, my heart racing not just from the impending chaos of service but from the unspoken connection hanging between us. "As ready as I'll ever be," I replied, taking a deep breath. "Let's make some magic."

The evening unfolded like a perfectly choreographed dance. Orders flew in, plates spun around, and the atmosphere crackled with energy. Each dish I plated felt like a step toward reclaiming my confidence, and I could feel Connor's presence beside me, anchoring me when I felt like I might float away. He had a knack for making the most mundane tasks feel exciting, as if each vegetable we chopped or each sauce we whisked was infused with a little bit of our collective spirit.

"Do you think we could get this dish on the menu?" he asked at one point, holding up a plate of my latest creation, a seared duck breast with a cherry reduction that shimmered like liquid rubies.

"Only if you promise not to tell anyone how much I cried while making it," I shot back, laughter bubbling between us like the simmering pots on the stove.

His laughter joined mine, filling the air around us. "Deal. Your secret's safe with me."

As the night wore on, I lost myself in the rhythm of the kitchen, momentarily forgetting the weight of my past. For those few hours, the worries of the world faded into the background, replaced by the symphony of sizzling pans and laughter. But the moment the last plate was served, reality crashed back in with the force of a tidal wave.

Connor and I stood side by side, sweat glistening on our foreheads, the remnants of our laughter still echoing in the bustling space around us. "We did good tonight," he said, his voice low, almost reverent as he surveyed the kitchen.

"Yeah, we did," I agreed, feeling a warmth bloom in my chest. Maybe this was what I needed—a reminder that I wasn't alone in this chaotic world, that there were others who understood the struggle, the passion, the desire to create something beautiful despite the shards that littered the path.

"Hey, how about we celebrate?" Connor suggested, his eyes bright with mischief. "I know a place nearby that serves the best post-shift drinks. Trust me, it'll be worth it."

The invitation hung in the air, heavy with possibilities. A part of me wanted to say no, to retreat to my small apartment and drown in my thoughts, but another part—the part that had been buried beneath expectations—begged to be heard. "Why not?" I found myself saying, my heart racing in anticipation.

"Great! I'll just grab my jacket," he said, flashing a smile that made my heart flutter again, and as he disappeared into the back, I couldn't shake the feeling that maybe, just maybe, tonight could be the first step toward piecing my broken self back together.

I followed Connor into the narrow alleyway behind the restaurant, the evening air cool against my flushed skin. The city had transformed into a symphony of lights and sounds, the distant murmur of laughter spilling from nearby bars, and the tantalizing scent of street food wafted through the air, mixing with the lingering aromas of our shift. Connor led the way, his strides long and easy, like he was used to navigating the labyrinth of city streets.

"So, tell me," he began, glancing over his shoulder, "what's your drink of choice? I promise not to judge if you say something like a dirty martini or a strawberry daiquiri."

I smirked, feeling the weight of the evening's stress slowly lift. "I think you'll find my taste is more sophisticated than that. A good whiskey sour is my go-to. It's sweet, but with enough of a kick to remind you that life isn't all sugar and spice."

Connor raised an eyebrow, a playful smile curling his lips. "Interesting choice. I'd have pegged you for something like a fancy gin and tonic, all highbrow and botanical."

"Well, you're wrong," I shot back, crossing my arms in mock offense. "A whiskey sour has depth. It's honest, like me."

"Honest, huh?" He chuckled, the sound warm and inviting. "So you're saying you're a complicated person?"

"Complicated? Absolutely. Just ask my father." The words slipped out before I could stop them, a sudden wave of vulnerability crashing over me. I immediately regretted opening that door, the weight of my relationship with him lingering like an uninvited guest.

Connor glanced at me, his expression shifting to something more serious. "Sounds like there's a story there."

"Isn't there always?" I countered, deflecting with a smile that felt more like a mask than anything else. "But enough about me. What about you? What's the secret life of Connor the sous chef? I can't imagine you've always been chopping onions in a kitchen like this."

He hesitated for a moment, a shadow flickering across his face, but then he shrugged, his easy demeanor returning. "Not much to tell. I grew up in a small town like you, always knew I wanted to be a chef. Took a few detours along the way, but here I am."

"Detours?" I pressed, intrigued. There was something about him that made me want to dig deeper, to uncover the layers he was hiding beneath that calm exterior.

"Let's just say I had a brief stint in the corporate world," he replied, his tone lightening. "I wore a suit and everything. Can you picture it? Me, in a tie?"

The image made me laugh. "I can't imagine you in a tie. You look much better with flour on your shirt and a knife in hand."

He grinned, a flicker of mischief in his eyes. "Fair enough. But let me tell you, nothing beats the rush of a dinner service compared to a three-hour meeting about spreadsheets."

As we turned the corner, I spotted the bar he had mentioned. It was a cozy place, strings of fairy lights draped lazily above the entrance, illuminating the small patio where patrons huddled around tables, drinks in hand. I felt a surge of excitement bubbling up inside me. This was a world I rarely ventured into after a long shift—places where laughter was effortless and joy was abundant.

Inside, the atmosphere was electric. The clink of glasses, the hum of conversations, and the occasional burst of laughter blended into a welcoming cacophony. Connor gestured toward a table in the corner, and as we settled in, I couldn't shake the feeling that this was the beginning of something unexpected.

"Two whiskey sours, please!" he called to the bartender, a friendly nod accompanying his request. "And maybe some snacks. We've just survived the dinner rush; we deserve it."

As the bartender disappeared to fulfill our order, I leaned back in my chair, taking in my surroundings. The walls were adorned with quirky art, and the scent of grilled meat mingled with something sweet, likely dessert. It was all so vibrant and alive, a stark contrast to the sterile environment of the kitchen.

"So, tell me, what do you think makes a great chef?" Connor asked, leaning forward, his elbows resting on the table.

I considered his question, tracing the rim of my glass with my fingertip. "It's about passion, I think. The ability to create something out of nothing. It's like magic—taking raw ingredients and turning them into a dish that tells a story. And if you can make people feel something when they eat your food, that's the real art."

"That's beautiful," he replied, his eyes sparkling. "You should put that in a book."

"Maybe I will," I said, a playful smile creeping onto my lips. "Right after I publish my memoir titled 'How to Break Wine Glasses and Relationships.'"

He threw his head back and laughed, the sound rich and contagious, and I felt a warmth spread through me that I hadn't experienced in a long time. The connection between us felt genuine, like we were peeling back the layers of our lives one conversation at a time.

Just then, the bartender returned with our drinks and a generous platter of sliders. "On the house," he said, winking before disappearing into the crowd.

I took a sip of my whiskey sour, the tangy sweetness dancing on my tongue. "This is incredible," I said, savoring the moment. "Who knew you had such excellent taste?"

"Well, I do have my moments," Connor replied, biting into a slider, his eyes narrowing in concentration. "And clearly, I have good taste in company, too."

The compliment made my heart skip a beat, and I felt a rush of warmth wash over me. But before I could respond, a commotion erupted from the entrance. A group of rowdy patrons stumbled in, their laughter loud enough to drown out our conversation. One of them, a tall guy with messy hair and a ridiculous Hawaiian shirt, spotted us and came over, a wide grin plastered on his face.

"Hey! Are you guys the chefs from that restaurant? We just had the most amazing dinner!" he exclaimed, his voice booming.

"Yes, that would be us," Connor said, his demeanor shifting to one of playful arrogance. "Did it live up to your high expectations?"

"Dude, you totally knocked it out of the park! I'm Brad, by the way." He extended a hand, and Connor shook it, glancing at me with an amused smile.

"Brad, the connoisseur of fine dining," I said, feigning seriousness. "Tell me, what was your favorite dish?"

"Honestly?" he replied, leaning in like he was about to share a secret. "The dessert! You guys serve that molten lava cake, right? It was like a hug from the universe!"

I laughed, enjoying the spontaneous energy he brought into our cozy corner. "Glad you liked it. We put a lot of love into it."

Just then, Connor's expression shifted, and I turned to see what had caught his attention. A woman stood at the entrance, her silhouette sharp against the warm glow of the bar lights. The moment our eyes met, a chill raced down my spine, recognition dawning as if I'd just opened a door I'd long tried to forget.

It was Clara, my best friend from high school—the one who had moved away without so much as a goodbye. The last time I'd seen her was the day I left Connecticut, and now she was standing there, looking just as surprised as I felt.

"Bree?" she called out, her voice slicing through the noise, an unexpected thread of familiarity tugging at my heart.

Before I could respond, Clara took a step forward, and I could see the shock morph into something darker in her eyes. Something I couldn't quite place. It felt as if the ground beneath me had shifted, unearthing old wounds and buried emotions I had thought safely tucked away.

"Is that really you?" she asked, her voice tight as she approached the table, tension hanging thick in the air.

The laughter, the warmth, the moments I had just shared with Connor vanished, replaced by an impending confrontation that threatened to upend everything I had built since leaving.

Chapter 2: Whispers of the Past

The air in the kitchen was thick with the scent of rosemary and garlic, a fragrant reminder of the delicate dance we performed daily with flavors and textures. As I stood there, my fingers trembling slightly over my phone, I could almost hear the spices whispering their secrets, urging me to reclaim my focus. It was ridiculous how the weight of my father's absence could overshadow everything—like a thunderstorm lurking just beyond the horizon, threatening to break at any moment.

"Hey, is everything okay?" Connor's voice broke through my fog. He wiped his hands on his apron, his dark curls falling over his forehead. I could see genuine concern etched across his face, and I felt a pang of something—gratitude, perhaps. Maybe even something deeper.

"Dad's in the hospital," I managed to croak out, the words tasting bitter on my tongue. His expression shifted, a blend of sympathy and surprise.

"Do you want to talk about it?" he asked, leaning against the counter, the tension of the moment dissipating just a little. There was something refreshing about his willingness to listen. Most people would have avoided eye contact, too wrapped up in their own worlds.

"Not really," I admitted, a small, defiant smile breaking through my mask of despair. "It's just... complicated. You know?"

"Complicated is my middle name," he replied with a smirk, and I couldn't help but laugh—a sound I desperately needed. "Just know you're not alone in the complicated department."

It was an odd connection we shared, this thread of unspoken understanding. Maybe it was the late-night shifts spent in a hot kitchen that forged bonds tighter than any family ties. The rhythm of chopping, sautéing, and plating made us a team, and somewhere in the midst of that chaotic choreography, I found myself surprisingly grateful for him.

"Do you want to talk about something else? I'm really good at distracting people," he offered, his eyes sparkling with mischief. I raised an eyebrow, daring him to be bold.

"Okay, Mr. Distraction. What's your strategy?"

"I could tell you about the time I mistook salt for sugar in a cake and ended up with the culinary equivalent of a tsunami," he said, his voice low and conspiratorial, and I leaned in, curious despite myself.

"Oh no, please tell me you didn't serve it to anyone."

"Let's just say it was the last time anyone took my baking requests seriously." He grinned, and for a moment, the weight of my father's absence felt a little lighter, like a backpack with just one too many rocks removed.

I glanced at the clock, aware that our break would soon end. The kitchen was already brimming with a medley of sounds—pots clanging, laughter bubbling up from the prep station. It was a symphony of chaos, and I realized how much I thrived in it. The hours spent here, away from my father's critical gaze, had become my refuge. I immersed myself in the rhythm of slicing, dicing, and stirring, finding solace in the heat of the flames and the dance of the ingredients.

But the thought of my father loomed like a storm cloud, and I knew I had to confront it sooner rather than later. The memories flooded back—his dismissive remarks when I'd shared my dreams of culinary school, the way he'd rolled his eyes at my culinary experiments. It was hard to ignore the voice that echoed in my mind, reminding me I was a disappointment. The shadow of his disapproval lingered like a heavy mist, suffocating any flicker of self-confidence I dared to nurture.

"Hey," Connor's voice broke my reverie again, a gentle reminder of the present. "You still with me?"

"Sorry, just got lost in my thoughts." I forced a smile, shaking off the melancholy like rainwater from a coat.

"Don't apologize. Just promise you'll let me know if you need to bail. Family stuff can be... a lot," he said, his tone dropping as if the weight of his own experiences hovered beneath the surface.

"Thanks. I appreciate it." It was an honest exchange, one that made me feel lighter, if only just a bit.

As the shift wore on, the kitchen pulsed with energy, each dish a testament to our hard work and dedication. I found myself slipping into a groove, a rhythm that allowed me to forget the ache in my chest, if only temporarily. The heat of the stove, the crispness of fresh herbs, and the vibrant colors of vegetables created a sensory feast, one I had grown to adore.

Just as I was plating a particularly exquisite ratatouille, my phone buzzed again. It was my mother this time. "Come to the hospital when you can. We need to talk." The finality of those words sent a chill down my spine, a reminder that the past was never truly buried, just lying in wait for the right moment to resurface.

"Everything okay?" Connor asked, sensing my shift in mood.

"I'm not sure," I replied, the pit of uncertainty growing. "It looks like I'll have to go see him."

"Do you want me to come with you?" His offer hung in the air, unexpected yet oddly comforting.

"No, I can't ask that of you," I said, my voice barely above a whisper.

"Really, I don't mind. Besides, someone needs to keep you grounded. Hospital visits can be a minefield." His sincerity tugged at me, the warmth of his presence becoming a lifeline.

I wanted to say yes, to take his hand and let him guide me through the chaos that awaited, but the reality of my father's expectations loomed large. "I'll be okay," I replied, though a part of me longed for the kind of companionship he offered.

"Okay, but remember—if you need a distraction afterward, I'm just a text away," he said, his smile radiating a warmth that seeped into the corners of my heart.

And just like that, with those simple words, he managed to carve a small space of light within my shadowed world, illuminating a path I had thought lost forever.

I stood at the counter, heart racing as I read the message again, each word like a punch to my gut. The clattering of pans and the sizzle of oil filled the kitchen, a chaotic backdrop to my swirling thoughts. What had my father done this time? I could already picture him lying in that sterile hospital bed, surrounded by white walls and too much fluorescent light. A thousand scenarios unfolded in my mind, each more dramatic than the last. The thoughts churned like a boiling pot, bubbling over with fears I hadn't wanted to confront.

"Are you really going to stand there and contemplate life while the rest of us are working?" Connor's voice pulled me from my reverie, sharp and teasing. He was wiping his hands on his apron, a bemused look dancing in his eyes. "You know they don't pay us to stand around looking like lost puppies."

"Funny, I thought this was a cooking school, not a comedy club," I shot back, attempting a smirk despite the tightness in my chest. "But thanks for the motivational speech, Coach."

He leaned in closer, that smirk growing into a grin. "Look, I'll even give you the whole 'rock star chef' vibe. But only if you promise to stop daydreaming about hospital food."

I couldn't help but laugh, a soft sound that momentarily eased my anxiety. "Deal. But if I end up making jello salads for a living, I'm blaming you."

"Just think of it as a potential side hustle," he quipped, his eyes glinting with mischief. "I hear jello is making a comeback."

The absurdity of his banter was exactly what I needed. It was as if he could sense the weight I carried, chipping away at it with humor. I focused on the rhythm of my work, finding solace in the familiarity of chopping vegetables and arranging them just so. Each slice and dice was a small act of defiance against my father's looming presence, a reminder that I had chosen this path, one steeped in vibrant flavors and colorful ingredients.

The hours passed in a blur, and just as I was beginning to feel anchored again, the phone buzzed at the edge of the counter. This time, it was a call from my mom. With a deep breath, I swiped to answer, the voice in my head screaming that I should have ignored it.

"Hello?" I said, trying to sound composed.

"Can you come to the hospital? We really need to talk," my mom's voice was shaky, the words tumbling out in a rush.

"About Dad?"

"Yes. It's important."

I didn't know how to respond. Important felt like a loaded word, brimming with implications I wasn't ready to unpack. I glanced at Connor, who was washing dishes, his back turned but ears obviously tuned in.

"Okay. I'll be there as soon as I can," I replied, my heart thumping a wild rhythm as I ended the call.

"Everything alright?" Connor asked, turning to me, the concern evident on his face.

"Not really. I have to go to the hospital," I said, trying to keep my voice steady.

"Do you want me to come?" he asked again, but this time with more intensity. It was as if he could see right through my bravado.

"No, really. It's fine," I insisted, not wanting to impose my family's mess on him. "I'll be okay."

"I'm not so sure about that," he replied, his eyes narrowing slightly. "Look, I get it. Family drama and all that. But sometimes, having someone there can make a difference. Especially if you're facing whatever news you're dreading."

He was right, of course. The thought of facing my father alone made my stomach twist. But I shook my head. "I appreciate it, but I think I need to do this on my own. Thanks for the offer, though."

Connor nodded, his expression thoughtful. "Just know you've got a kitchen full of people who have your back. If you need anything, just text me."

"Got it," I said, a warm feeling spreading through me despite the uncertainty hanging over my head. "If I don't return, send a search party, okay?"

He chuckled, and I was grateful for the small moments of levity amidst the storm that was my life. I grabbed my bag and stepped out of the kitchen, the world outside feeling oddly surreal as I walked towards the hospital. The city buzzed around me, a cacophony of honking cars, distant laughter, and the rich aroma of street food wafting through the air. But all of it felt muted, like I was watching it from behind a glass wall, separated from the vibrancy of life by my swirling emotions.

When I arrived at the hospital, the fluorescent lights seemed to buzz louder, and the antiseptic smell hit me like a wall. My mom was waiting in the lobby, her face drawn and weary, a stark contrast to the vibrant woman I knew. I took a deep breath, steeling myself for the conversation to come.

"Mom," I said softly, walking over to her.

"Hey, sweetheart," she replied, pulling me into a quick hug. There was something fragile about her, as if she might shatter under the weight of whatever news she had to share.

"Is it bad?" I asked, pulling back to look at her.

"Let's go sit," she said, leading me to a small waiting area. The muted TV flickered in the corner, but it felt more like a backdrop to our tension than anything else.

We settled into the stiff chairs, the silence stretching between us, thick and heavy. "Your father had a fall," she began, her voice trembling slightly. "He's stable now, but..."

"But what?" I pressed, my heart racing.

She hesitated, and I could see the fear in her eyes. "He wants to talk to you, and there's more. He's been diagnosed with some health issues."

The words hung in the air like a lead weight, the implication hitting me hard. My father—my complicated, often cruel father—was facing his own mortality. "What kind of health issues?"

"Heart problems, they think," she replied, the tremor in her voice betraying the calm facade she was trying to maintain. "He was supposed to see a doctor weeks ago, but... well, you know how he is."

"How long does he have?" I asked, my voice barely above a whisper.

"We don't know," she said, tears welling in her eyes. "But it's serious. He wants to make things right with you."

I blinked, confusion mixing with a flood of emotions. My father wanted to make things right? That was new. "Why now?"

She shook her head, clearly grappling with her own feelings. "I don't know, but he's asked for you. He wants to apologize."

"Apologize?" The word felt foreign, slipping through my fingers like sand. It was the last thing I expected. "What could he possibly say that would change anything?"

"Maybe it's not about changing anything, but starting over," she replied, a hint of hope flickering in her eyes.

"Starting over," I echoed, the weight of that phrase pressing heavily against my chest. Could we really begin anew? Could I really face him?

Before I could respond, a nurse walked by, glancing at us with a knowing look. "You can see him now," she said gently, her voice soothing but firm.

My heart raced as I stood, a mix of dread and anticipation swirling within me. This was it—the moment I had both dreaded and longed for.

"Are you ready?" my mom asked, her eyes searching mine.

I opened my mouth to respond, but nothing came out. Instead, I squared my shoulders and nodded, the silence of the waiting area a deafening precursor to the storm that awaited. Together, we walked toward the room, each step echoing like a drumbeat, leading me toward a confrontation I couldn't avoid any longer.

The door creaked open, revealing my father lying in the hospital bed, looking smaller and more fragile than I remembered. As he looked up, our eyes met, and in that moment, the weight of the past and the uncertain future collided in a silent standoff.

"Hey, kid," he said, a hint of his old bravado flickering in his gaze. "We need to talk."

But before I could respond, a sudden crash echoed from the hallway, followed by frantic voices. My stomach twisted as I turned to see what was happening, a sense of dread washing over me. Whatever facade I had built around this moment was about to shatter.

Chapter 3: Burnt Edges

The city had taken on a peculiar glow under the hazy light of dusk, with streetlights flickering to life like hesitant stars. I walked the cracked pavement, feeling every uneven stone as if it were a metaphor for my life. Each step echoed the hollow rhythm of my heart, a syncopation of unease and anticipation. The air was thick with the scent of impending rain, mingling with the faint whiff of fried food from a nearby diner, reminding me that life continued its relentless march even as everything felt suspended in limbo.

I wasn't sure where I was headed; perhaps my legs just wanted to carry me far away from the sterile walls of the hospital and the weight of all that unsaid. I slipped into a small coffee shop, the kind with mismatched chairs and walls plastered with local art, where the chatter of caffeine addicts filled the air. The barista, a bright-eyed woman with a cascade of curls and an infectious smile, greeted me like an old friend. I barely returned the sentiment, my mind still entangled in the thrum of my father's hospital room.

"Hey there! What can I get for you?" she chirped, her enthusiasm almost jarring.

"Just a black coffee, please," I replied, my voice lacking the luster it usually had.

As she bustled around the espresso machine, I noticed a couple at a nearby table. They were animated, the man's hands slicing through the air as he spoke, his laughter mingling with hers like a favorite song. I couldn't help but feel the sting of envy prick at my heart—a reminder of what I had lost, of the warmth of human connection that had evaporated over the years.

"Here you go!" The barista slid my cup across the counter, and I clutched it like a lifeline, savoring the heat radiating from the ceramic. "Everything okay?" she asked, concern shadowing her bright demeanor.

"Just... family stuff," I muttered, casting my gaze to the floor, suddenly feeling exposed under her scrutiny.

"Yeah, I get it. Life can throw some real curveballs," she said, leaning in a bit, her voice softening. "If you need someone to talk to, I'm here."

I offered a small smile, not quite ready to unravel my heart to a stranger, no matter how friendly. Instead, I took my coffee and sank into a corner seat, a cozy nook wrapped in the scent of roasted beans and sugar. I pulled out my phone, scrolling through messages that felt like echoes from another life. Friends texting about dinner plans and weekend getaways, all mundane details that felt worlds away from my reality.

As I stared into the dark depths of my coffee, I realized how many years had slipped through my fingers, much like the grains of sand that the universe had so carelessly scattered. I had been so wrapped up in my own survival, my own dreams, that I hadn't noticed how much I had left my family behind. My father had become a ghost in my life, and now, with his health hanging in the balance, I felt the weight of my neglect pressing heavily on my chest.

With each sip of coffee, bitterness mixed with my thoughts, leaving a strange aftertaste. The burn of caffeine was a stark reminder of my own life choices—each one a decision that had brought me to this very moment. I thought about how I had sprinted toward my ambitions, leaving behind the very people who had rooted for me all along. My career, my goals—they felt like hollow trophies now, glimmering but devoid of warmth.

Suddenly, the door swung open, and a gust of wind rushed in, bringing with it a flurry of raindrops that tapped against the windows like an impatient child. My eyes flickered toward the entrance, and there he was—Jake. He was drenched, his shirt clinging to him like a second skin, but still managing that disarming grin that had first captivated me years ago.

"Didn't think I'd find you here!" he exclaimed, shaking off the rain like a dog, his wet hair falling into his eyes. He spotted me and made his way over, leaving a trail of dripping water in his wake.

"Surprise!" I said, forcing cheer into my voice despite my earlier melancholy.

"Mind if I join you?" He didn't wait for an answer, sliding into the seat across from me. His energy was infectious, a contrast to the weight I'd been dragging around.

"Sure, but fair warning, I might be in a bit of a mood," I admitted, gesturing toward my coffee cup.

"Hey, if you need to mope, I'm an expert in moping," he winked, and I couldn't help but chuckle, the tension in my chest loosening slightly.

We chatted, and for a while, the weight of my worries receded into the background. Jake shared his latest misadventures—getting lost on his way to a meeting, accidentally sending a client an embarrassing meme instead of a report. The absurdity of it all was a balm for my troubled soul, and as I listened, I felt the layers of my own worries peel back, revealing the heartache beneath.

But just as laughter danced on the edge of my lips, a sobering thought tugged at my heartstrings—my father lay fighting for his life, and here I was, indulging in a moment of levity. The guilt bubbled up like the froth atop my coffee, threatening to spill over.

"Hey," Jake said, his voice suddenly serious, cutting through my spiral. "You okay? You've gone quiet."

"Just... thinking," I murmured, forcing a smile that felt more like a grimace.

"Thinking's dangerous. You know what they say about thinking too much?" he teased, his eyes narrowing playfully.

"Can't say I do," I replied, genuinely curious.

"It leads to overthinking, which leads to bad decisions, like texting your ex or calling your mother to ask for a life plan," he said, grinning.

I laughed, but it was a sound laced with sadness. "Maybe I should avoid that last one."

"Or maybe you should call her. You never know when it might be the right time," he said, his tone shifting, the sincerity wrapping around my heart like a warm embrace.

And just like that, I found a small spark of courage igniting within me, flickering against the shadows that had clouded my thoughts.

The café had transformed from a sanctuary into a trap, the rich aroma of coffee now twisted with guilt and the shadows of past decisions. Jake sat across from me, his cheerful banter providing a welcome distraction from the tempest brewing inside my mind. Yet even as I laughed at his antics—his dramatic retelling of the time he accidentally spilled a drink on his boss—I could feel the tightness in my chest, the ache of unresolved family ties, pulling me back into the depths of my worries.

"Seriously, though," he said, leaning back in his chair, his smile fading slightly. "You've got to talk to her. It doesn't have to be a big thing. Just... check in, you know? Sometimes those little conversations can change everything."

"Right, because nothing says 'family bonding' like a heart-to-heart over the phone while my dad's lying in a hospital bed," I replied, my tone sharper than intended. Jake raised an eyebrow but didn't flinch.

"Look, I know it's messy," he replied, an understanding softness creeping into his voice. "But you have to face it sooner or later. You can't keep running away from them, especially not now."

"Running away? Is that what you think I'm doing?" I scoffed, rolling my eyes. The accusation felt like a pebble lodged in my shoe, irritating and insistent. "I'm just... busy. I'm building my life. I have responsibilities."

"And what's the cost of that life?" he countered, his gaze steady and unyielding. "You're building all these walls, and what if you look up one day and there's nobody left on the other side?"

The question hung between us, heavier than the rain that had begun to patter against the windows. It was a truth I couldn't deny, yet acknowledging it felt like staring directly into the sun—too bright, too painful. I forced a laugh, a feeble attempt to lighten the mood, but it fell flat.

"I didn't realize I'd signed up for an existential crisis over coffee," I said, shaking my head, trying to brush off his words like crumbs from my shirt. "You've really got a talent for that, you know?"

"Hey, someone has to keep you grounded," he shot back, but his smile was genuine, the kind that made my insides twist in an unfamiliar way.

Before I could respond, the door swung open again, and a gust of wind ushered in a rush of cold air. The bell above the entrance jingled, announcing the arrival of a figure I recognized too well—my mother. She strode in, her coat pulled tightly around her as if it could shield her from the world's harsh realities. The moment her eyes met mine, I felt a shiver run down my spine. It was the kind of moment that brought with it a flood of memories, both beautiful and painful.

"Emily," she said, her voice wavering as she approached. The warmth of the café felt suddenly stifling, and I couldn't tell if it was the steam from the coffee machine or the tension between us.

"Mom," I replied, my heart pounding against my ribcage. Jake shifted in his seat, instinctively sensing the change in the atmosphere.

"What are you doing here?" she asked, her eyes darting to Jake, then back to me, a flicker of confusion in her gaze.

"Just... taking a break," I managed, glancing at Jake, who looked like he was weighing the right moment to excuse himself.

"I didn't know you were meeting someone," she said, and the edge in her voice was unmistakable.

"He's just a friend," I replied quickly, desperate to defuse the situation before it spiraled. "We were talking, and—"

"Talking? About what?" Her tone hardened, and I could see the worry lines etched deeper on her forehead.

"About life," I said, hoping to keep it vague enough to avoid a full interrogation. "You know how it is."

"Oh, I do," she shot back, crossing her arms defensively. "Life has a way of throwing things at you when you least expect it."

Jake cleared his throat, sensing the tension rising. "I should probably get going," he said, standing up. "Nice to meet you, ma'am." He flashed a quick smile before turning to me. "Call me later? We can chat."

"Yeah, sure," I replied, but the words felt heavy, caught in my throat as I watched him leave. The door shut with a soft thud, sealing off the warmth and comfort he brought with him. Suddenly, the café felt smaller, the walls closing in around us as my mother's gaze intensified.

"What were you really talking about?" she pressed, her voice low but fierce.

I hesitated, suddenly feeling like a child caught in a lie. "Just... work stuff. It's been a rough week."

"A rough week?" She shook her head, disbelief flickering in her eyes. "You're not the only one dealing with rough weeks, Emily. You've shut us out for so long. Do you even realize that?"

"I'm trying to build something for myself!" I shot back, my voice rising. The barista glanced over from the counter, her eyes wide as she caught the undercurrents of our conversation. "I have to focus on my career. I thought you'd understand."

Her expression hardened, and I felt the words hanging between us like a wall, sturdy and unyielding. "And what about your father? He needs you now, more than ever."

"Don't you think I know that?" I retorted, each word laced with frustration. "What do you want from me? I can't just drop everything and rush to your side every time something goes wrong!"

"I want you to care!" she shouted, the words spilling out like a dam breaking. "I want you to be part of this family. But you're always too busy for us."

The café fell silent around us, every head turning in our direction, the air thick with a mix of coffee and conflict. I could feel the heat rising in my cheeks, humiliation mixing with anger. "I'm here, aren't I?" I shot back, my voice barely above a whisper now, trembling with the weight of her words.

"Barely," she said, her voice steadying, but the hurt was evident. "You think those phone calls and occasional visits make it better? It's not enough. It never has been."

A heavy silence descended between us, each moment stretching into eternity. I felt the weight of her disappointment settle on my shoulders, and for the first time, I truly recognized the depth of our estrangement.

"I don't know what you want me to say," I finally admitted, my heart racing. "I'm trying to figure things out just like you are."

"Maybe try showing up for once?" she said, her eyes glistening with unshed tears. "Your father..."

But before she could finish, her phone buzzed insistently in her pocket, a sound that shattered the tension hanging in the air. She fished it out, glancing at the screen, and her expression shifted—panic mixed with confusion.

"What is it?" I asked, suddenly alert, my heart hammering as the atmosphere shifted once more.

"It's the hospital," she said, her voice trembling as she answered the call. "Hello? Yes, this is Rachel Anderson."

I held my breath, the world around us fading into a blur as her face paled, the color draining from her cheeks. Whatever was being said on the other end of the line, it struck her like a bolt of lightning.

"No... No, no. You can't be serious."

The coffee shop, with its warm lights and cheerful chatter, felt worlds away as I grasped the unfolding horror. Time slowed, and every heartbeat echoed in my ears, a countdown to the unknown.

"What's happening?" I demanded, my voice cracking as dread coiled around my throat.

But she was already backing away, her hand trembling as she hung up, her eyes wide with fear. "Emily..."

And just like that, the ground beneath me seemed to shift, the very foundation of our lives trembling under the weight of a single word, pregnant with implications. The atmosphere crackled with tension, and I was left teetering on the edge, the unthinkable looming ever closer.

Chapter 4: The Taste of Something New

Returning to the restaurant felt like coming up for air after being underwater too long. Each swing of the kitchen door ushered me into a world bustling with energy, where clattering pans and sizzling ingredients provided a soundtrack that eased my anxious heart. I buried myself in the work, losing track of time as I prepped for the evening's menu. There was something calming about the rhythm of chopping, sautéing, tasting—actions that required focus but freed my mind from everything else, a form of meditation amidst the chaos.

The kitchen was a mosaic of scents and sounds: the sweet, earthy aroma of roasted garlic mingled with the sharpness of fresh herbs, creating a fragrant haze that enveloped me like a comforting blanket. The overhead lights cast a warm glow over the stainless steel surfaces, illuminating my station as I lined up my ingredients like soldiers ready for battle. Each blade slice felt purposeful, each chop a beat in my personal culinary symphony.

Connor was there again, moving through the kitchen with the kind of ease that comes only from years of experience. His presence was both familiar and disquieting, a mixture of comfort and intrigue. He had been a mystery since the day he arrived—quiet but intense, his focus akin to a hawk's. There was a raw intensity about him that seemed to both draw and repel, as if he were a magnet repelling the very metal that called out to him. As he deftly maneuvered between stations, I couldn't help but steal glances, curious about the thoughts that flitted behind his deep-set eyes.

Tonight, something felt different. The air hummed with an electricity that neither of us could ignore. As we worked side by side, a tense silence settled between us, the kind that thickened the atmosphere, making the routine motions feel charged with unspoken words. I had been perfecting my signature sauce for weeks, each iteration painstakingly crafted, and Connor watched me with an intensity that made my stomach flip.

"Why don't you add a hint of lemon zest?" he suggested, his voice low and unassuming, but there was a spark in his eyes. I hesitated, the weight of my own stubbornness colliding with the budding curiosity. Lemon? In my sauce? It felt sacrilegious, like suggesting pineapple belongs on pizza—a blasphemy I wasn't ready to entertain. Yet, there was something in his tone, a blend of confidence and gentleness, that made me trust him.

I took a breath, set aside my initial reluctance, and zested a lemon with deliberate care, feeling the bright yellow rind give way to the fragrant oils that burst forth. As I folded the zest into my simmering pot, a magical transformation began. The vibrant acidity brightened the dish, pulling the rich flavors together like a conductor bringing an orchestra to life. I tasted, and the flavors danced on my tongue, the dish elevated beyond anything I had expected.

Looking at him in surprise, I felt a surge of gratitude mingling with something else—a giddy thrill that made my heart race. And then, for the first time, he smiled—a real smile that reached his eyes, momentarily peeling away the layers of mystery that surrounded him. In that fleeting moment, something shifted between us, something I couldn't name. But it was there, undeniable, like the taste of something new and unexpected.

"I didn't think you'd go for it," he said, that sly grin tugging at the corners of his lips, lighting up his otherwise serious demeanor. "Guess I underestimated your adventurous spirit."

"Adventurous? Hardly," I shot back, the challenge sparking a fire in my chest. "I prefer my recipes tried and true."

"Sometimes the best things happen when you take a risk," he countered, leaning against the counter, arms crossed, a playful glint in his eye. "You might find you like it."

I rolled my eyes, pretending to dismiss his wisdom, but the truth hung in the air between us, heavy with possibilities. Here I was, trapped in my routine, and yet, in this bustling kitchen surrounded by pots and pans, I felt a new door creak open just a crack, hinting at something that could flourish if only I had the courage to push through.

The night unfurled like the waves of a gentle tide, each ticket calling out for attention as I fell into the rhythm of service. The dining room hummed with laughter and clinking glasses, the kind of atmosphere that wrapped around me like a warm hug. The smells wafted through the air, enticing diners and drawing them deeper into a culinary journey.

As plates flew from the kitchen, I noticed Connor drifting in and out, slipping a taste of this dish here or adjusting a garnish there, as if the kitchen was a dance floor and we were partners moving in sync, each adjusting to the other's rhythm. My heart raced at the unexpected exhilaration of it all. I had always thought I preferred solitude in the kitchen, the quiet hum of my own thoughts guiding me, but tonight, with Connor beside me, everything felt different.

He caught me staring again, an eyebrow raised in mock challenge. "What's the matter? Never seen someone work?" His voice dripped with playful sarcasm, the kind that made my cheeks heat in embarrassment.

"More like I'm trying to figure out how someone can seem so annoyingly perfect," I shot back, unable to suppress a smile.

"Perfect? Me?" He feigned shock, placing a hand dramatically over his heart. "You must be mistaking me for someone else."

A laugh bubbled up, breaking the tension that had woven itself tightly around us. It was a sound that echoed in the kitchen, mixing with the sizzling pans and bustling footsteps, creating a melody that felt exclusive to this moment. There was something undeniably charming about him, a mix of wit and warmth that disarmed me in ways I didn't know I craved.

As the night wore on, I found myself drawing closer to him, the gap between us narrowing in a way that felt both natural and charged. Each shared laugh, each quick glance held a promise of something more. I couldn't shake the feeling that the universe was nudging me toward an unfamiliar path, one that felt deliciously risky—like the unexpected lemon in my sauce.

The rhythm of the kitchen wrapped around me, a comforting cocoon as orders flew in, the buzz of the dining room permeating the air like a distant melody. Each plate we sent out became a part of an elaborate choreography, my pulse syncing with the thud of the chef's voice calling out commands. I watched Connor move with purpose, a ballet dancer in a crisp chef's coat, weaving through the chaos as if it were a second skin. The way he handled each task with grace and precision only heightened my admiration—and perhaps a burgeoning attraction.

I had always considered myself a lone wolf, finding solace in solitude rather than in company. But tonight, the camaraderie in the kitchen felt intoxicating. Connor's presence sparked something within me, a need to be seen, to connect, a desire that frightened and thrilled me all at once. As the night wore on, the banter between us flowed effortlessly. Each exchange felt layered with undertones, a silent understanding brewing between the clever quips and shared laughter.

"Are you always this charming, or is it just the garlic in the air?" I quipped, wiping my brow with the back of my hand after ladling a generous portion of sauce onto a plate.

"Depends on who I'm working with," he replied, leaning closer, his breath warm against my cheek. "I think I might need to change my recipe." His eyes sparkled with mischief, and I fought the urge to blush.

We were in our element, creating not just dishes but a connection that felt electric. I found myself looking forward to his suggestions, eager to see how he might elevate my next creation. When he slipped me a taste of the duck he was preparing, the smoky richness and sweet glaze ignited my senses. "See?" he said, eyes twinkling, "You should be more adventurous. Life's too short for boring food."

"Boring food? You don't know the half of it," I shot back, a grin breaking across my face. "My taste buds have seen more action than a reality TV show."

The night continued to unfurl, and as we worked side by side, it felt like we were crafting more than just meals; we were mixing ingredients of life—spontaneity, laughter, trust. The last table's order arrived, and as I plated the final dish, a sense of triumph swelled within me. But as I stepped into the dining area, a familiar face in the crowd froze me in place.

Lena. My sister. She hadn't been part of my life for years, and yet there she was, sitting at a table with a man I didn't recognize. My heart raced, a mixture of shock and dread flooding my senses. Our last conversation had been a whirlwind of unresolved emotions, and now here she was, like a specter from the past, stirring up all the things I thought I had buried.

I forced myself to breathe, turning my back on the table as I moved through the dining room, my composure wobbling. I felt Connor's gaze follow me, a silent question hanging in the air between us. It was as if I had stumbled into a shadow I couldn't outrun.

"Hey," he said, stepping up beside me as I returned to the kitchen, my heart hammering against my ribs. "You okay?"

I managed a nod, though the unease knotted my stomach. "Yeah, just... an old ghost." My voice was shaky, and I hated the vulnerability it exposed.

"Ghosts can be tricky," he remarked, his expression turning serious. "Want to talk about it?"

I hesitated, caught between the desire to confide in him and the instinct to protect my own wounds. "It's just family stuff," I finally replied, hoping my vague answer would suffice.

"Family can be a minefield," he offered, his tone gentle yet filled with understanding. "But you don't have to go through it alone."

I glanced up at him, surprised by the depth of his empathy. It was rare to find someone who not only understood the complexities of familial ties but was willing to share in the burden. "Thanks, but I'm fine. Really." The words slipped out a little too quickly, almost defensively.

"Fine, huh?" He crossed his arms, a smirk teasing his lips. "That's what everyone says just before they go and blow something up."

"Are you saying I'm a ticking time bomb?" I raised an eyebrow, both amused and annoyed.

"Just saying you might want to consider defusing the situation before it blows up in your face," he countered, a playful glint in his eyes. "You know, culinary tips and life advice, all in a day's work."

I couldn't help but chuckle, despite the tension still swirling inside me. The door to the kitchen swung open, and as the last order came in, I plastered on a smile, pushing my concerns aside. The shift was almost over, but the image of Lena remained etched in my mind, a constant reminder of unfinished business.

The evening wound down, the laughter and chatter fading into a gentle hum as we cleaned up the kitchen together. Connor and I fell into a rhythm, the banter flowing naturally between us as we stacked dishes and wiped surfaces. But the weight of the encounter with my sister loomed large, casting shadows I couldn't ignore.

Just as I thought I had escaped the night without another confrontation, the kitchen door swung open once more. It wasn't a diner or a server; it was Lena. Her gaze locked onto mine, a mixture of surprise and something else swirling in her expression. My heart dropped as the air shifted, anticipation crackling between us.

"I—" she began, her voice a hesitant whisper, but the words hung unformed in the space between us, heavy with years of unresolved history. The kitchen felt suddenly small, the ambient noise fading to a dull murmur as I took a step forward, unsure of what to expect.

Before I could gather my thoughts, Connor shifted beside me, his stance protective yet curious, as if sensing the shift in dynamics. "Do you two need a moment?" he asked, his voice low but clear.

"Actually, yes," Lena said, her eyes darting from me to him, uncertainty etched across her features.

And just like that, the fragile veneer of my evening began to crack, the tension in the air palpable as the past collided with the present. As I stood there, the familiar scent of garlic and herbs fading into the background, I felt an impending storm gathering, a whirlwind of emotions waiting to burst forth, leaving me on the precipice of a decision that could change everything.

Chapter 5: Flames and Friction

The kitchen was a cauldron of chaos, its heat wrapping around me like a thick, suffocating blanket. The hiss of sautéing vegetables mingled with the sharp clatter of knives against cutting boards, creating a symphony of culinary discord. It was a rhythm I had come to love, yet tonight it felt different, charged with an electricity that crackled in the air, threatening to explode. I wiped the back of my hand across my forehead, feeling the slick sheen of perspiration, but it wasn't just the heat that had my heart racing.

Tony's voice boomed through the cramped space, drowning out the usual sounds of clinking glasses and sizzling pans. "I don't care how good you think you are; this isn't your kitchen!" The words echoed off the stainless steel walls, and I felt the weight of every pair of eyes trained on us, the rest of the staff standing still as statues. The tension felt palpable, as if the air itself was thickening, waiting for the inevitable clash.

I had never been one to shy away from confrontation, but facing Tony was like standing at the edge of a precipice, the ground crumbling beneath my feet. His weathered face, taut with anger, was a stark contrast to the warmth I had grown accustomed to in the kitchen, where the smell of garlic and herbs often embraced me like an old friend. But this wasn't about friendship; it was about evolution.

"Maybe it's time for something different," I shot back, my voice steady despite the fluttering in my chest. "The same old dishes won't bring in new customers."

There was a beat of silence, a collective intake of breath from the team, and I could almost hear the gears turning in their heads. In a kitchen like ours, tradition held as much power as the knives we wielded, and here I was, daring to suggest we cut through it like a hot knife through butter.

Tony's face turned an alarming shade of crimson, his frustration palpable as it bled into the air. For a moment, I thought the simmering resentment would boil over, that I would find myself packing my knives and walking out the door. But then Connor, my rock and ally amidst the storm, stepped forward, his presence a balm against the simmering tension.

"She's right," he said, his tone calm but firm, a steady lighthouse in the midst of the chaos. "We need to evolve." His gaze met mine, and a spark of encouragement ignited between us, infusing my resolve with a new energy.

Tony glared at him, his eyes narrowing into slits of irritation, and I held my breath, the room teetering on the edge of a precipice. Would Connor's intervention diffuse the situation or fan the flames of Tony's ire? My heart raced, caught between hope and dread.

After a long, heavy moment, the tension in the room morphed into something almost tangible, like a thick fog wrapping around us. Tony's jaw clenched, his brows knitting together in a stormy scowl. "You think changing the menu will bring in new customers?" he scoffed, the derision dripping from his words like poison.

I straightened, determination igniting my veins. "I don't just think it; I know it. Look around, Tony. We're losing regulars. They want excitement, something fresh. We can't keep serving the same dishes and expect things to change."

His eyes flashed with irritation, and for a moment, I thought he might strike back with a retort sharp enough to cut through the air. Instead, he crossed his arms, the gesture a fortress of defiance. "You want excitement? Fine. Show me."

"Show you?" I repeated, disbelief mingling with excitement. "You mean—"

"Get in the kitchen, make something new, and if it's worth it, I'll consider adding it to the menu." His voice had hardened, but beneath it, I sensed a glimmer of grudging respect. Perhaps I wasn't entirely off base. Perhaps there was room for my vision amid the fiery crucible of tradition.

"Fine," I said, a fierce grin spreading across my face. "Consider it done." The challenge hung in the air, ripe with promise and peril.

As I moved into the kitchen, my heart drumming a chaotic beat against my ribs, Connor sidled up next to me, his presence both reassuring and electric. "You're brave, you know that?" he said, a hint of admiration lacing his voice.

"Or just stupid," I shot back, but a smile tugged at my lips.

"Stupid can be brave," he replied, the corner of his mouth lifting in that way that made my heart do an uninvited flip. "What are you thinking?"

The gears in my mind whirred with possibilities, colors and flavors colliding like fireworks in my imagination. "Something bold, something that would make Tony's head spin." I glanced around the kitchen, spotting fresh ingredients scattered like confetti—vibrant heirloom tomatoes, fragrant basil, a rainbow of peppers. "Let's play with heat and flavor, something unexpected."

As I dove into my work, chopping, sautéing, and experimenting, the world around me faded into a blur. The kitchen became my sanctuary, each ingredient a note in a grand symphony I was conducting. I imagined the flavors dancing together, merging into something extraordinary. The knives glided through the vegetables, each slice a step closer to unveiling the culinary masterpiece that simmered in my mind.

"Let's add some chorizo for spice," I suggested, tossing a few pieces into the sizzling pan. The aroma erupted like a firework, an intoxicating blend of savory and spicy that filled the air, wrapping around me like a warm embrace.

"Now we're talking!" Connor exclaimed, a twinkle in his eye that mirrored the excitement coursing through me.

For a moment, everything felt right, the kitchen alive with the potential of what I was creating. Yet, lurking in the shadows was the reality that awaited me—the possibility of failure and the looming specter of Tony's judgment. But tonight, I was determined to seize the moment, to fight for a future where flavors could soar as high as my aspirations.

The clang of pots and pans formed a chaotic symphony around me, blending with the scents of the sizzling chorizo and the sweetness of sautéed bell peppers. I lost myself in the rhythm, the world narrowing to just me and the ingredients dancing on the hot grill. With each chop, I imagined the excitement in the customers' eyes, the delight in their voices as they savored something new and bold.

Connor leaned against the counter, watching me with an expression that was half amusement, half admiration. "You know, if Tony doesn't explode, this could be the start of something fantastic," he said, a teasing lilt in his voice.

"Or the end of my culinary career," I shot back, trying to keep the anxiety at bay. "But if I'm going down, I'm going down swinging."

"Good motto," he replied, smirking. "Just don't take out the whole kitchen while you're at it."

I couldn't help but chuckle, even as the stress curled around my shoulders like a tight knot. I was knee-deep in a whirlwind of flavors, layering spices, and coaxing the ingredients into a harmony that would make even Tony reconsider. The heat of the chorizo began to mingle with the acidity of the heirloom tomatoes, creating a sauce that shimmered in the pan, enticing in its vibrant colors.

But then Tony's heavy footsteps echoed in the distance, each step a reminder of the looming storm. I glanced over my shoulder, catching a glimpse of him watching from the entrance, arms crossed and expression a storm cloud. "You think you can just waltz in here and change everything? It's not that simple," he barked, his voice slicing through the kitchen chatter like a cleaver.

I took a deep breath, wiping my hands on my apron before turning to face him. "I'm not trying to change everything; I'm trying to elevate what we already have. We can keep the essence of our dishes while adding a twist, a touch of excitement."

"You mean chaos," he snapped back, his eyes narrowed into slits.

"Chaos can be delicious," I countered, a challenge hanging in the air between us. "Look, why don't you taste what I'm making? If you don't like it, then I'll concede. But if you do..." I let the unspoken promise linger, hoping it was enough to convince him to at least take a bite.

"Fine," he huffed, the battle of wills igniting a fire in the pit of my stomach. "But don't expect me to like it just because you threw in a few fancy ingredients."

"Noted," I replied, suppressing a grin. It was a small victory, a spark of hope igniting in the suffocating atmosphere.

As I plated the dish, I felt like a magician pulling a rabbit from a hat. The vibrant colors danced on the plate—a mosaic of reds, greens, and golden browns. I added a sprig of fresh basil on top, the final touch that tied the whole creation together.

"Here goes nothing," I murmured, presenting the dish to Tony like it was a delicate piece of art. "One chorizo heirloom tomato medley, with a twist of spice and a dash of love."

He took the plate from my hands, his fingers brushing against mine for just a heartbeat, igniting a flicker of warmth in my chest. I watched, heart racing, as he brought the fork to his lips, and for a moment, time slowed.

His expression was inscrutable as he chewed, and I held my breath, the kitchen noise fading into an echo around us. I exchanged glances with Connor, who stood close by, a mix of anxiety and excitement mirrored in his eyes. Tony finally swallowed, his brow furrowing as he contemplated the flavors, and I could almost see the gears in his mind grinding against one another.

"It's... different," he said slowly, the words thick on his tongue.

"Different good or different bad?" I pressed, unable to keep the tension from weaving its way into my voice.

"Different like a kid who discovers a new way to ride a bike," he replied, a hint of grudging respect creeping into his tone. "It's thrilling, but there's the risk of falling flat on your face."

I nearly laughed, the relief washing over me like a refreshing breeze. "I'll take thrilling over safe any day."

He rolled his eyes but couldn't hide the smirk threatening to break through. "Let's just see if the customers feel the same way. You're not out of the woods yet."

The challenge hung in the air, but I could see a crack forming in Tony's armor of tradition. "How about we put it on the special menu for this weekend?" I suggested, the excitement bubbling in my chest.

"Fine," he grumbled, though the way his lips quirked betrayed the satisfaction brewing beneath his tough exterior. "But if the customers riot over it, don't come crying to me."

I couldn't help but grin, my heart soaring. "I'll take my chances."

As the kitchen buzzed with renewed energy, I felt a surge of hope. Perhaps this was the turning point I'd been yearning for, a moment where flavors and passion collided. I dove back into my work, infusing new life into other dishes, experimenting with textures and tastes, invigorating the entire menu. The kitchen transformed into a whirlwind of creativity, where laughter and playful banter mingled with the aroma of rich sauces and baked bread.

"Are you this passionate about everything, or just the food?" Connor quipped, his eyes twinkling with mischief as he tossed a handful of fresh herbs into the air, letting them rain down like confetti.

"Only the things that set my heart on fire," I shot back, the banter dancing between us like a well-rehearsed duet.

"Good to know," he said, stepping closer, his shoulder brushing against mine. "I might need to step up my game if I want to keep up with you."

Just then, the door swung open, and a new figure stepped inside—Nina, our pastry chef, her face flushed and her eyes wide with a mix of urgency and excitement. "Guys, you're not going to believe this! We've got a food critic coming in tonight. I overheard it in the market!"

The kitchen erupted into a frenzy of activity, the atmosphere shifting from playful to tense as we scrambled to ensure everything was perfect. My heart raced again, but this time it was tinged with an exhilarating thrill. A food critic could be the breakthrough we desperately needed.

"Okay, people!" Tony barked, taking charge. "We need to pull out all the stops. I want this place to shine."

I glanced at Connor, whose expression mirrored my excitement. This was our moment. The challenge of a lifetime, and I was ready to rise to the occasion. As the clock ticked down, I focused on the dishes I'd created, the flavors melding into something that could truly showcase our kitchen's potential.

But just as I thought we were on the verge of greatness, I caught Tony's eye across the bustling kitchen. His expression shifted, an unexpected storm brewing behind his eyes. "Wait," he said, his voice dropping to a whisper as he leaned toward me, urgency threading through his words. "What's in that special dish you made? I can't shake the feeling that there's something else at play here..."

A chill ran down my spine as his words hung ominously in the air, and I realized that the twist I had crafted might lead to more than just culinary applause. As I opened my mouth to respond, the door swung open once more, and the figure that stepped through made my blood run cold—an old rival from culinary school, her eyes scanning the room like a hawk.

She was here, and with her presence came the reminder that the stakes were higher than I had anticipated. My heart dropped, and suddenly, the kitchen felt smaller, the air thicker, as if the walls themselves were closing in around me.

Chapter 6: Scars Beneath the Surface

The clatter of dishes had faded into a hush, replaced by the soft hum of the refrigerator and the occasional sigh of the exhaust fan. It was a strange tranquility, one that settled over the restaurant like a warm blanket after a storm. I leaned against the cool metal of the prep counter, absentmindedly wiping down the surfaces with a rag that had seen better days. The restaurant was my sanctuary, a place where the chaos of my life felt almost manageable. But tonight, the calmness was different; it had a weight, a gravity that pulled me into Connor's orbit.

He stood at the sink, his hands submerged in soapy water, the steam curling around him like a lingering ghost. It was almost a ritual, this moment we shared, washing away the remnants of a busy shift. I had always found solace in these small, mundane tasks, but there was something about his presence that turned the ordinary into the extraordinary. The way his fingers danced in the water, how he occasionally glanced over at me with a half-smile—it stirred something deep within, a feeling I couldn't quite place but recognized as familiarity.

I hesitated before breaking the silence. "What happened to your hand?" I gestured toward the scar, a jagged line that marred his otherwise perfect skin, a stark reminder of a past I wanted to uncover.

Connor paused, his brow furrowing slightly as he looked down at the scar as if it were a relic of another lifetime. "I used to work in a place like this," he murmured, the words barely above a whisper. "But things went wrong. I made mistakes."

His voice was thick with unspoken memories, each word laced with a tension that made me lean closer, urging him to continue. It was an unexpected intimacy, this late-night confessional, and I could feel the world outside the restaurant—the city humming with life—fade away into the background. "What kind of mistakes?" I asked, curious yet cautious, not wanting to push too hard, but yearning for him to let me in.

He sighed, the weight of his thoughts hanging between us like a delicate glass ornament, fragile yet beautiful. "I was young and stupid, overconfident. I thought I could handle everything. One night, during a rush, I got distracted, and everything spiraled. Someone got hurt because of my carelessness." The admission fell heavy in the air, and I could see the pain etched in the lines of his face, the way his shoulders slumped as he recalled the memory.

I swallowed hard, my own scars rising to the surface in sympathy. "We all have our battles," I said softly, trying to reassure him that he wasn't alone in his pain. "Mine are a bit different, but they still haunt me."

He turned to face me fully, his eyes searching mine for understanding, and in that moment, I felt an undeniable connection, as if we were two broken souls finding solace in each other's company. "What do you mean?" he asked, his tone genuine, urging me to share my own burdens.

The words bubbled up, and before I could second-guess myself, I spoke. "I lost my brother a few years back. He was my anchor, my everything. One night, he just... didn't come home. I still see him in every shadow, hear his laugh in every corner of this place." I could feel the familiar ache in my chest, a hollow pit where my brother used to reside, and for the first time in a long time, I let someone see that vulnerability.

Connor's expression softened, empathy spilling from his eyes. "I'm sorry," he whispered, the sincerity cutting through the heaviness of the room. "That's a pain I can't imagine."

Our stories wrapped around each other, two threads weaving a tapestry of shared grief and resilience. The more we talked, the more layers I peeled away from him, revealing a complexity I had never anticipated. He was a man forged in the fires of his past, shaped by loss and regret, yet there was a warmth about him that invited me in, a light that flickered defiantly against the dark.

"You know," he said, a wry smile breaking through the solemnity, "I didn't expect my night to end with a therapy session in a dishroom."

I laughed, the sound a little too bright against the backdrop of our shared melancholy. "Welcome to my world. Next time, we can charge for admission." The banter lightened the mood, but beneath the playful exchanges, I felt the spark between us intensify, crackling like static electricity in the air.

The clock on the wall ticked steadily, but the time felt suspended, stretching and folding around us. I could have stayed there, lost in conversation with him, for hours, unraveling our pasts like a tangled ball of yarn. But just as I felt we were building something real, something that could take us beyond our scars, the moment shifted.

The door swung open, the bell jingling cheerfully, shattering the intimacy of our bubble. A couple of regulars stumbled in, loud and boisterous, pulling Connor back to reality. I felt a pang of disappointment as he straightened, the warmth between us retreating like a tide, leaving behind only the cold residue of unfinished conversations.

"Hey, guys! We're closed!" he called, but the couple waved him off, oblivious to the late hour and the magic that had just ignited between us.

I cleared my throat, the remnants of our conversation still hanging in the air, but now feeling foreign. The tension shifted as laughter echoed in the restaurant, swallowing our shared vulnerability whole. I wanted to reach out, to remind him of the bond we had begun to forge, but the moment had slipped away like water through fingers.

"Guess I'll finish up here," Connor said, the smile on his face morphing into something more professional, more distant. The connection we had begun to explore felt like it was being pulled back into the shadows, and I could feel the chill of it settling in.

"Yeah, I should—" I started, but the words caught in my throat, lost in the chaotic energy that suddenly filled the room. I watched him put on his mask of indifference, the walls he had let down just moments before snapping back into place.

And just like that, the night shifted, leaving behind the echoes of our stories, the warmth of our shared scars. It felt like a haunting promise lingering in the air, a reminder that beneath the surface of our lives, there were wounds that ran deep, waiting for the right moment to resurface.

The laughter of the couple echoed off the walls, a loud intrusion that broke the fragile spell we had woven between us. I stood there, half-anchored to the past, half-drifting into the future, watching Connor shift back into his role as a server, his demeanor transforming like a chameleon slipping into its natural colors. The walls he had lowered now fortified against me, rising to obscure the intimate conversation we had begun.

The couple, blissfully unaware of the emotional tension they had interrupted, commandeered the table closest to the kitchen, their loud voices shattering the silence like a well-thrown plate. Connor shot me a quick, apologetic glance, a fleeting connection that told me he felt it too—this abrupt return to reality. He resumed his routine, filling glasses and offering menu recommendations, his smile bright but detached. It was as if the warmth of our previous conversation had become a distant memory, replaced by the mundane ritual of serving food and appeasing patrons.

I busied myself with cleaning the counter, wiping away the traces of our shared moment, wishing I could bottle it up, preserve it for later. Yet, as I squeezed the rag tightly, the water pooling at the edge mirrored the unsettled feelings swirling within me. I wanted to shout at the couple to leave, to take their happy chatter somewhere else, but that would hardly be fair. They were just looking for a late-night bite, and here I was, mired in my emotional turbulence.

"Can I get you anything else?" Connor asked, flashing his server smile at the pair as they perused the menu. I noticed how his laughter rang just a bit hollow, as if he were playing a part he didn't quite believe in anymore. It tugged at my heart, that hint of vulnerability, buried beneath layers of charm and professionalism.

"Just the check, please!" one of the women chirped, flipping her hair over her shoulder with a casual flick, oblivious to the shifting dynamics at the back of the house.

"Right away," he replied, though the words felt like they were slipping from his mouth rather than flowing. The glint in his eyes had dimmed, and for a moment, I longed to reach out, to remind him that the person standing behind the counter was still the one who had shared pieces of himself just moments before.

As he punched the order into the register, I leaned back against the counter, crossing my arms and watching the interplay of his features—the slight crease in his brow, the way his lips tightened when he concentrated. He was a puzzle, an enigma, and I wanted nothing more than to unravel it, piece by piece.

When he finally came back to me, a plate of leftover garlic knots in hand—our unspoken midnight snack ritual—I tried to coax the previous warmth back into our atmosphere. "You know, if you wanted to share more about those mistakes, I'm all ears. I mean, look at me, I'm practically a walking disaster."

Connor chuckled lightly, but the shadows in his eyes remained. "You're not a disaster," he said, his tone playful yet serious. "You're just a work in progress. Aren't we all?"

"True, but I'm a bit more of a construction zone, complete with bright orange cones and caution tape." I rolled my eyes for effect, hoping to lighten the mood. "I'm surprised I haven't caused an accident yet."

"Don't worry," he said with a smirk, "I'll take care of you. I have experience with chaos." He gestured dramatically, like a magician unveiling his best trick, and for a heartbeat, we both shared a laugh, the weight of our conversations dissipating like steam from a pot left on too long. But even in laughter, I sensed a flicker of something deeper lingering beneath his humor, a vulnerability he wasn't quite ready to expose.

Just as the atmosphere began to shift again, the door swung open, a rush of cold air flooding the warmth of the restaurant. I glanced up to see a figure silhouetted against the harsh streetlight outside—a tall man with wild hair and an unkempt coat, his features obscured by the shadows.

"Connor!" he bellowed, the voice grating like metal on metal, cutting through the evening's camaraderie. "You in here?"

Connor's face paled slightly, a flash of recognition crossing his features. I noticed the way his posture stiffened, the light in his eyes dimming once more. "What are you doing here, Alex?" he asked, trying to keep his voice steady.

"Just checking in," the newcomer replied, stepping further inside, the door swinging shut behind him. There was a casual confidence in his stride, yet an air of menace lingered in the wake of his presence. My pulse quickened, caught off guard by the sudden shift in our already turbulent night.

"Really? Because it looks like you're crashing a party." Connor's words dripped with sarcasm, though the edge in his voice betrayed an underlying tension I hadn't seen before.

Alex shrugged, looking around the dimly lit restaurant. "I figured you'd be here, working late as usual. Heard you're making quite the splash in the culinary scene."

"Yeah, well, some of us have to work to pay the bills," Connor replied, his tone clipped. I could feel the undercurrent of unease between them, thick enough to slice through with a knife.

"Still, man, you can't keep hiding in this place forever." Alex leaned against the counter, a smirk playing at the corners of his lips, while

Connor's jaw tightened. "What's it going to take to get you out of this rut?"

"Not interested," Connor shot back, the tension escalating with every passing moment. I shifted on my feet, caught in the crossfire of an argument that felt far too personal.

"Come on, Connor," Alex pressed, his voice lowering conspiratorially. "You can't run from your past. It's only going to catch up with you."

I stepped forward, the instinct to defend Connor bubbling up. "Maybe he doesn't need to hear that right now," I interjected, crossing my arms and casting a determined glance at Alex. "Why don't you back off?"

"Look, lady," he began, but I held my ground, unwilling to let this interloper disrupt the fragile connection Connor and I had begun to forge.

Connor shot me a grateful look, but the tension was palpable. "This isn't your fight," he murmured, but his eyes betrayed a hint of gratitude.

"Actually, it is," I replied, my heart racing. "If you want to talk about running, maybe it's time for you to face whatever it is you're avoiding, instead of letting some loudmouth walk all over you."

The words hung in the air, daring them both to respond. Connor opened his mouth, then closed it, clearly wrestling with his emotions. But before he could reply, Alex laughed, the sound a mix of disbelief and annoyance. "Aren't you a little out of your depth here?"

"You'd be surprised how deep I can swim," I shot back, unwilling to back down.

The tension crackled between us, thickening like a fog rolling in over the city. Just as I thought Connor would step in, Alex's phone buzzed in his pocket, a welcome interruption. He pulled it out, glancing at the screen, and for a moment, the weight in the room shifted.

"Looks like you're not the only one with baggage," he said, his tone shifting as he read whatever was on his phone. The color drained from his face, and he quickly turned to Connor. "I need to go. We're not done talking."

With that, he strode toward the door, the bell jingling as he exited, leaving a heavy silence in his wake. I turned to Connor, who looked as if he had just been caught in a storm he couldn't escape. The electricity in the air hadn't dissipated; it had only thickened, becoming more charged and unpredictable.

"What just happened?" I asked, a mix of curiosity and concern flooding my voice.

"Just... someone from my past," Connor replied, his voice tight, the familiar walls rebuilding around him. "I thought I had put that behind me."

"But it looks like he's not done with you," I said softly, stepping closer. The gulf between us felt insurmountable, yet I wanted to reach across it. I wanted to know what haunted him, what shadows were creeping back into his life.

He ran a hand through his hair, frustration etched across his features. "No, he's not." His gaze flickered to the door, the lingering chill of Alex's presence still hanging in the air.

"I know you don't want to talk about it, but—"

"I really don't," he interrupted, the sharpness in his tone slicing through the room. I flinched but held my ground, determined to peel back the layers of this man who intrigued me more with every passing moment.

The atmosphere shifted again, a weighty silence settling between us, thick and pregnant with unspoken words. I wanted to fight for him, for us, but he looked so lost, so afraid. Just when I thought he might open up again, his phone buzzed in his pocket, breaking the tension like a sharp crack of lightning in a still sky.

He glanced at the screen, his expression changing rapidly from confusion to something resembling dread. "I have to take this," he said, his voice clipped, as he stepped away, his back turned to me.

"Connor—" I started, but the tension was palpable, a wall rising once more between us.

"Just a minute," he said, his tone shutting me out, and I felt a chill race down my spine. Something had shifted irreparably

Chapter 7: Salt in the Wound

The sun struggled to break through the slate-gray clouds, as if even the sky felt the weight of my loss. It cast a muted light over the kitchen, where I had spent countless hours chopping, sautéing, and plating, the comforting rhythms of cooking now drowned beneath an overwhelming silence. I sat at the small wooden table, a solitary figure surrounded by a chorus of unwashed dishes and half-prepared ingredients, remnants of a life that felt achingly normal, yet painfully out of reach. The scent of garlic lingered in the air, a reminder of the last dinner I had cooked for my father—one of those meals that had always been a celebration of his favorite flavors, but had turned bittersweet in the wake of his absence.

A dull ache throbbed in my chest, the kind that clung stubbornly, refusing to fade. I traced the rim of my coffee mug, the porcelain cool against my fingers, as I replayed every moment from the last few days in my mind. The hospital room had been sterile and stark, the fluorescent lights buzzing overhead as my father slipped away, his hand limp in mine. I remembered the way he looked at me just before the end—a flash of something like recognition or perhaps relief, and then nothing. Just silence, thick and suffocating.

I pulled my knees to my chest, wrapping my arms around them like a shield against the world. The phone buzzed, startling me from my reverie. Connor's name flashed on the screen. I hesitated, fingers hovering above the device, thoughts swirling in a storm of regret and guilt. He had been my anchor during this tumultuous time, the one voice that dared to penetrate the fog I had wrapped myself in. But how could I explain to him the depth of my despair? How could I let him in when I was still trying to understand it myself?

With a sigh, I swiped the screen to silence the call, retreating deeper into the cocoon of my solitude. A moment later, I heard a soft knock on the door. I froze. I wasn't ready to face anyone. The world outside felt too loud, too bright, too full of reminders of the life I was supposed to be living. Another knock, firmer this time, coaxing me from my shadows. It was a persistent sound, one that chipped away at my resolve.

"Emma, it's Connor. Please, let me in."

His voice wrapped around me like a warm blanket, but I resisted. I didn't want to face his concern, the way his brow would furrow when he saw the pain etched across my features. I wanted to keep the walls high, the fortress secure. After what felt like an eternity, I let out a shuddering breath and swung the door open, revealing him standing there, drenched in the drab light of the overcast day.

His expression morphed from anxiety to relief, a small smile breaking through the shadows of his worry. "Hey," he said softly, stepping inside. The weight of his presence filled the space, grounding me even as I felt myself begin to unravel.

"Hey," I echoed, my voice barely above a whisper. I glanced away, suddenly aware of the chaos around us. The kitchen felt like a crime scene, with dishes piled high and remnants of my attempts at normalcy scattered like breadcrumbs leading to a darkness I didn't want to confront.

"I brought lunch," he announced, pulling a takeout container from his backpack, a small smirk dancing on his lips. "Your favorite—pad Thai. I thought maybe we could eat it together?"

"Thanks, but I'm not really hungry," I replied, waving my hand dismissively, though the scent of the spices danced in the air, teasing my senses.

Connor set the container on the table, unfazed by my rejection. "Emma, you need to eat. You can't just shut everyone out. I know it feels easier, but—"

"But what?" I shot back, my voice rising. "You don't understand. You don't know what it's like to lose someone like that. To watch them fade away, piece by piece, until there's nothing left but memories." The words tumbled out, raw and jagged, a reflection of the turmoil swirling within me.

His expression shifted, a flicker of understanding igniting in his eyes. "You're right. I don't know what that feels like, but I want to be here for you. Please, just let me in, even a little."

The tension hung in the air, thick and palpable. I could see the sincerity in his gaze, the way he was willing to fight for me when all I wanted to do was retreat. It stirred something deep within me, a flicker of hope battling against the tide of despair.

"I don't know how," I admitted, my voice trembling. "I feel so lost."

He took a step closer, the warmth radiating from him a comforting balm against the chill that had seeped into my bones. "Then let's figure it out together. One step at a time."

I swallowed hard, his words both a lifeline and a challenge. The thought of leaning on him was terrifying, yet liberating. I didn't want to burden him with my grief, but as I met his gaze, I saw the determination to stand by me, no matter how difficult the path ahead might be.

"I don't want to fall apart in front of you," I confessed, my voice barely above a whisper.

"Then don't," he replied with a wry smile. "We'll do it together, piece by piece."

In that moment, something shifted within me. The walls I had built started to crumble, and for the first time since my father's death, I felt the stirrings of connection. Perhaps I didn't have to navigate this storm alone. Perhaps there was room for both grief and healing, light and darkness, in this complex tapestry of life.

Connor remained, his presence a steadying force as I stood on the precipice of my grief, the world swirling around me like a watercolor painting left out in the rain. "You know, I could always whip up my famous avocado toast," he offered, attempting to lighten the mood with a hint of humor. "It's scientifically proven to cure sadness. At least, that's what I tell myself every Sunday."

I couldn't help but let out a half-hearted chuckle, the sound surprising me. "You really think avocado toast is the answer to everything?"

"Absolutely," he said, crossing his arms with mock seriousness. "Not only is it delicious, but it also has those omega-3 fatty acids. Perfect brain food for when you need to think about—let's say, not isolating yourself like a hermit crab."

There was a glimmer in his eyes that hinted at his determination to break through my barriers. I was acutely aware that I had inadvertently crafted a fortress out of my sorrow, and here he was, willing to hurl himself against the walls.

"I could use a little brain food," I admitted, the weight of his gaze softening my defenses. "But you'll have to make it. I can barely function, let alone create something edible right now."

"Deal," he grinned, immediately rummaging through my pantry like he was on a scavenger hunt, pulling out what seemed like a never-ending supply of half-empty jars and expired packets. "You really need to take inventory around here. I think I just found a jar of pickles from when your dad thought he could make homemade giardiniera. Spoiler alert: it did not end well."

The corners of my lips twitched up. "His pickles were legendary... for all the wrong reasons."

As he clattered about, I leaned against the counter, my heart lightening slightly as the rhythm of our banter began to knit together the frayed edges of my thoughts. The kitchen was transforming from a wasteland of grief back into a place of warmth, the familiar chaos of cooking encroaching on my solitude like a welcome guest.

"Alright, let's see what we're working with," he declared, and in the next few moments, he had transformed the space, chopping and mixing as if he had never left. The sizzle of onions hit the air, a sound I had once found soothing but now felt foreign.

"How do you do that?" I asked, fascinated as he tossed ingredients into a bowl like a magician pulling rabbits from a hat.

"Do what? Cook? It's just a little patience and a lot of practice," he replied, grinning at me over his shoulder, a playful glint in his eye. "And a touch of fear. You should see my kitchen at home. It looks like a food war zone after I'm done."

"Your secret is safe with me," I laughed, the sound filling the room like a long-lost melody. "As long as you promise to share the end product."

"Oh, I don't know," he teased, flicking a stray strand of hair out of his eyes as he stirred a mixture. "What if it turns out terrible? I could just leave you with my culinary catastrophe, and you'll never let me in your kitchen again."

"Too late for that," I countered, a hint of challenge in my tone. "You've already breached my defenses."

"Glad to hear it," he said, his voice low and sincere, the lightness briefly fading. "I don't want to be a burden, Emma. I want to be someone you can lean on. Grief is a heavy load to carry alone."

The weight of his words settled between us, and I felt a stirring within me. A nagging voice in my mind warned me to guard my heart, but the warmth of his sincerity was a balm I hadn't realized I needed. "I appreciate you, you know. For being here."

He paused, his back still turned, and I wondered if he could hear my heart thudding in the stillness. "You've got a lot of love to give. It's okay to let some of it back out. Just remember you're not alone in this. Not now, not ever."

As the fragrant aroma filled the kitchen, I took a moment to absorb the reality of his presence, a palpable comfort in a space once filled with despair. Suddenly, the front door creaked open, and my heart raced with a mix of anticipation and dread.

"Emma?" My mother's voice cut through the warmth like a chill breeze, and I felt my stomach twist.

"Great timing," I murmured under my breath, wishing I could conjure a spell to erase the tension from the air. Connor's eyes met mine, a flicker of concern crossing his features.

"Mom, I'm in the kitchen!" I called out, bracing myself for her arrival.

The door swung open wider, revealing her silhouette framed in the harsh light of the hallway. She stepped inside, her eyes scanning the room before landing on me. The moment seemed suspended in time, her gaze locking onto the chaos of the kitchen—the signs of life, the signs of healing—and the realization hung heavy between us.

"Emma," she said softly, her voice thick with unspoken words. "I didn't know you were... busy."

"Just cooking," I replied, forcing a smile. "Connor's helping."

Her expression shifted, an intricate blend of surprise and uncertainty. "Helping, or...?"

"Cooking," I insisted, a little too quickly. "Just cooking."

"What's for lunch?" she asked, her eyes darting to the makeshift meal, and I could sense the awkwardness settle like a thick fog.

"Pad Thai," Connor interjected, ever the social maestro, stepping into the fray with confidence. "It's scientifically proven to lift spirits. Well, at least according to my Sunday brunch ritual."

"Connor!" My mother's tone was surprised yet delighted, a reminder of the connection we had almost lost. "It's nice to see you! I hope you've been taking care of Emma. She needs all the help she can get right now."

I shot Connor a look, a silent plea to steer clear of the impending storm that brewed in my mother's eyes. He nodded, a hint of amusement dancing on his lips as he whisked a handful of herbs into the bowl.

BREAKING THE MOLD

"Speaking of help, I brought some things for you," my mother said, her voice suddenly stern, producing a paper bag that had seen better days. "Thought you could use a little home cooking yourself."

"Thanks," I replied, my voice trailing off as I noticed the familiar containers spilling over. Chicken soup, her infamous lasagna, a dessert I didn't dare ask about—her attempts at reaching out, yet somehow missing the mark.

"You're still a mess," she said, her gaze piercing through me. "You can't just hide away. You need to face the world."

"I'm trying!" I exclaimed, the frustration bubbling to the surface. "But it's hard when the world feels like it's caving in."

Before she could respond, Connor stepped in. "Maybe we can all face it together? Food always makes things better, right?"

The air thickened with tension, and I could feel the precarious balance teetering. "How about we sit down and eat?" he suggested, trying to usher us towards the table as if to smooth over the jagged edges.

"Sure," I said, but even as I spoke, an unease settled into the pit of my stomach. I glanced at Connor, who was still attempting to maintain a lighthearted atmosphere, but the heaviness from my mother loomed like a storm cloud ready to unleash its fury.

"Emma, we need to talk about your father's arrangements," she stated, her voice grave and deliberate, slicing through the air like a knife.

At that moment, I realized the fragile peace we had built was on the brink of collapse. The conversation I had been avoiding was about to unravel, and I could feel the ground shifting beneath me. The weight of her words hung in the air, and I knew there was no escaping it. As I opened my mouth to respond, the doorbell rang, an unexpected interruption that sent my heart racing.

"Who could that be?" My mother asked, eyes narrowing as she turned towards the door.

"I'll get it," I said, relief flooding through me. I needed a moment to breathe, to collect my thoughts before facing the inevitable discussion. I hurried towards the door, my heart pounding with a mix of anxiety and hope, unaware that beyond the threshold lay a twist that would alter everything.

Chapter 8: A Recipe for Healing

The soft hum of my mixer echoed in the kitchen, its comforting whirr blending with the fragrant aromas swirling around me. I had taken to midnight cooking like a moth drawn to a flickering light. The air was thick with the sweet scent of vanilla and melting butter, my old friends in a time of uncertainty. As the clock ticked past eleven, the world outside faded into a hushed lull, leaving me alone with my thoughts and the vibrant chaos of my kitchen.

Chopping onions with a precise determination, I allowed the rhythm of my knife against the cutting board to drown out the cacophony of doubts swirling in my head. Each slice was a reminder that I was capable of creation, a flicker of confidence in the shadows that had loomed over me for far too long. The tears from earlier hung in the back of my throat, a stubborn knot that refused to dissolve. I had thought they would have been released in the cathartic embrace of cooking, but they clung on, lurking like unwelcome guests at a party where I was desperately trying to keep the mood light.

Connor leaned against the doorway, arms crossed, a faint smile playing on his lips as he watched me. His presence had become a strange comfort—like a warm blanket that I wasn't quite ready to wrap myself in. I glanced up, catching his gaze, and a flicker of something ignited between us, something both exhilarating and terrifying. "You know, if you keep chopping those onions like that, they might start to fear for their lives," he said, his voice teasing yet warm, breaking the tension that had woven its way into the room.

I shot him a playful glare, though it couldn't mask the grin tugging at my lips. "Well, they should consider themselves lucky. It's either this or being sautéed into submission. I prefer my onions with a little bit of fear. Adds character."

"Character, huh?" he mused, stepping closer. "Is that what you're going for? A dish with a dark past?"

"More like a dish with a dark present," I replied, my voice lighter than the weight in my heart. "I'm trying to create something that tastes like freedom—something that'll help me reclaim my own."

The words lingered between us, an uninvited truth in a space we had filled with laughter and banter. He seemed to ponder my statement, his expression softening as he stepped further into the kitchen. The warmth from the oven illuminated his features, creating a halo effect that made him look almost angelic. "Then how about we make this a little more adventurous? What about adding a pinch of risk? Maybe even a dash of unpredictability?"

I raised an eyebrow, intrigued. "Are you suggesting we throw in something wild? Like chili flakes?"

"Or perhaps something a little more unexpected," he suggested, a glint of mischief in his eyes. "Like pineapple. On pizza."

"Absolutely not," I said, recoiling with exaggerated horror. "That's where I draw the line. That's not culinary adventure; that's culinary treason."

He chuckled, the sound warming the space between us, easing the tension I hadn't even realized I was holding. "You know, some people swear by it. You might be surprised."

"Oh please, I'm already surprised that you're here." I turned back to the bowl of batter, hoping to distract myself from the magnetism pulling us closer. The way he stood so close made it difficult to concentrate, the air thickening with unspoken words and thoughts that I wasn't ready to confront.

"Why is that?" he asked, his curiosity piqued. "You think I'm just here for the free food?"

"Food, yes," I said, carefully measuring out the flour, "but more likely to witness my impending kitchen disaster. I swear if I set off the smoke alarm, it'll be a testament to my cooking skills—or lack thereof."

Connor stepped in beside me, nudging me with his shoulder. "I think you're underestimating your skills. This looks promising." He gestured to the myriad of ingredients spread out like a painter's palette, the colors bright and inviting. "But I think you're avoiding something. You haven't told me what you're really cooking for."

My heart lurched at the directness of his words. He had a way of cutting through the banter, exposing the raw nerve I desperately tried to shield. I stirred the batter, watching the way it transformed, the ingredients melding together, each twist of the spoon mirroring the chaos within me. "I'm just trying to keep busy," I finally admitted, my voice barely above a whisper. "To distract myself from… everything."

His silence was weighty, pressing against the air like a summer storm cloud, ready to burst. "You know, distraction can only take you so far. You can't hide forever."

I paused, meeting his gaze, feeling the shift in the atmosphere. "And what would you suggest I do instead? Face my demons with a side of garlic bread?"

"Maybe start by acknowledging that they exist. You don't have to battle them alone, you know." His sincerity cut deeper than I had anticipated, a reminder that my facade was starting to crack.

The weight of his words settled between us, an open invitation to dive deeper, to shed the layers I had built around myself. But the kitchen was my refuge, my safe space where the chaos of my thoughts could simmer on the back burner, undisturbed. I let out a nervous laugh, attempting to deflect. "Okay, how about you help me with this dish instead of dissecting my life?"

He smiled, a knowing grin that hinted he wouldn't let me off that easily. "All right. What do you need? A pinch of courage? A cup of honesty?"

"Just a handful of love," I replied, hoping the playful tone would mask the vulnerability lurking beneath. "And maybe a sprinkle of patience. I've got enough courage for both of us."

As we worked side by side, the tension began to dissolve, replaced by the warmth of shared laughter and the comfort of companionship.

I poured the batter into a pan, feeling a renewed sense of purpose flow through me. With each passing moment, the layers of my defenses began to peel away, exposing a longing I hadn't realized was there—a desire for connection, for understanding, for someone to see the messy, imperfect version of me that I had kept hidden for far too long.

"Okay, I think we're ready to bake," I announced, wiping my hands on a dish towel, trying to shake off the weight of what had been said. "Now, we just have to wait."

"Waiting is the hardest part," he replied, leaning back against the counter, his expression contemplative. "But the end result is worth it."

"Yeah," I murmured, glancing at the oven. "Just like life, I guess. Full of unpredictable heat and unexpected flavors."

As the oven door closed, sealing in the potential of our creation, I realized that the heat of the kitchen mirrored the warmth of something new brewing between us—something both terrifying and exhilarating. In that moment, amid the chaos of flour and sugar, I felt a flicker of hope, a recipe for healing, simmering just beneath the surface.

The oven timer chimed, breaking the spell of silence that had enveloped the kitchen. The sound was both a welcome jolt and an unexpected reminder that time was a relentless force, moving forward whether I was ready or not. I pulled the door open, letting a cloud of warm, fragrant air wash over me, and the sight that greeted me was nothing short of magical: a golden-brown cake, its surface glistening as though it were wearing a crown of sugary glory.

Connor leaned in, peering over my shoulder with an eagerness that was almost boyish. "Well, would you look at that? It's a masterpiece!" His enthusiasm wrapped around me like a cozy blanket, momentarily dispelling the nerves simmering beneath my skin.

"Masterpiece or not, it's still got to cool before we can dig in," I replied, teasing him with a mock-seriousness that didn't quite conceal my own excitement. "Patience, remember?"

"Patience is overrated," he shot back, crossing his arms and casting me an exaggeratedly disapproving glare. "I say we take a slice while it's still warm. If you wait too long, it'll just become a sad little lump of cake, mourning the glory it once had."

"Now you're just being melodramatic," I laughed, swatting him playfully with a dish towel. "This isn't some Shakespearean tragedy, Connor. It's a cake."

"Right, but even cakes have feelings. You know how fragile they are. A few minutes can change everything." His eyes sparkled with mischief, igniting a playful challenge between us.

"Fine, but if we do this, we have to dress it up first. A plain slice just won't do." I rummaged through the pantry, pulling out powdered sugar, berries, and whipped cream, determined to elevate our late-night indulgence to something truly special.

"I'll take a slice with all the frills," he grinned. "I'm all about the drama tonight."

"Then you're in luck," I said, pouring a generous amount of cream into a mixing bowl, "because I happen to have a flair for the theatrical when it comes to dessert."

As I whisked, the sound of the beaters mixing with the quiet moments between us felt like a soothing balm. The kitchen filled with a symphony of scents—the rich, sweet notes of vanilla and the tangy brightness of fresh strawberries. For a fleeting moment, the burdens of the outside world dimmed, and it was just us in our little culinary bubble, crafting something beautiful together.

Once the cream was whipped to perfection, I started assembling the plates, layering slices of the warm cake with clouds of cream and the vibrant berries. "Voila! The dramatic dessert of the evening," I proclaimed, placing the plates on the counter between us.

He picked up a fork, eyeing the cake with the kind of reverence usually reserved for fine art. "This is definitely a dish worthy of a standing ovation."

"Careful, or I might expect you to throw flowers at my feet," I shot back, my heart fluttering at the ease of our banter.

He took a bite, his eyes widening in delight. "This is incredible! If I knew you could cook like this, I might have spent more time hovering around your kitchen."

"Is that a hint?" I teased, enjoying the way our chemistry simmered under the surface like a well-spiced broth.

His gaze held mine, unyielding yet playful. "Only if it means I get to share more of your culinary masterpieces—and maybe your company."

The weight of his words settled in the air, and for a moment, the lightness of our exchange transformed into something deeper. The brief silence hung between us, charged with unspoken possibilities, but I quickly turned back to the counter, busily arranging more berries as a distraction.

"Let's not get too carried away with the sweetness," I joked, breaking the tension, "I don't want you to get any crazy ideas about moving in or anything."

"Who says I'm not already plotting to take over your kitchen? I can be a fantastic sous chef, you know. I can even peel potatoes with the best of them."

"Ah yes, a true culinary virtuoso," I replied, smirking as I dabbed cream on his nose with my finger. "The greatest chef of the century, known for his mastery of potato peeling."

"Hey! That was uncalled for!" he exclaimed, mock outrage spilling from his lips, but his laughter filled the space, and I felt my heart lighten.

In that moment, I caught a glimpse of what could be, a tantalizing prospect that made my pulse quicken. But then, like a shadow creeping across sunlight, doubt rushed in, a reminder of all that I had yet to face. Could I really allow someone into my life again, into the chaos of my heart?

"I'm serious," he said, breaking the spell of my reverie, "You're more than a talented cook. You're someone who brings joy into this kitchen. And if that means occasionally getting cream on my face, I'd call it a fair trade."

His sincerity sliced through my uncertainty, and I felt a warmth spreading through my chest, tempting me to lean closer, to explore the contours of this growing connection. Yet, the ghosts of my past whispered caution, urging me to hold back, to keep my heart wrapped tightly in layers of protective armor.

"Thank you," I said softly, my voice barely above a whisper. "That means a lot, especially considering how... messy things have been for me."

"Messy is part of life. It's where all the good stuff happens," he replied, leaning forward as if to bridge the distance I had erected between us. "You've been through a lot, but you're stronger than you realize. And if you let me, I'd like to help you through it."

The invitation hung in the air, thick with unspoken promises and undeniable chemistry. It was tempting, and I could feel the walls I had built around myself beginning to shake under the weight of his earnestness. But just as I opened my mouth to respond, my phone buzzed on the counter, shattering the moment into shards of reality.

I reached for it, my heart sinking as I saw the name flashing on the screen. It was my mother, and the anxious knot that had been loosening in my chest tightened once more.

"Sorry, I need to take this," I said, my voice wavering slightly as I turned away from him, suddenly feeling exposed.

"Of course," Connor replied, though the disappointment was evident in his eyes. "We can pick this up after you're done."

I nodded, trying to shake off the sense of dread curling in my stomach. I answered the call, and my mother's voice spilled out, a tidal wave of concern and urgency flooding through the line. "Honey, we need to talk. It's about your father..."

Her words pierced the cozy atmosphere of the kitchen, dragging me back into a world I had hoped to escape, a world filled with complications and unresolved pain. As I listened, the reality of the situation settled like a lead weight on my chest, threatening to drown out the light I had felt just moments ago.

"Mom, I—" I started, but her voice cut through my thoughts, sharp and demanding.

"No, you need to hear me out. It's important. I know you've been distant, but this... this is serious."

As she spoke, I felt Connor's gaze on me, his eyes searching, curious, and concerned. I wanted to share this moment with him, to lean on him as I had begun to trust him, but the darkness of my family's turmoil loomed large, a shadow that threatened to eclipse everything else.

I bit my lip, trying to focus on my mother's words, but all I could think was that the kitchen, once a sanctuary, was now teetering on the edge of chaos once more. My heart raced, caught in a whirlwind of anxiety and uncertainty as I turned to look at Connor, whose expression had shifted from playful to serious.

"Mom, just tell me what's going on," I finally managed, knowing full well that whatever she had to say would change everything.

As I braced myself for the news, the air crackled with tension, the sweet aroma of cake fading into the background as my life hung in the balance, poised on the edge of uncertainty, waiting for the other shoe to drop.

Chapter 9: Stirring the Pot

The hum of the restaurant was a comforting backdrop, an orchestra of clinking glasses, sizzling pans, and the soft murmur of patrons indulging in their meals. I stood in the kitchen, apron slightly askew, my hair pulled into a haphazard bun, a sense of purpose filling the air around me. The heat radiating from the stovetops wrapped around me like a warm embrace, its intensity igniting my passion for cooking. I was lost in my world of simmering sauces and freshly chopped herbs when the bell above the kitchen door jingled, jolting me back to reality. I glanced up just as Tony stormed through, his face a canvas of fury painted in vivid strokes.

"It's a disaster!" he exclaimed, his voice booming like a thunderclap. I turned my attention to the clock, the ticking hands mocking the frantic rhythm of my heart. It was far too early for chaos, and yet, here it was, uninvited and relentless. I wiped my hands on the apron, suddenly aware of the tension tightening in the pit of my stomach.

"What happened?" I asked, hoping the answer would be something manageable—maybe a table of unruly customers or a missing shipment of heirloom tomatoes. But as Tony thrust his phone toward me, I knew I was grasping at straws. The screen glared back with a single line of text, and my breath hitched in my throat.

"The risotto was a soggy mess, lacking any discernible flavor. A true disappointment in a sea of pretentious dining."

My dish—the very creation I had poured my heart and soul into—was now publicly dissected by someone who didn't even know the joy of fresh basil or the symphony of garlic and onion dancing in the pan. I felt a weight crashing down, pressing against my chest as I fought the urge to crumble.

Tony paced, his footsteps heavy with frustration. "This critic has the power to make or break us! We can't afford a bad reputation. We need to figure this out, and fast!"

In the midst of Tony's ranting, a familiar face appeared at the doorway, effortlessly cutting through the turmoil. Connor strolled in, his calm demeanor a stark contrast to the whirlwind swirling around us. The slight upturn of his lips suggested he was oblivious to the chaos enveloping the restaurant. It was as if he was a walking beacon of light in our stormy kitchen.

"What's with the commotion?" he asked, his voice low and soothing, as if he were speaking to a spooked animal rather than two frantic restaurateurs.

"Just the usual, Connor," I replied, forcing a smile despite the gnawing anxiety clawing at my insides. "A scathing review that could ruin everything we've built."

His expression shifted, seriousness cutting through the light-hearted facade. "Let me see." He reached for Tony's phone, scanning the text with narrowed eyes. "This guy has no idea what he's talking about."

"Tell that to our customers," Tony shot back, frustration bubbling over like a pot on the brink of boiling.

Connor's brow furrowed slightly, and I could see the wheels turning in his mind. "Maybe we can turn this around. A bad review doesn't have to be the end; it can be a catalyst for change. We can improve, show them what we're really made of."

There was something about his conviction that struck a chord deep within me. It resonated louder than the critic's words, reminding me why I loved cooking in the first place. The kitchen was my sanctuary, my canvas, and it had the power to create joy—even in the face of adversity. I straightened my posture, wiping my hands on the apron once more, this time feeling the fire within reignite.

"You're right," I said, my voice stronger now. "We can fix this. We need to revisit the dish, refine it, and maybe even turn it into something new altogether."

BREAKING THE MOLD

Tony stopped his pacing, his eyes widening. "Are you serious? You think we can bounce back from this?"

"I know we can," I insisted, my heart racing with renewed determination. "Let's gather the team, brainstorm, and make this risotto sing."

Connor's smile returned, brighter and more genuine. "That's the spirit! Let's stir the pot, literally and figuratively."

As we gathered the staff, the atmosphere began to shift. It was like watching a storm dissipate, replaced by a fragile but hopeful calm. Laughter filled the air as we exchanged ideas, each voice adding its own flavor to the mix. We dissected the review, discussed the critics' possible expectations, and even debated the merits of adding a splash of white wine or experimenting with new ingredients.

Amidst the brainstorming, a vibrant idea bloomed. "What if we infuse the risotto with saffron?" I suggested, the thought rolling off my tongue like a fine wine. "And pair it with a tangy lemon zest to brighten the flavors?"

"Now you're talking!" Connor chimed in, his eyes glinting with enthusiasm. "Let's elevate this dish. We can create something unforgettable."

The energy surged through me, pulling me into a creative whirlwind where every suggestion felt like a piece of a puzzle snapping into place. We chopped, stirred, and sautéed with a fervor that turned the kitchen into a bustling hive of activity. My heart swelled with every bubbling pot and sizzling pan, reminding me that in moments of crisis, the kitchen became a family—a collective spirit fighting against the odds.

As the new risotto simmered gently, the aroma wafting through the kitchen was intoxicating, wrapping around me like a warm hug. The vibrant yellow color was a promise of rebirth, a testament to our resolve to not only withstand the storm but to thrive within it. Connor and I shared a moment, a brief glance filled with unspoken understanding. In that fleeting second, I realized how much he had become a part of my journey—not just as a colleague, but as someone who believed in me, even when I struggled to believe in myself.

The final dish, a stunning medley of colors and aromas, glistened under the warm kitchen lights. It was our masterpiece, born from the ashes of failure, and it was time to present it to the world. With Connor's hand on my shoulder, I felt an electric thrill of anticipation. Whatever came next, we would face it together, and I knew we wouldn't back down. We were ready to show the world what we were truly capable of.

The clatter of utensils echoed in the kitchen as the team rallied around our newfound mission, energized by the collective determination that had ignited. Each chef moved with purpose, their usual banter transformed into a focused dialogue that buzzed with excitement and creativity. I glanced over at Connor, who was deep in conversation with Tony, his hands gesturing animatedly as he laid out a plan. The sight of them collaborating brought a warm glow to my chest, a reassurance that we were truly in this together.

"Okay, team! Let's break this down," I called, my voice cutting through the rhythmic sound of chopping. "What's our strategy for the new risotto? We want to make sure it's not just better, but unforgettable."

A chorus of ideas erupted, some sensible and others wildly ambitious. Marcus, our sous-chef, suggested infusing the broth with roasted garlic, while Lisa, the pastry chef, chimed in about a possible herb-infused oil drizzle for that extra flair. As we shared laughs and culinary experiments, the initial weight of that harsh review began to lift, replaced by a buoyant sense of camaraderie.

"Let's make sure we're not just cooking for the critic but for the people who walk through those doors every day," I said, my enthusiasm palpable. "They're the heart of this restaurant."

"Are we really making risotto for the people?" Connor teased, an eyebrow raised in mock seriousness. "What if they're just here for the breadsticks?"

I feigned shock, clutching my chest dramatically. "Never! The breadsticks are merely the prelude to the main event. We're here to wow them with culinary brilliance!"

The laughter that followed filled the kitchen, reminding us all why we had chosen this chaotic, unpredictable life of service. I knew the criticism stung, but we had a chance to redefine ourselves, to rise from the ashes of the critic's words. Each laugh, each shared suggestion, was a step closer to what we wanted to achieve.

With the recipe taking shape, we moved into a rhythm that felt electric. I had always thrived in high-pressure situations, and today was no different. The clanging of pots and pans became a soundtrack to our unyielding spirit, the sizzling sound of the risotto coming together echoing my heartbeat.

I glanced at Connor, who was hunched over the stovetop, testing a spoonful of our latest concoction. His face shifted from concentration to sheer delight as he savored the flavor. "This is amazing!" he exclaimed, his eyes sparkling with the thrill of discovery. "I think we're onto something here."

"Glad to hear it. You're my taste-tester extraordinaire," I quipped, a playful smile dancing on my lips. "Though I must admit, I'm a bit worried you might get used to this."

His laughter resonated through the kitchen, mixing with the fragrant steam that curled around us like a comforting hug. "What can I say? It's a tough job, but someone's got to do it."

As the final touches came together, I felt an overwhelming surge of pride. This risotto wasn't just a dish; it was a symbol of resilience, a testament to our collective effort. We worked late into the night, perfecting every nuance, until the golden risotto glistened under the kitchen lights like a sunset captured in a bowl.

The next day dawned with a crispness that seemed to promise change. As the restaurant opened its doors, I could feel the tension in the air—thick and electric, mingled with the scent of freshly baked bread and rich espresso. The usual morning chatter felt subdued, as if everyone was holding their breath, waiting for the inevitable verdict on our new creation.

As the lunch rush hit, we hustled through orders, each plate a delicate dance of balance and flavor. The risotto made its debut, garnished with a swirl of lemon-infused oil and fresh herbs, the vibrant colors inviting patrons to indulge. The initial reactions were promising, whispers of delight creeping from table to table.

"I'll take a risotto," a voice rang out, sharp and demanding, cutting through the kitchen's melody. I glanced up just in time to see a figure striding through the restaurant, a woman exuding confidence and an air of authority that made even Tony straighten his posture. It was Marissa, a food blogger with a reputation for being brutally honest.

"Here we go," Connor murmured beside me, an eyebrow cocked in a mixture of amusement and apprehension. "Is it bad form to offer her a complimentary dessert if she doesn't like the risotto?"

"Definitely bad form," I shot back, rolling my eyes playfully. "But we'll just have to impress her. If she thinks this is a soggy mess, we'll have more than just her bad review to deal with."

As Marissa settled at a corner table, her eyes scanning the menu with the keen gaze of a hawk, I could feel my pulse quicken. The restaurant buzzed with energy, but my focus narrowed on her. It was time to show her the magic we had conjured, to prove that we were not just another eatery that would fold under pressure.

When the moment came for her to try the risotto, the world around us faded into a blur. I held my breath, watching as she took the first bite. Her expression was inscrutable, a carefully crafted mask that revealed nothing. The seconds stretched into eternity as her fork

BREAKING THE MOLD

hovered over the bowl, the weight of my hopes hanging on that single moment.

"What do you think?" I ventured, my voice breaking the silence like a knife slicing through tension.

Her gaze flickered up, and I searched for a spark of appreciation, a glimmer of approval. Instead, her lips twisted into a wry smile that sent an inexplicable chill down my spine. "It's certainly... something."

Before I could respond, a commotion erupted from the front of the restaurant. The door swung open, and in rushed a group of people, the clatter of heels and laughter ricocheting off the walls. I barely recognized them at first—our regulars, faces full of anticipation, clutching their phones as if they were holding the winning lottery ticket.

"Did you hear?" one of them shouted, eyes wide with excitement. "The critic is here again! They're going to review the new risotto!"

My heart sank, a boulder crashing into the depths of my stomach. Not just any critic, but the critic—the one who had ripped my dish to shreds just days before. I glanced at Connor, panic etched across his face as we both grasped the enormity of the situation.

Marissa's smile widened as she leaned back in her chair, clearly amused by the unfolding drama. "Well, this just got interesting," she said, her voice laced with mischief.

The atmosphere shifted, the air thickening with anticipation. My fingers tightened around the edge of the countertop, and I took a deep breath, steeling myself for the storm that was about to unleash. We had fought to rise above the ashes, but now we stood on the brink of potential disaster, the scales of fate teetering uncertainly.

Would we rise again, or was this moment about to be our undoing?

Chapter 10: Fire in the Sky

The city below shimmered like a mosaic of fractured glass, each window reflecting the fiery hues of dusk. I could almost hear the laughter and the clinking of glasses wafting up from the patio below, where patrons indulged in the vibrant nightlife, blissfully unaware of the turmoil swirling inside me. "It's just one critic," Connor continued, a hint of impatience threading through his tone. "You know how it is; they're looking for drama, not the truth. Your food speaks for itself."

"Sure," I said, allowing a bitter laugh to escape my lips. "If only it could talk back, then maybe it could defend itself." I glanced sideways at him, hoping to catch a glimmer of the confidence I so desperately wanted to absorb. But his gaze was fixed ahead, the shadow of a smile just brushing his lips as if he were secretly enjoying my internal monologue.

We had danced this dance before, Connor and I. Always hovering on the edges of something unspoken, always too afraid to leap into the unknown. I shifted my weight, the metal of the fire escape vibrating beneath us. It was a balancing act, this fragile equilibrium between our friendship and something deeper, something that made my heart race like the thrum of an electric current.

"It's easy to get lost in the criticism," he said, finally turning to me, his eyes reflecting the last glimmers of sunlight like twin beacons in the gathering dusk. "But look at what you've built. This place is amazing, and people love it."

"Do they?" I shot back, my voice sharper than I intended. "Or are they just pretending to like my food because it's trendy? Maybe they're all just caught up in the hype, and once the novelty wears off, they'll abandon ship."

He raised an eyebrow, the corner of his mouth quirking up in that way that always made my stomach flutter. "So, you're saying your culinary creations are like a Tinder date? One swipe and they're gone?"

"Exactly!" I exclaimed, folding my arms defiantly. "One minute, they're craving my spicy shrimp tacos, and the next, it's all about the newest trendy food truck down the street. My culinary heart can't take it."

"Then stop making it so easy for them to leave. Make it unforgettable." His tone shifted from playful to serious, the intensity in his eyes compelling me to meet his gaze. "Create something that lingers in their minds, something that demands attention. Like that time you experimented with those roasted beet and goat cheese crostinis. They were like little works of art, and you know it."

The memory bubbled to the surface, and I couldn't help but smile. Those crostinis had been a labor of love, each slice of beet meticulously roasted to perfection, the creamy cheese a dreamy contrast. They had sparked genuine conversation, moments of delight around the tables that stretched far beyond mere sustenance. But that was the problem, wasn't it? I had chased those moments, constantly seeking validation through others' tastes.

"Every time I try to create something bold, it feels like I'm walking a tightrope," I admitted, my voice lowering as the weight of my insecurities bore down on me. "One misstep and it's a disaster, and everyone's there to witness the fall."

"Then learn to embrace the fall," he replied, a smile dancing across his lips as if he was inviting me into some secret. "Because it's part of the journey. Besides," he added, nudging me playfully with his shoulder, "I'll be there to catch you. Even if I have to dive into a vat of crème brûlée."

The thought of Connor splashing into a dessert was absurd enough to coax a genuine laugh from me. It was always a reminder that he brought a lightness to my world, a willingness to embrace the chaotic beauty of life.

"Maybe you're right," I said, a spark of determination igniting within me. "I'll show that critic that I'm not going anywhere. I'll make something so ridiculously memorable they won't have a choice but to remember my name."

"Now that's the spirit!" he said, his enthusiasm contagious. "So, what's the plan, Chef?"

I squinted into the horizon, the city unfolding beneath us like an infinite canvas just waiting for bold strokes of color. "How about a twist on classic comfort food? Something nostalgic but with a spin that'll catch them off guard."

"Like?" he prompted, leaning in closer, his excitement palpable.

"Macaroni and cheese," I declared, feeling a thrill race through me. "But not just any mac and cheese. I'll infuse it with roasted garlic and truffle oil, sprinkle in some crispy pancetta, and top it all with panko breadcrumbs for that perfect crunch. It'll be like a cozy hug, but with an edge."

"Now you're talking!" he exclaimed, his eyes sparkling. "You'll turn that critic into a loyal fan faster than you can say 'al dente.'"

As I began to outline my culinary masterpiece, my heart raced not only from the thought of the upcoming challenge but from the way Connor's unwavering support made me feel seen and heard. I could sense the potential swirling around us like an invisible energy, fueling my resolve. And though the night was falling, I felt an undeniable spark igniting within me—a fire that demanded to be shared.

We stood together in that fading light, surrounded by the hum of the city and the promise of possibilities. Connor leaned closer, our shoulders brushing, and I could feel the warmth radiating from him, wrapping around me like a warm embrace. In that moment, I realized that maybe, just maybe, I wasn't alone in this fight. And for the first time, the uncertainty didn't feel so overwhelming; instead, it felt like the beginning of something worth chasing.

The city transformed as the sun dipped below the horizon, each light twinkling to life like a star awakening from slumber. I took a deep breath, letting the scents of roasted garlic and sautéed onions mingle in the air, infusing me with a sense of purpose. "Okay, let's put this into motion," I declared, excitement bubbling within me like the boiling pot of pasta I envisioned in my mind. "I'm going to reinvent comfort food in a way that will make even the most discerning critic weep."

Connor turned to me, his expression a blend of admiration and amusement. "And here I thought we were just going to dive into those tacos again. You really are feeling bold, huh?"

"Just wait until you taste this mac and cheese," I said, punctuating my words with a dramatic wave of my hand. "It will be a culinary love letter, but with a sharp twist that leaves them craving more."

He chuckled, leaning against the railing, his confidence in me radiating like the heat from the kitchen. "Let's see if your love letter can get through the critic's wall of indifference."

"I'll make sure it does," I promised, my determination hardening like the crust of a perfect crème brûlée. "Let's head inside; I have a million ideas buzzing around in my head. And I'll need your taste buds to help guide me."

We hurried down the fire escape, our laughter mingling with the growing symphony of the city below. The kitchen was alive, a chaotic dance of chefs and servers darting back and forth, each focused on their part of the evening's performance. The clanging of pots and pans, the sizzle of ingredients hitting hot oil—it was a rhythm I had come to love.

As I set about gathering ingredients, Connor slipped into the role of my sous-chef, his enthusiasm infectious. "So, what's the first step in your grand culinary opera?" he asked, cracking open a bottle of truffle oil with an exaggerated flourish.

"First, we need to make the béchamel sauce," I replied, my voice brimming with excitement. "The creaminess will be the foundation of this masterpiece. But let's add a layer of roasted garlic to elevate it."

"Roasted garlic? Now we're talking. Nothing says 'I love you' like the lingering scent of garlic." He winked, and I couldn't help but roll my eyes at his dramatics.

We worked side by side, chopping, stirring, and laughing, our movements flowing effortlessly. With each bite of pasta I tasted, I could feel the weight of the review lifting, replaced by a burgeoning sense of pride in my craft. Connor's playful banter filled the space with warmth, as if he were somehow channeling the fiery sunset outside.

"Alright, it's time to add the cheese," I declared, surveying the array of varieties laid out before us. "A mix of sharp cheddar and creamy Gruyère for that gooey factor."

Connor leaned in, his expression mock-serious. "You do realize this is the part where we either create magic or unleash culinary chaos, right?"

"Only if you don't keep your hands steady," I shot back, tossing a handful of shredded cheese his way. "The stakes are high, Connor. Can you handle the pressure?"

He feigned an exaggerated gasp, clutching his chest. "I may not survive this kitchen showdown. But for you, I'd sacrifice my taste buds."

As the macaroni cooked and the sauce thickened, I felt a familiar thrill coursing through me. This was my world, my domain, and I was ready to reclaim my passion. The flames of doubt flickered like embers in the background, but the exhilaration of creation drowned them out.

"Now for the secret ingredient," I said, my eyes twinkling with mischief. "The crispy pancetta. It adds that savory punch that will have them dreaming of this dish long after the plates are cleared."

"Ah, the drama continues," he teased, sprinkling the pancetta with flair. "I can already hear the critic singing your praises."

We both laughed, but there was a tension beneath it, a realization that this wasn't just about the food. It was about standing tall despite the fear of falling. It was about creating a moment that mattered, both in the culinary world and in my own heart.

Once the dish was assembled, I carefully transferred it to the oven, the anticipation making my heart race. "Forty-five minutes and we'll have our masterpiece," I said, tapping my fingers against the counter, my excitement palpable.

While we waited, Connor leaned against the counter, observing me with an intensity that made my cheeks flush. "You know, I've seen you at your best, but tonight feels different. It's like you're on fire."

"Fire in the sky, right?" I quipped, the connection between us electric. "Or is it just the oven heating up?"

"Maybe both," he replied, his voice dropping to a conspiratorial whisper. "But I think it's more than just the cooking. You're passionate about this, and it shows."

Before I could respond, the kitchen door swung open, and in strode our head chef, a whirlwind of authority and energy. "What's this I hear about a culinary showdown?" he boomed, his presence commanding instant attention. "And why am I not invited?"

"Just a little project between me and Connor," I said, trying to keep my tone casual while my heart raced. "I'm reinventing mac and cheese for the next big review."

He raised an eyebrow, clearly intrigued. "I'd love to see what you've come up with. Show me this mac and cheese of yours."

Panic surged through me. This wasn't just the critic; this was the head chef, the gatekeeper of our culinary world. I shot Connor a look, and he nodded encouragingly, as if silently telling me to rise to the occasion.

"Alright, give me a moment," I said, forcing my nerves aside. The oven timer chimed, and I pulled out the bubbling dish, the aroma filling the kitchen, enticing and rich. I plated it with precision, the melted cheese stretching like a delicious tapestry over the crispy pancetta.

"Bon appétit," I declared, placing the dish in front of the head chef, my heart pounding in my chest.

He took a moment, examining it like an art critic before taking a forkful. The kitchen fell silent, the air thick with anticipation. His expression remained inscrutable as he chewed, the tension in the room coiling tighter with each passing second.

Finally, he swallowed and met my gaze, his eyes alight with something I couldn't quite read. "This is...interesting," he said, his tone neutral yet unyielding.

"Interesting?" I repeated, dread pooling in my stomach. "That's it?"

"Interesting can be good or bad," he replied, the corners of his mouth lifting in an enigmatic smile. "But let's see how the rest of the staff feels about it."

As he turned to gather the others, I felt Connor's hand on my back, steadying me. "You've got this," he whispered, his faith in me a lifeline.

But just as the kitchen door swung open again, an unexpected figure stepped in—a familiar face I had hoped to avoid. The food critic, resplendent in her tailored jacket and sharp demeanor, scanned the room, her eyes landing directly on me. My stomach dropped.

"Is this the famed mac and cheese I've heard whispers about?" she asked, her voice slicing through the kitchen's buzz like a knife.

I could only stare, my heart racing. In that moment, I knew my carefully constructed world was teetering on the brink of chaos, the flames of uncertainty licking at the edges. And as her gaze locked onto mine, I realized that everything I had worked for was about to be tested in the most unpredictable way imaginable.

Chapter 11: A Bitter Aftertaste

The kitchen hummed with an electric intensity, the kind that makes you question your sanity as you stand over a stove, flame licking at the edges of your pan like a ravenous beast. The metallic scent of sautéed onions mingled with the sharp aroma of garlic, creating an olfactory symphony that usually filled me with glee. Today, however, it felt more like a funeral dirge, a lament for the once-vibrant atmosphere that had been replaced by a morose silence. Tony's discontent brewed like the espresso he never allowed to over-extract, each moment of tension echoing the grinding gears of a machine on the verge of collapse.

"Why do you insist on letting every little thing get to you?" I finally ventured, my voice softer than I intended, slipping out like a shy guest at a party. "You know what the review said wasn't—"

"Wasn't what? Fair?" Tony shot back, his brow furrowed, deep lines forming like fault lines on his forehead. "It doesn't matter if it was fair or not! It was a blaring siren that announced to the world we've slipped, and I'll be damned if I let this place drown because of one bad service!"

He slammed his hand down on the counter, the clatter of metal echoing through the kitchen like the chime of a judgment bell. I bit my lip, resisting the urge to snap back. Who knew that one review could cause such chaos? For a moment, I considered what might have happened had the critic sampled a different dish, one of our signature creations. But then again, the plate I had crafted with passion—tender, herb-crusted lamb served over a bed of creamy polenta—had been met with silence, the kind that cuts deeper than a well-placed critique.

Connor, my steadfast ally in this chaotic world, leaned against the counter, arms crossed, his brow slightly raised as if daring me to engage further. "How about we focus on making the next dish a showstopper?" he suggested, his voice smooth and calming, like a balm on a raw wound. I appreciated his unwavering faith in my abilities, but today it felt like attempting to kindle a fire in a rainstorm.

"I'm not sure I can even cook up a proper soufflé," I admitted, glancing at the heavy-duty mixer that loomed in the corner. "Every time I step foot in the kitchen, all I taste is bitterness."

"Then don't. Taste something else." Connor stepped forward, his eyes brightening with mischief. "You've got a ton of other flavors at your disposal, and the critics can't take that away from you. Just show them what you're made of, and let the sauce simmer on their opinions."

His encouragement sent a small spark of hope igniting within me, even as I winced at the thought of the review hanging over my head like a dark cloud. I knew I could cook; I'd spent my childhood baking cookies with my grandmother, an experience that left an imprint on my soul. The way her hands moved—each twist of the whisk and pat of dough—created a rhythm that danced in my heart. I didn't want to let that rhythm falter now.

As the shift wore on, I found myself moving through the kitchen with renewed vigor, chopping, sautéing, and plating with a fierceness that came from desperation. I craved redemption. The smell of roasted garlic filled the air, the promise of something magical wafting as I combined ingredients with newfound purpose. I focused on every detail, from the texture of the sauce to the vibrant colors on the plate, desperate to prove that I could rise above the recent disaster.

"Wow, look at you," Connor teased, nudging me as I adjusted the garnish on my latest creation. "Going all Gordon Ramsay on us, are we?"

"Only if I can be the good Gordon, not the one that shouts," I shot back, a playful smile breaking through my earlier gloom. The laughter that followed felt like a burst of sunlight breaking through the murkiness, reminding me of the camaraderie that made this place feel like home.

Just then, the restaurant door swung open, and a familiar face stepped in, the light from the street casting a halo around her. It was Clara, our resident food blogger, and unofficial cheerleader. She was known for her penchant for praising local gems and her almost uncanny ability to sniff out the hidden culinary treasures of the city.

"Hey, kitchen wizards!" she called out, her voice a sweet melody amidst the chaos. "I'm here to see if the rumors about your recent mishap are true!"

Before I could even attempt to mask my dread, Tony straightened up, smoothing his apron as if preparing for battle. "Come in, Clara! You're just in time for something special," he said, his tone shifting, attempting to embrace her warmth.

"Special? I can already feel the delicious vibes in the air!" she chirped, moving closer to where I stood, my hands momentarily frozen over a plate I had just finished.

With Clara's arrival, the atmosphere in the kitchen lightened, a breath of fresh air in an otherwise stifling day. Her enthusiasm was infectious, and as I plated up a dish infused with a sprinkle of creativity, I realized that perhaps today wasn't just about surviving the storm. It was about dancing in the rain.

"Try this," I said, nudging the plate toward Clara, my heart racing. "It's a new take on our classic mushroom risotto, but with a twist of lemon zest and a hint of truffle oil."

Her eyes widened, the glint of genuine excitement sparking there, and I held my breath as she took her first bite. A few seconds passed, a lifetime of anticipation building until finally, her eyes lit up.

"This is divine! It's like a flavor explosion in my mouth!" she exclaimed, the sincerity in her voice washing over me like a soothing wave.

As I watched her enjoy the dish, I could feel the embers of my confidence reigniting. Perhaps it was time to rise from the ashes, time to turn that bitter aftertaste into something sweet. And with Clara's glowing approval, the kitchen buzzed back to life, the laughter flowing like the wine we served. I felt lighter, buoyed by the chance to transform our fate—and maybe, just maybe, it wouldn't be the last laugh after all.

The rhythm of the kitchen resumed, albeit with a new cadence that thrummed with a mix of apprehension and resolve. I lost myself in the steady clinking of utensils and the hum of conversation, clinging to the notion that I could silence the echo of that review with every stir of my spoon and slice of my knife. The faces around me were a mosaic of frustration and expectation, and I could feel their gazes lingering on my back as I moved, as if I were a tightrope walker inching across an unseen chasm.

"Hey, superstar," Connor whispered, sidling up beside me as I poured stock into the simmering pot, steam curling around us like a friendly embrace. "You've got this. Just channel your inner chef and let the flavors do the talking."

"I think I've misplaced my inner chef somewhere between the sauté pan and the cutting board," I replied with a half-hearted grin, but the warmth in his gaze reminded me that I wasn't alone in this.

As the clock ticked closer to service, the door swung open again, and in walked a group of diners, their chatter cutting through the haze of tension. Clara, ever the radiant presence, was at the front, her laughter filling the space as if she were an artist painting vibrant strokes on a muted canvas. My heart fluttered with a mix of anxiety and hope as she made her way to the bar, her enthusiasm infectious.

"Looks like I brought a little crowd with me!" she called out, waving to the staff like a seasoned diplomat rallying her troops. "Hope you've got something special cooking back there!"

The patrons settled into their seats, their chatter rising and falling like the tide. With each passing moment, I felt the weight of expectation grow heavier, as if the atmosphere itself were daring me to rise to the occasion.

"I can't believe how busy it's getting!" I said to Connor, my voice rising above the clamor. "What if we can't deliver? What if we fail again?"

He leaned in, his expression serious but his eyes dancing with mischief. "Then we'll just have to blame it on the weather. After all, it's not your fault if the universe decided to throw a tantrum."

A giggle bubbled up, breaking through my trepidation. The chaos of the kitchen spun around me, and I found myself diving into the orders, each plate a step toward redemption. I plated the risotto with precision, adding a flourish of fresh herbs as if each sprinkle could wash away the ghosts of my recent failures.

Service began, and the kitchen erupted into a whirlwind of shouts and laughter, my heart racing with each order that flew in. I moved fluidly, like a dancer on the stage, lost in the music of sizzling pans and clinking glasses. The tension began to ebb, replaced by a sense of purpose.

"Order up!" I shouted, pushing a beautifully plated dish toward the pass, feeling a thrill of adrenaline surge through me.

"Looking good! You're on fire tonight!" Tony's voice rang out, and for the first time that day, I caught a glimpse of a smile creeping across his face.

Just as the rhythm of the evening settled into a groove, the front door swung open again, and in walked a figure clad in a tailored suit, exuding an aura of confidence that drew every eye in the room. I froze, a mix of curiosity and apprehension flooding through me. He strode toward the bar with purpose, his gaze sharp as he surveyed the restaurant, a knowing smile creeping across his lips.

"What's going on?" I muttered to Connor, who had been standing by the grill, flipping burgers as if they were delicate soufflés.

"I have no idea, but I think we just entered a plot twist," he replied, his eyes glued to the newcomer.

The man approached Clara, leaning casually against the bar, a confident grin lighting up his face. I caught snippets of their conversation, her laughter intertwining with his words like a duet, and something inside me twisted with an inexplicable unease.

"Who is that?" I asked, a note of irritation lacing my tone. "He's got the vibe of someone who's just walked off the cover of a magazine."

"Probably someone important, but don't let it distract you," Connor replied, shaking his head as he focused back on the sizzling pans.

But it was too late; my focus fractured as I watched Clara lean in closer to the man, a playful glint in her eyes. My stomach twisted in knots, and I forced myself to return to the task at hand, plating another dish with unsteady hands.

As the night wore on, the newcomer remained a constant presence at the bar, his laughter echoing through the kitchen like a siren call. Clara seemed enthralled, her attention fully captured, and I couldn't help but feel a strange pang of jealousy twist in my gut.

The orders continued to roll in, but I couldn't shake the feeling that something was off. My usual rhythm faltered, the dishes feeling heavier as I struggled to concentrate. The moment I heard Clara's laughter again, I glanced up, and my breath caught in my throat. The man had taken her hand, holding it with an intimacy that sent an icy dagger straight through my resolve.

"Hey, chef! You okay?" Connor's voice pulled me from my spiral, his brow furrowed with concern.

"Yeah, just peachy," I said, forcing a smile that felt more like a grimace.

But the night turned on a dime. As the last few tables finished their meals, the atmosphere shifted, the din of laughter morphing into a chorus of whispers. I caught sight of the man standing, looking over the bar with a glimmer of mischief in his eyes.

"Hey, kitchen!" he called out, his voice rich and smooth. "Who's in charge of this culinary circus?"

"Don't engage him!" Connor whispered fiercely, a warning in his tone, but I was already stepping forward, compelled by something deep inside.

"That would be me," I declared, summoning a bravado I didn't quite feel as I wiped my hands on my apron and faced him.

"Ah, the chef herself! I must say, I've heard quite a lot about you and your little establishment," he said, a sly smile spreading across his face, revealing just enough charm to keep me on edge.

"Well, I hope it's all good things," I shot back, trying to keep my tone light despite the tension swirling in the air.

"Oh, it's mostly good," he replied, his eyes gleaming with an amused challenge. "Though I wonder what would happen if I reviewed you myself."

My heart raced. "Is that a threat or an invitation?"

His smile widened, and I could feel the weight of every gaze in the room resting on us, anticipation thickening the air. Suddenly, the din of the restaurant faded into a muted backdrop, the world around us narrowing down to just the two of us and that playful smirk.

Before I could respond, Clara bounded up beside him, a mixture of admiration and exasperation dancing in her eyes. "You can't just swoop in here and start making demands! We're trying to enjoy our night, and you're stealing the show!"

"Ah, but isn't that the fun of it?" he countered, his gaze shifting back to me. "Besides, I like a good challenge."

My heart skipped a beat, but just as I opened my mouth to reply, the door swung open again, and a familiar figure stepped inside, their silhouette stark against the ambient glow of the restaurant. It was Tony, and the thunderous silence that followed his arrival felt like a storm brewing on the horizon.

"Are we having a party without me?" he asked, his voice heavy with authority as he approached, the tension in the room thickening with every step he took.

The newcomer straightened, the charming grin replaced by a more serious demeanor. "Just a friendly conversation about food, nothing to worry about."

"Good," Tony replied, his gaze scanning the room before landing on me. "Because we've got work to do."

A chill coursed through me at the edge of his tone, and as he turned back toward the kitchen, I caught the glance between him and the stranger, something unspoken crackling in the air like static electricity.

And just as quickly as the atmosphere had shifted, the door swung open again, but this time, it was a delivery driver holding a large box. "Delivery for the chef!" he called, and I felt a sinking feeling in my stomach as the eyes of everyone in the restaurant turned toward me, the weight of expectations and tensions crashing down as I realized the evening was far from over.

Chapter 12: Ghosts in the Kitchen

The restaurant felt like a forgotten relic, its once-vibrant atmosphere reduced to a ghostly echo of laughter and clinking glasses. As I wiped down my station, the flickering fluorescent lights above cast long shadows, each one whispering secrets of the night. I tried to focus on the task at hand—stacking plates, scrubbing the remnants of someone's half-hearted attempt at a gourmet meal—but my thoughts spiraled into the depths of memories better left buried.

The soft whoosh of the dishwasher behind me was almost comforting, a steady rhythm that drowned out the haunting silence. But as I rubbed at a stubborn stain on the counter, I found myself lost again in the recollection of my father's final days. His face had been a canvas of unspoken apologies, a silent plea for understanding. I could still hear the machines beeping in that sterile hospital room, the smell of antiseptic clinging to my skin as I fought back tears. The regret in his eyes had mirrored my own, a fragile connection severed by stubborn pride and words left unspoken.

"Lena," Connor said, his voice breaking through my reverie like a lifeline thrown into turbulent waters. I glanced up to find him standing there, arms crossed, brow furrowed. His green eyes searched mine with a concern that was both endearing and irritating. I loved that about him—his ability to read me like a book, even the chapters I hadn't written yet. "You've been off all night. What's going on?"

I opened my mouth to brush him off, to conjure some excuse about the chaotic dinner rush or the way the chicken had gone dry, but the truth bubbled to the surface unbidden. "It's...my dad," I finally admitted, the words tasting bitter and foreign on my tongue. "I keep thinking about him. The last time I saw him..."

"What happened?" he asked, gently probing, his expression softening as he leaned against the counter, bringing him closer to my world. The faint scent of lemon and thyme lingered on his apron, a reminder of the evening's specials and the effort we'd both put into them.

I took a deep breath, my heart pounding like a frantic drummer in my chest. "He looked at me like he wanted to say something, but the words just wouldn't come. It was like we were trapped in this moment of silence, both of us scared to shatter it." I let the memories wash over me, a tide of grief that I had tried to ignore. "I thought I'd have more time. Time to make things right, to tell him how much I wanted his approval. How I wanted him to see me, really see me, not just the daughter he had imagined."

"Maybe he saw you more than you realize," Connor said, his voice steady as he leaned closer. The warmth of his presence wrapped around me, shielding me from the cold fingers of regret. "Sometimes, people can't express what they feel, but it doesn't mean they don't care. It's just...complicated."

I swallowed hard, fighting the knot that formed in my throat. "It doesn't feel complicated. It feels like a weight I can't shake." The kitchen lights flickered again, casting erratic shadows on the walls as if even the building was responding to my turmoil. "I thought I could just move on, throw myself into work, distract myself. But it's like he's always there, a ghost haunting my kitchen."

Connor chuckled softly, breaking the tension with a flicker of mischief in his eyes. "Well, if you're going to have a ghost, at least make it a culinary one. I bet he'd whip up a mean soufflé." His lighthearted banter made me smile, the corners of my mouth tugging up despite the heaviness in my heart.

"I wish he had taught me how to cook," I said, the thought bursting forth. "All those years, and he never once let me step foot in the kitchen with him. I remember begging to help, but he'd just shake his head and tell me to focus on my studies. 'Cooking isn't for dreamers,' he'd say. He thought I was wasting my time."

"Maybe he was just scared," Connor suggested, his tone softening again. "You're a dreamer, Lena. You chase after things that scare most people. Maybe he didn't want you to get hurt in a world that doesn't always appreciate ambition."

The insight struck a chord deep within me, resonating like a tuning fork. "But that ambition has cost me so much," I admitted, letting my vulnerability hang in the air between us. "I've sacrificed relationships, even my own happiness, chasing after this ideal of success. And for what? To feel his disappointment more keenly?"

"You're not your father's disappointment," Connor said, his voice steady and strong. "You're not a ghost in his kitchen—you're carving your own path. Don't let his past shape your future."

I looked up, meeting his gaze, and in that moment, I felt a flicker of hope amidst the lingering shadows. Perhaps Connor was right. Perhaps it was time to stop hiding from my father's expectations and start embracing my own journey. The weight of grief still pressed on my chest, but it didn't feel quite so suffocating anymore.

As we stood there, the distant hum of the city outside a gentle reminder of life beyond these walls, I felt the kitchen shift around me. It was no longer just a place of work; it was a canvas for my growth, a stage for my transformation. I was ready to confront the ghosts of my past—not to banish them but to invite them to the table and share a meal.

Connor's eyes narrowed with understanding, as if he could see beneath the surface of my turmoil, peeling back layers I had so carefully constructed. "You know," he said, tilting his head slightly, "it's okay to feel lost sometimes. It doesn't mean you're weak or failing. It just means you're human."

I exhaled a shaky breath, gratitude mixing with frustration. "Human? Right. Tell that to the ghosts that seem to think I'm their personal chef. They don't leave me alone, especially when I'm elbow-deep in prep work. Just last week, I could've sworn I heard my dad's voice reminding me how to chop an onion. As if I needed a refresher course at this point in my life."

He chuckled softly, a rich sound that warmed the cool kitchen air. "At least he chose a useful lesson for a ghost. Just wait until he starts critiquing your plating. Then you'll know he's really watching."

I shook my head, unable to suppress a grin. "I'd be happy to take the feedback if it came with a side of his famous béchamel sauce."

For a moment, the banter pushed the shadows back, and the weight on my shoulders lightened. But the glimmers of joy were brief, like the flickering lights above, battling against the encroaching darkness. "You know what? Maybe you should cook something for him," Connor suggested. "A dish that represents all the things you couldn't say to him. You're a chef, Lena; turn your emotions into flavor. It could be cathartic."

The idea hung between us, tantalizing and terrifying. Could I really channel my grief into something tangible? I glanced at the kitchen, the knives gleaming under the lights like sharp little sentinels waiting for orders. "I could try, but what would I even make? Something like 'Sorry I didn't become a doctor, Dad' soup?"

Connor leaned in, a grin playing at his lips. "You'd have to add a pinch of 'I should have listened to you' salt for authenticity."

I laughed, the sound both a release and an invitation to further explore this newfound idea. "Maybe a 'Just because I'm not a doctor doesn't mean I can't make a killer risotto' dish would be more appropriate."

His smile faded into contemplation. "What would it taste like?"

I pondered for a moment, the gears in my mind whirring to life. "Creamy, rich, maybe a little nutty. The kind that wraps around you like a hug but has just enough zing from fresh lemon to remind you of all the challenges. It needs depth, you know? Just like life."

"Sounds delicious," he replied, his eyes glinting with interest. "Let's do it. Tomorrow, after the lunch shift, we'll gather the ingredients and make your homage to dad."

Just as I felt a spark of excitement ignite within me, the swinging door to the kitchen flew open, and in walked Delia, our head chef and resident hurricane. "You two lovebirds planning a culinary rendezvous without me?" she teased, her voice dripping with playful sarcasm.

Connor straightened, his grin fading into a more professional demeanor. "Just brainstorming some new recipes, Delia."

"Oh really? I hope that includes something that can actually go on the menu and not just 'I wish my father loved me' pasta."

"Hey!" I protested, the warmth from our previous conversation quickly dousing under her playful jab. "I happen to think that's a winning dish."

"Only if you serve it with a side of self-reflection," she quipped, throwing a towel over her shoulder as she surveyed the kitchen chaos. "Look, can we keep the drama to a minimum tonight? We're on the brink of a new menu launch, and I need every able-bodied chef on deck."

"Drama? What drama?" I replied, my voice tinged with faux innocence.

Connor snorted, and I shot him a sideways glance that said, "Let it go." He flashed a smile that seemed to say, "You're not fooling anyone."

Delia rolled her eyes but softened her expression. "Just make sure you're back in line before the next order. And, Lena, keep the ghosts out of the kitchen. I need my staff functioning at full capacity, not haunted by childhood regrets."

"Noted," I replied, raising my hands in mock surrender. As Delia whirled around, her energy sweeping through the kitchen like a summer storm, I felt the ghosts of my past retreating once again. But as the door closed behind her, my thoughts returned to my father, the missed opportunities, the whispers of what could have been.

"Are you really going to do it?" Connor asked, breaking the silence that settled in the wake of Delia's exit.

"Cook something for him? I don't know..."

"Why not? You've got nothing to lose except maybe the tears you'd drown in while you're at it."

His words ignited a sense of determination within me, a flicker of resolve that felt almost new. "Okay, then. Tomorrow, I'm turning my memories into something delicious. But you're helping," I added, jabbing a finger in his direction.

"Absolutely. I'll be your sous-chef, even if it means my knives will be on ghost duty."

As the night wore on and the restaurant quieted, I could almost envision it—a dish steeped in memory, flavor, and a touch of bitterness, served with a side of hope. The mere thought electrified me. I began gathering the remnants of the evening, moving with newfound energy as I arranged the disarrayed tables and cleared the last of the half-finished glasses.

Then, as the last customer slipped out the door, a sharp sound echoed through the kitchen. A clatter that didn't belong. My heart raced as I turned toward the noise, an involuntary shiver racing down my spine. The industrial refrigerator hummed softly, but something else was off, a strange rustling sound emanating from the pantry.

"Connor?" I called out, my voice wavering as I stepped cautiously toward the pantry door.

No answer.

With each creak of the floor beneath my feet, the sense of dread tightened its grip. My instincts screamed for me to turn back, but curiosity and fear wove an intoxicating thread that pulled me closer. I reached for the handle, my fingers trembling as I prepared to confront whatever lay inside.

The door swung open, revealing the dimly lit pantry stacked with ingredients and supplies. At first, it seemed empty, shadows dancing playfully in the flickering light. But then, I caught a glimpse of movement in the corner, a shape that shouldn't be there.

"Connor?" My voice barely rose above a whisper.

The pantry felt alive, vibrating with unspoken secrets and the echoes of the past. My heart raced as I stepped inside, the smell of spices and aged wood swirling around me, both familiar and unsettling. And just as I turned, the flickering light cast a shadow across the floor, revealing the unmistakable outline of a figure, hidden in the corner—a ghost in my kitchen, as real as the pain I thought I had locked away.

"Who's there?" I demanded, my pulse quickening as the figure moved closer, and the air thickened with an inexplicable tension.

Chapter 13: Unraveled Threads

The days blended into a monotony that felt both endless and strangely comforting, like the simmering sauce that bubbled on the stove—a constant hum in the background of my chaotic mind. Each morning, I would step into the restaurant, the aroma of sautéed garlic and fresh herbs swirling around me like an embrace, yet it was an embrace laced with suffocating tension. The kitchen was a symphony of clattering pans and sizzling meats, the rhythm almost hypnotic. I moved through this world as though I were a ghost, tethered to the physical but ever slipping through the cracks of the emotional chaos that consumed me.

Tony had morphed into something sharper, his presence a dagger wrapped in silk. He had always been demanding, but now his criticism flowed like wine at a bad dinner party—too much, too strong, and impossible to avoid. Each remark about my incompetence felt like a splash of cold water, shockingly invigorating yet leaving me shivering and unsettled. "You really think that's how you should be chopping those onions?" he'd say, voice dripping with that sugary condescension that made me want to roll my eyes and retreat into a corner. "Maybe you should try watching the technique again."

Connor, my steadfast anchor in this storm, would catch my eye from across the kitchen, and with a quick, reassuring smile, he would remind me that I wasn't alone. But even his support felt inadequate against the tide of Tony's relentless onslaught. It was as if the man could sense the cracks forming in my facade, and with each pointed jab, he worked to deepen them. I'd spend my breaks pacing the tiny alley behind the restaurant, the scent of day-old trash mixing with the sweetness of blooming jasmine, trying to convince myself that I was stronger than Tony's barbs. But with each day, my confidence felt more like a mirage, receding just as I thought I was reaching it.

And then there was the shadow of my father looming over everything. Connor had become a confidant in my grief, a person with whom I could finally share the weight that had settled on my shoulders since that fateful call. I had thought opening up about him would free me from the shackles of guilt and sorrow, but instead, it felt like laying bare the very essence of my vulnerability. "You can't carry it alone," Connor had said softly, his eyes reflecting a depth of understanding that took my breath away. "Talk to me. Let me help."

I had nodded, tears gathering in the corners of my eyes, and let the words spill out—about my father's illness, the suffocating fear of loss, and the guilt that gnawed at me for the choices I had made. But even with his kindness wrapping around me like a warm blanket, the haze did not lift. Instead, I found myself slipping deeper into a cycle of resentment and despair, a trap woven with the threads of disappointment and unmet expectations.

"Are you going to let him walk all over you like that?" Connor's voice was edged with frustration one evening after another particularly biting comment from Tony. We were cleaning up after service, the clinking of plates and the buzzing of the neon lights casting shadows across the darkened dining room. "You deserve better, you know?"

The fire in his tone lit a flicker of rebellion in me. I turned, leaning against the cool marble countertop, and searched his face for the strength I lacked. "What if I can't get better? What if I'm just not cut out for this?"

"You're smarter than you give yourself credit for," he insisted, leaning closer. "And just because Tony thinks he's a culinary god doesn't mean he gets to dictate your worth. You're talented, and you've got heart." His words wrapped around me like the thick smoke rising from the grill, warm and suffocating, igniting something inside.

But the deeper I sank into the whirlwind of my emotions, the more I noticed the subtle shifts around me. I was becoming aware of the small, insidious ways that Tony's venom seeped into the cracks of my confidence. I found myself second-guessing every decision, even the simplest ones, like whether to add a pinch of salt or a dash of pepper.

Suddenly, the act of cooking—once a passionate dance of creativity and joy—had morphed into a minefield of self-doubt.

One evening, after a long shift, I lingered in the kitchen while the other staff trickled out, their laughter echoing against the walls as they departed. The sound was a reminder of camaraderie I felt increasingly estranged from. Alone, I stood at the stove, stirring a pot of risotto, the creamy consistency beckoning like an old friend. I poured myself into the dish, every stir a plea for validation, each grain of rice a whisper of hope. But as the minutes ticked away, the risotto became a reflection of my spiraling thoughts—clumpy and off-balance, no longer the masterpiece I had envisioned.

Just as I was about to toss it and start anew, Tony appeared in the doorway, his figure silhouetted against the fluorescent lights. "What are you doing?" he asked, his tone surprisingly soft. "You should've cleaned up by now."

"Working on a special," I replied, forcing a smile that didn't quite reach my eyes. "Thought I'd try something different."

He stepped closer, peering into the pot as if he could dissect my failures with the keen eye of a judge. "It looks... interesting. But I wouldn't serve that to anyone if I were you." The faintest hint of a smirk crossed his lips, and my heart sank further into the pit of my stomach. "You need to keep things simple. You're trying too hard to impress."

It felt like he had reached in and twisted the knife, the very thing I had feared all along. In that moment, I realized that it wasn't just my cooking that was under attack—it was my spirit. The delicate threads of my confidence were unraveling, and the more I fought against it, the more I felt like a marionette with fraying strings.

As he turned to leave, the weight of his words hung in the air, thick and suffocating, a tangible reminder of my struggle. But as I stirred the risotto, I made a silent vow. I would not let him win. Somewhere beneath the layers of doubt, a spark still flickered, and I was determined to fan that flame back to life.

Evenings turned into a blur of flickering fluorescent lights and the relentless clang of pots, but beneath the din, a quiet resolve was brewing in me. I had decided that if Tony wanted to cut me down, I would refuse to bend. I began to approach my work with an invigorated focus, each chop of the knife echoing my determination. The culinary world was my canvas, and I wouldn't let it be painted over with his condescension.

"Hey, are you ready to rock the service tonight?" Connor called out as he entered the kitchen, his presence like a burst of sunlight piercing through a dreary sky. He wore an apron with a quirky slogan that read, "Kiss the Cook, But Don't Expect a Meal," a playful rebellion against the serious atmosphere Tony cultivated.

"Ready as I'll ever be," I replied, rolling my shoulders back and letting the warmth of his smile wash over me. "I've got some new dishes I want to test out."

He raised an eyebrow, intrigued. "Is it the risotto again? Because I think the last batch was trying to start a rebellion."

"Ha! No risotto tonight. I'm going with a roasted beet salad and a spiced butternut squash soup. Something to brighten the menu," I said, my excitement bubbling to the surface. It was strange, the way a spark of creativity could shift the air around me, even if just a little.

"Now we're talking! Just don't let Tony get his hands on it, or he'll smother it in something boring like mayonnaise," Connor teased, laughter dancing in his eyes. It felt good to joke, to find lightness in a place that had felt so heavy for far too long.

As the evening unfolded, the restaurant pulsed with energy, the chatter of patrons mingling with the sizzling sounds of the kitchen. I moved seamlessly among the chaos, dishing out plates with newfound confidence. With every compliment from the servers—"This salad is stunning!" "I can't believe how good this soup tastes!"—I felt a piece of that heavy fog lifting, revealing glimpses of clarity and purpose.

But Tony was never far from my mind. I could feel his gaze, sharp and assessing, as I plated each dish. It was like a predator waiting for the moment I'd slip, poised to pounce. I was determined not to let that happen. If he wanted a fight, I'd give him one, armed with my creativity and passion.

Just as the dinner rush reached its peak, a chaotic flurry of orders swept through the kitchen. "Table twelve wants another round of that beet salad!" one of the servers shouted, urgency lacing her voice.

"On it!" I called back, heart racing with adrenaline. I grabbed the vibrant beets, slicing them with a precision I hadn't thought I still had. My mind focused entirely on the rhythm of cooking, blocking out the storm of doubts swirling around me.

In that moment, I was in my element. I had become a conductor, orchestrating a symphony of flavors and textures that could draw in even the most jaded diner. As I reached for the balsamic glaze, a sudden commotion erupted near the entrance, drawing my attention.

I turned just in time to see Tony storming toward me, an unsettling energy radiating from him. "What is this?" he barked, pointing a finger at the salad I was plating. "You think you can just throw whatever together and call it gourmet? That's a joke, right?"

His words were venomous, yet the room felt surreal, as if I were watching a play unfold. "Actually, it's a roasted beet salad, and the reviews have been—" I began, but he cut me off.

"Listen, it's not about what you think it is. It's about what I want it to be. Get back to the basics, or you'll be back at square one. No one here cares about your 'creative flair.'" His voice was low and menacing, an undercurrent that sent a chill down my spine.

For a moment, everything fell silent, the chatter of the restaurant fading into a dull hum. I could feel the weight of the moment pressing down on me, the eyes of my coworkers shifting between us like spectators at a tense drama. I straightened my spine, fighting the urge to shrink back.

"You know, Tony, sometimes the basics aren't enough. People want to taste something new, something real," I shot back, my voice steady despite the tremor in my hands. "If you think a little creativity is too much for this place, maybe you should consider the bigger picture."

His expression shifted, surprise flickering in his eyes before a sneer overtook it. "You really think you're ready for the bigger picture? Newsflash: you're not. You're just a cook with delusions of grandeur."

A bead of sweat trickled down my back as my heart raced. The kitchen felt like it was closing in on me, each breath a struggle as adrenaline flooded my veins. This wasn't just about food anymore; it was about respect, about standing my ground.

Before I could respond, a loud crash echoed from the back of the kitchen, snapping our attention. The door swung open, and a figure stumbled in, eyes wide and frantic. It was Matt, the new dishwasher, his apron splattered with a kaleidoscope of colors.

"Fire! In the storage room!" he gasped, his voice thick with panic.

Chaos erupted. The mood shifted from tense to frantic as the kitchen staff rushed to assess the situation, leaving Tony and me in an uneasy standoff. My instincts kicked in, adrenaline surging as I turned toward the source of the commotion. The faint smell of smoke wafted into the kitchen, a pungent reminder that our world was on the verge of being upended.

"Everyone, stay calm! We need to evacuate!" I shouted, already moving toward the back door, where the flames were beginning to lick up the walls.

In the rush, I caught Connor's eye across the room, his expression mirroring my alarm. He moved to join me, determination etched across his features, but Tony remained frozen, caught between fear and anger.

"We can't just leave!" he barked, but I could barely hear him over the growing roar of the flames. The smoke was thickening, curling into the kitchen like an insidious serpent.

"Move!" I urged, grabbing Connor's arm and tugging him toward the door. There was no time for hesitation. If we were going to get everyone out alive, I had to act fast.

But as I glanced back, Tony stood rooted in place, a conflicted expression on his face. And then, just as I was about to turn away, I noticed something—a glimmer of something in his eyes, a flicker of fear that mirrored my own.

"Tony! Come on!" I yelled, heart pounding as the smoke began to cloud my vision. But he seemed lost in thought, staring at the fire as if it were a reflection of all the battles we had fought, all the words we had exchanged.

As the urgency of the situation escalated, I felt the walls closing in. A part of me wanted to turn back, to pull him from his reverie and into the reality of our situation, but the weight of his anger and disappointment held me back. It was maddening, the way the fire danced behind him, illuminating the lines of tension on his face.

Just then, the lights flickered, and I knew we had mere moments left before all hell broke loose. In that instant, I made a choice, one that might alter everything. "I won't leave you behind!" I shouted, taking a step toward him, but the ground shook beneath us, a warning that time was running out.

The moment stretched like a taut string, and as the flames crackled ominously, I could see the choice etched on Tony's face. Would he follow me, or would he stay trapped in the blaze of his own making? My heart raced, uncertainty swirling like the smoke around us, and I braced myself for whatever would come next.

Chapter 14: A Fork in the Road

The chaos of the kitchen swirled around me, a cyclone of sizzling pans, shouting chefs, and the sharp scent of garlic, mingling with the sweet, stubborn aroma of burnt edges and spilled dreams. Each day was a lesson in resilience, but the lessons had begun to feel like punishment, leaving me raw and frayed at the edges. I could hear the metal clanging against metal, a rhythm that once felt like home but now echoed the relentless urgency of a sinking ship. Tony's voice cut through the noise, an impatient growl that stirred an unsettling mix of nostalgia and dread in my chest.

"Who put the salt in the chocolate mousse?" he shouted, his tone slicing through the air like a chef's knife through overcooked spaghetti. I could see the tension coiling around him, each command wrapped tighter than the last. The young line cooks exchanged uneasy glances, their brows slick with sweat, their enthusiasm dulled under the relentless scrutiny. They weren't just scared of Tony; they were scared of failure, scared of disappointing the man who had taken them under his wing, even if his wing felt more like a storm cloud lately.

I shifted my weight, leaning against the doorframe as I watched the turmoil unfold. My heart thudded in my chest, matching the erratic rhythm of the chaotic kitchen dance. Connor sidled up beside me, his presence a calming force against the backdrop of chaos. "You look like you've seen a ghost," he teased, attempting to draw a smile from the corners of my mouth, which felt as heavy as the lead weight of uncertainty I carried.

"Or maybe I'm just haunted by bad decisions," I retorted, glancing sideways at him. His messy hair and soft eyes offered a refuge amidst the storm. Connor had become my tether in this tumultuous sea, a grounding reminder that I wasn't just a cog in this machine. He leaned in closer, the warmth of his shoulder brushing against mine, a small comfort in the raging tempest.

"Decision time?" he asked, his voice dipping low, a secret shared between us. I could see the concern etching deeper lines on his forehead, a silent plea for clarity.

"Yeah. I can't keep pretending everything's fine," I admitted, my voice trembling slightly. "It's like being stuck in quicksand. The harder I fight, the deeper I sink." The truth of my situation settled in my stomach like an unwelcome guest, reminding me of every late night and early morning, every risk I had taken in the name of a dream that felt increasingly unattainable.

Connor watched me with an intensity that felt almost like an embrace, as if he understood the tempest swirling within. "You have options, you know. It doesn't have to be this way." His words were soothing, but they only deepened the turmoil inside me.

"I don't know if I want to explore those options. What if I fail?" The question hung in the air, thick with the weight of unspoken fears and what-ifs. The thought of walking away from the restaurant was both exhilarating and terrifying, like standing on the edge of a diving board, staring into the unknown depths below.

"Failure is just a step toward finding what really matters. You have to trust yourself," he said, his voice steady, each word a deliberate step toward my heart. It was easy to get lost in his eyes, deep pools of understanding that reflected back all the hopes I'd tucked away.

But Tony's roar cut through our moment, pulling me back into the fray. "Can we please get it together? We can't afford another screw-up tonight!" His frustration ricocheted off the walls, an unwelcome reminder that my indecision was but a small piece of a much larger puzzle that was crumbling under pressure.

I felt the weight of the restaurant on my shoulders. The dreams I'd cultivated alongside the recipes, the laughter echoing through the dining room, the intoxicating smell of a perfect risotto, now felt like memories slipping through my fingers like grains of sand.

"I should probably—" I started, but Connor interjected gently, "You should do what's best for you."

He was right, of course. But the thought of leaving the restaurant felt like leaving a part of myself behind, an act of betrayal against the community we had built. I pictured the faces of our regulars, the joy in their eyes when they took that first bite of a new dish, the connection we fostered through food. Yet, as the tension simmered in the kitchen, I also pictured myself—lost, tired, and unfulfilled.

"Do you think it's possible to love something so much that it becomes toxic?" I asked, my voice barely above a whisper, the question curling in the air like smoke.

"I think it's not just possible; it's common," Connor replied, a flicker of understanding flashing across his face. "But love shouldn't hurt like this."

His words settled over me, a quiet revelation that illuminated the chaos around us. I realized then that love, in all its forms, should uplift, not suffocate. My heart raced as I felt a stirring deep within me, a flicker of hope amidst the uncertainty.

With each heartbeat, the tension in my chest began to shift, reshaping into a realization I could no longer ignore. Maybe the fork in the road wasn't something to dread but an opportunity to carve out a new path. Perhaps it was time to reclaim my voice and find a direction that would lead me back to the joy I had once found in this place.

"Let's talk," I said finally, my voice steady as I turned toward Connor. "I think I need to figure out my next move."

And as the kitchen continued its chaotic dance around us, I felt a surge of determination, a sense of clarity slicing through the fog.

I took a deep breath, the air thick with the scent of garlic and simmering sauces, a once-comforting aroma now tinged with resentment. "I need to see if I can still breathe without it," I said, my voice barely above a whisper. Connor's brow furrowed, the worry etched on his face deepening. He had always been the cautious one, while I'd embraced the heat of the kitchen like a moth drawn to a flame, reveling in the chaos that now felt more suffocating than exhilarating.

"Then maybe you should," he said, his tone firm yet soft, as if trying to cradle my uncertainty. "But you don't have to make that decision tonight. Sleep on it."

"Sleep?" I laughed, a sharp sound that caught even me off guard. "Sleep hasn't been an option since Tony started referring to his spice cabinet as 'the vault.'"

The corners of Connor's mouth twitched, and for a moment, the heaviness in the air lifted. "What's next, a secret code to enter the pantry?" he quipped, his eyes dancing with a mischief that momentarily banished the shadows looming over my thoughts.

"Oh, you'd better believe it. And if we fail to unlock the 'vault' correctly, we're destined to be banished to the 'Dungeons of Dishes.'"

Connor snorted, the tension around us dissolving into laughter. I savored that moment, knowing it was a temporary reprieve from the decisions swirling in my mind like leaves caught in a gust of wind. As we shared a laugh, I felt the warmth of camaraderie envelop us, a fleeting reminder of what had once made this place feel like home.

But the laughter faded too quickly, replaced by a silence thick with unspoken words. I couldn't ignore the gnawing sensation in my gut—the unsettling realization that I was at a crossroads, and one wrong step could lead me down a path I wasn't ready to face.

"I think I need a sign," I confessed, my voice now tinged with vulnerability. "Something to tell me which way to go."

"I'm not sure they make road signs for this kind of thing," Connor replied, his expression serious yet soft. "But maybe it's not about a sign. Maybe it's about trusting yourself."

"Trusting myself is the last thing I'm good at," I sighed, running a hand through my hair, which had begun to frizz from the heat of the kitchen.

"That's a lie," he countered. "You've trusted yourself enough to stand in this kitchen every day, to pour your heart into the dishes, to make it a place people love."

As he spoke, I felt the weight of his words settle over me, like a comforting blanket. But just as quickly, that warmth was pierced by the harsh reality of the chaos unfolding behind me. Tony's voice rose again, escalating into a full-blown rant about the state of the kitchen, and I could almost hear the sound of his dreams crumbling under the pressure.

It was then I noticed the clock hanging above the prep station, its hands inching toward midnight. Time felt both infinite and fleeting, and with every passing second, the urgency of my decision pressed harder against my chest.

"I'll figure it out," I said finally, though I wasn't sure I believed myself. "I just need to see what's out there, what else I'm capable of."

"Just promise me you won't let fear make the decision for you," Connor said, his gaze steady, a tether pulling me back from the abyss of doubt.

"Fear has been my roommate for too long," I admitted with a wry smile. "Maybe it's time for me to kick it out."

We shared a moment of silence, the atmosphere thick with the understanding that change was brewing, waiting to burst forth like the perfect soufflé. But just as I was about to lose myself in that comforting thought, the kitchen door swung open, and Tony stormed in, his face a storm cloud threatening rain.

"Where's the fresh basil?" he barked, eyes scanning the room as if seeking someone to blame.

Connor and I exchanged glances, the playful banter we'd just shared evaporating under the weight of Tony's ire. "It was right next to the tomatoes," Connor said, trying to diffuse the tension.

"Next to the tomatoes? It's always next to the tomatoes! What is it with you people?" Tony shot back, his voice grating against my nerves like fingernails on a chalkboard. I felt my skin flush with irritation.

"Tony, maybe if you took a minute to breathe—" I began, but he cut me off, the sharpness in his tone echoing through the kitchen.

"Breathe? We can't breathe when we're drowning in incompetence!"

His words were a slap, and I felt the anger bubbling up inside me like a pot ready to boil over. "You know what, Tony?" I said, surprising even myself with my boldness. "Maybe it's not just incompetence. Maybe it's you."

The silence that followed was deafening, the kitchen momentarily frozen in time. The cooks glanced at one another, wide-eyed, and Connor shifted uncomfortably beside me.

"Excuse me?" Tony's tone dripped with disbelief, his hands on his hips, daring me to continue.

"You heard me," I replied, a surge of adrenaline pumping through my veins. "You've turned this place into a war zone, and it's suffocating everyone. It's not just about the food anymore; it's about the atmosphere you create."

The tension was palpable, a taut line ready to snap. I could see Tony's face flush with anger, his jaw tightening as he wrestled with my words. This wasn't how I'd imagined our conversation going, but the truth had slipped out like a wayward soufflé, and there was no putting it back.

"Maybe you should take a look in the mirror," he said finally, his voice low and dangerous.

I could feel the kitchen holding its breath, the anticipation wrapping around us like a thick fog. I had crossed a line, and the other side looked dark and daunting.

But before I could respond, the door swung open again, this time revealing a figure silhouetted in the doorway. I squinted into the bright light, my heart racing as I tried to make out the shape. It was someone I hadn't expected to see, someone who would change everything.

The air crackled with an unexpected tension, and just like that, the atmosphere shifted, a new twist in this unfolding story that was about to turn my world upside down.

Chapter 15: The Sound of Breaking Glass

The decision came to a head one night during the busiest dinner service we'd had in weeks. The kitchen was a frenzied symphony of sizzling pans and the rhythmic clatter of utensils, punctuated by the occasional shout from the waitstaff as they relayed orders that came in thick and fast. A fragrant haze of garlic and rosemary hung in the air, wrapping around us like a comforting blanket, yet tension crackled, sharp and electric, beneath the surface.

Tony, our head chef and tyrant wrapped in a chef's coat, had been on edge all night, his temper simmering just below the surface. I watched him through the haze of steam, his brow furrowed, hands moving with the precision of a surgeon, yet his eyes darting like a hawk searching for weakness. I'd never seen him this volatile, but I sensed that the pressure of the service was squeezing him, and the moment one of my dishes returned with a minor complaint—a sauce that was perhaps a shade too thick for the diner's delicate palate—it was like lighting a match to a fuse.

His eruption was instant. "You're not cut out for this," he snarled, his voice slicing through the clamor of the kitchen like a knife through butter. "You're dragging us all down."

His words, jagged and unforgiving, hit me square in the chest, sinking in like a punch to the gut. I stood frozen, the heat of the kitchen suddenly turning ice cold around me. The busy rhythm of service dulled into a distant echo, and I felt the world shrink down to that moment, that accusation. I had poured everything into this job, my passion simmering alongside the sauces I perfected, and now, with a single phrase, Tony was attempting to boil it all down to nothing.

But in that moment, something deep within me snapped. Perhaps it was the bubbling anger that had simmered for too long, or the crushing weight of doubt that had followed me through my shifts like an unwelcome shadow. Whatever it was, I found my voice—raw, unwavering, and loud enough to drown out the chaos around me.

"No," I said, my voice shaking with the heat of anger and frustration. "I'm done." The words rang out, a declaration that felt foreign yet liberating. I slammed the nearest pan down onto the counter, the sound of metal meeting stone erupting into the air like a gunshot, freezing the entire kitchen for a heartbeat.

I could feel the eyes of my coworkers on me—some wide with surprise, others narrowed in judgment—but I didn't care. The adrenaline coursed through my veins, propelling me forward as I stepped closer to Tony, who wore a mask of disbelief that slowly morphed into something darker.

"What did you just say?" he demanded, his voice low and dangerous.

"I said I'm done," I repeated, the fire in my chest igniting anew. "I've had enough of your bullshit, Tony. This isn't just a job for me; it's my passion. But you treat it like a prison yard, where everyone is a potential threat. I'm not going to let you take my joy and twist it into fear anymore."

The room hung heavy with my words, a mix of astonished silence and the faint sound of sizzling pans continuing their work, as if the kitchen itself held its breath. I didn't back down; I couldn't. The thought of leaving this culinary world, this intoxicating place that felt like home, sent a shudder through me, but so did the thought of enduring another shift under Tony's suffocating rule.

His lips curled into a sneer. "You think you can just walk away? You're not ready for this world. It chews you up and spits you out. You're too soft, too fragile."

"Maybe that's what you want to believe," I shot back, the heat of our confrontation igniting an unexpected sense of power within me. "But you've never seen me at my best. You only see the mistakes, the little things that don't matter in the grand scheme of cooking. What matters is the heart you put into each dish, and you wouldn't know anything about that if it jumped up and bit you."

His eyes blazed with fury, and for a split second, I feared I had pushed him too far. But then the weight of the moment shifted, and I realized the truth. I wasn't afraid of him; I was afraid of what I might miss out on by staying. I had dreams that stretched beyond these walls, aspirations that demanded I take risks.

I turned to the rest of the staff, who stood as silent witnesses to our escalating conflict. "If anyone else wants to join me, I'd love the company. But I refuse to stay in a place where my worth is measured by my ability to withstand a verbal onslaught."

Tony opened his mouth, perhaps to deliver another round of vitriol, but a sound came from behind me—a soft, hesitant clapping. I turned to see Marie, one of the prep cooks, a shy smile creeping across her face as she joined in. "You're right," she said, her voice gaining strength. "We deserve to be treated with respect."

One by one, heads began to nod, the tension in the air morphing into solidarity. It was as if the walls of our kitchen had shifted, letting in fresh air, a sense of camaraderie blossoming amidst the chaos.

Tony stood there, mouth agape, as I took a step back, my heart racing not from fear but exhilaration. Perhaps I had just set myself free, breaking the glass that had held me captive for too long. As I turned to leave, I caught a glimpse of my reflection in the stainless steel—a woman transformed, ready to carve her own path in a world that no longer felt daunting but full of possibility.

The moment hung like a suspended note in a song, teetering on the brink of resolution or disaster. The air pulsed with an electrifying mix of shock and liberation. My coworkers stood frozen, eyes darting between me and Tony as if waiting for the aftermath of a storm to reveal itself. The sizzle of pans continued in the background, a stubborn reminder that life, and dinner service, went on. But for me, time had stalled.

Tony's face twisted into a grimace, his eyes narrowing into slits that promised retribution. "You think this is a game? You think you can just walk away from this kitchen, from us? You don't even know what it means to be dedicated!"

"Dedicated?" I shot back, my voice rising in pitch, fueled by a sudden clarity that burned through my earlier doubts. "You mean dedicated to being treated like a punching bag? This isn't dedication; it's toxic. You can't expect respect from us when you don't show it."

A fleeting moment of uncertainty flickered across his face, but he quickly masked it with indignation. "You think you're the first to challenge me? I've seen plenty of aspiring cooks crumble under pressure. You'll be no different."

"Is that a challenge or just a sad attempt to scare me?" I smirked, relishing the surprise etched on his features. The momentum was shifting; I could feel it. "Because I'm not going to crumble. I'm going to grow."

"Grow?" he scoffed, the sound dripping with disdain. "Where will you go? What will you do? You're a dime a dozen in this city."

"Perhaps," I replied, taking a breath to steady my racing heart. "But every dime can be turned into a dollar, and I'm not just going to sit here while you try to grind me down."

With that, I turned away from him, my heart pounding like the beat of a drum in my ears. I had no plan, no safety net, but I could feel my courage building with each step. I had carved out a niche for myself here; I had poured love and energy into every dish, every ingredient, and now it was time to take that energy elsewhere.

As I slipped through the kitchen doors into the night, the familiar sounds of clanging pans and sizzling meat faded behind me. The cool night air wrapped around me like a comforting embrace, and I felt lighter, buoyed by a rush of adrenaline and the thrill of uncertainty. I was free—at least for the moment.

The city stretched before me, its pulse thrumming like a heartbeat, the lights twinkling like stars fallen to Earth. I wandered aimlessly, seeking solace in the vibrant energy of the streets, feeling as though I could finally breathe without the weight of Tony's toxic shadow looming overhead.

Lost in thought, I turned a corner and stumbled upon a small café, its warm glow spilling out onto the sidewalk, inviting and full of life. The sound of laughter wafted through the open door, a melody of familiarity that tugged at my heart. I hesitated, the thought of stepping into a place that promised warmth and camaraderie pulling me in.

Inside, the atmosphere buzzed with a delightful mix of clinking cups and animated conversation. I scanned the room, noting the eclectic crowd: a couple sharing a slice of decadent cake, a group of friends huddled over steaming mugs, and a lone figure in the corner, lost in the pages of a thick novel.

As I walked to the counter, a friendly barista greeted me with a bright smile, the kind that felt like sunshine breaking through clouds. "What can I get for you?"

"Just a coffee, please," I replied, grateful for the normalcy of the exchange.

As I waited, I caught a glimpse of my reflection in the shiny espresso machine—hair slightly askew, cheeks flushed from the intensity of my earlier confrontation. I almost laughed at the sight of myself, a culinary warrior stepping out of the chaos and into the light.

"Here you go!" the barista chimed, handing me a steaming cup. "It's a house blend; it'll kick you into gear."

I took a sip, the rich flavor enveloping my senses, grounding me in the present. Just as I was about to find a corner to sit and reflect, a voice from the other side of the counter drew my attention.

"Is that a new look for the kitchen's resident rebel?"

I turned, surprised to see Jake, a fellow chef from my old workplace, leaning casually against the counter. His dark hair was tousled, and his signature grin was as charming as ever, making it impossible for me to remain irritated.

"I wouldn't say rebel," I replied, rolling my eyes. "More like... emancipation."

"Ah, the sweet taste of freedom," he teased, leaning in closer. "You don't know how good it is to see someone finally take a stand against Tony. He's been running that place into the ground for ages."

"Glad I could provide some entertainment," I quipped, but beneath the surface, a thrill of uncertainty danced in my stomach. "What brings you here? Didn't you work the late shift?"

"Just finished up and thought I'd grab a drink before heading home. It's nice to see you out in the wild, so to speak." His eyes sparkled with mischief. "You do know there's a whole world outside that kitchen, right?"

"More than you know," I said, taking a deep breath, emboldened by the conversation. "I'm exploring my options."

"Is that so? You've got talent, and I can't help but think the right kitchen could really use you."

"Do you have one in mind?"

The corner of his mouth quirked up. "Maybe. But I wouldn't want to steal you away too soon. I think you might still be worth a few more showdowns with Tony."

"Let's not get carried away," I laughed, feeling the tension of the night start to ease. But as I glanced around the café, a shadow slipped through the door, catching my eye. My heart raced when I recognized the figure striding in—a figure I'd hoped to avoid for a long time.

Tony stood at the entrance, scanning the room, his expression a mixture of anger and disbelief. Our eyes met, and in that instant, the air crackled between us, thickening with unresolved tension.

"Uh-oh," Jake said, his tone shifting. "Looks like your emancipation might be short-lived."

I couldn't move, the weight of the confrontation I'd left behind pressing against my chest as I braced for the inevitable clash. The thrill of newfound freedom collided with the dread of facing my past, and in that moment, I was trapped between two worlds—one promising growth and possibility, and the other steeped in control and fear.

The café buzzed on around me, oblivious to the storm brewing in the corner, and I knew then that whatever came next would either seal my fate or set me truly free.

Chapter 16: A Leap into the Unknown

The neon lights flickered like erratic fireflies, illuminating the cracked pavement beneath our feet. The hum of traffic blended with distant laughter, creating a symphony of chaos that oddly soothed my frayed nerves. Connor's brow was knitted in worry, but I could see the flicker of admiration in his gaze, as if I'd just performed some daring stunt instead of merely stepping away from a table of half-hearted conversation and stale ambitions.

"What did you say to him?" he asked, stepping closer, the warmth of his body a grounding force against the chill of the night.

"Nothing that mattered," I replied, brushing a loose strand of hair behind my ear. The scent of grilled cheese wafted from the diner across the street, but my appetite had vanished along with the weight of my confession. "Just... it was all so predictable. I didn't want to spend another evening rehearsing lines for a play I never auditioned for."

Connor's mouth quirked into that half-smile that made my heart race and my stomach flutter. "So, you decided to go off-script? Brave move."

"Or foolish," I admitted, shoving my hands deep into my pockets, my fingers brushing against the cool metal of my keys, grounding me. "But if I stay in that life any longer, I might forget who I am entirely. And I can't let that happen."

The city breathed around us, a pulsating organism filled with stories, dreams, and regrets. I could feel the energy of it seeping into my bones, igniting something deep within. Connor leaned against the brick wall of the building beside us, his eyes glimmering with mischief. "You know, for someone who just walked away from a dinner with the future of her career, you look a bit too... happy."

I laughed, the sound bubbling up like champagne, bright and effervescent. "Am I not allowed to be happy after making a life-changing decision?"

"Sure, but you might want to rethink that choice if you want to avoid the rabid horde of professionals who will chase you down the street. There's a certain thrill in knowing you've sparked something in the middle of a city that's otherwise busy drowning in its own expectations."

As I gazed at him, a realization hit me like a lightning bolt. This wasn't just a moment of courage; it was an invitation to embrace the unknown. The prospect of not knowing what came next filled me with both dread and exhilaration. "What if I fail?" I asked, my voice barely above a whisper.

Connor shrugged, his demeanor casual, yet his eyes betrayed a flicker of understanding. "Failure is just a plot twist in your story. You can't have an interesting book without a few unexpected turns, right?"

"Right." I studied him, the way his hands were shoved into the pockets of his jacket, how the faintest hint of a smirk danced on his lips. He had a knack for simplifying life's complexities into digestible morsels, and for that, I adored him even more. "And what about you, Mr. Expert on Plot Twists? What's your next move?"

He paused, the smile fading slightly, and I could almost see the gears turning in his mind. "Honestly? I'm trying to figure that out. I'm stuck between what's expected of me and what I actually want. It's a pretty cramped space."

"Want to break out together?" I proposed, the words tumbling out before I could catch them.

"What did you have in mind?" His curiosity piqued, the playful glint returning to his eyes.

"Maybe we should take a road trip. Just us, no plans, no itinerary—just a map and our ridiculous taste in music."

"Road trip?" His tone was incredulous, but I saw the spark ignite behind his brown eyes. "You really are jumping off the deep end, aren't you?"

I nodded, feeling the pulse of my heart echo the rhythm of my adventurous spirit. "I need to feel alive again. It's time to escape this predictable script. How about it? What's stopping us?"

"I mean, besides the fact that I don't have a car and can barely keep my plants alive?"

"Details, details," I teased, shoving him playfully. "But seriously, we can figure it out. I'm tired of waiting for life to happen when I can just... make it happen."

He studied me, a silent conversation passing between us. I could sense the cogs in his mind turning, the tension of possibility hanging in the air like an unfinished symphony. "Okay," he finally said, his voice steady. "I'm in. But we have to pick the music."

"Deal," I replied, a rush of exhilaration washing over me. "And I get the aux cord first."

We shared a laugh that echoed through the empty street, the sound weaving itself into the fabric of the night, binding us in this moment of shared spontaneity. As we stood there, illuminated by the kaleidoscope of city lights, I realized that this wasn't just a leap into the unknown—it was a leap toward rediscovery, an opportunity to redefine our paths.

A sense of hope flickered in my chest, mingling with the adrenaline coursing through my veins. For the first time in ages, I felt ready to embrace whatever chaos life threw my way. With Connor by my side, the future seemed limitless, and the notion of freedom transformed from a distant dream into an exhilarating reality.

As the laughter and chatter from the restaurant faded behind us, the urban night wrapped us in its cozy embrace, alive with the distant blare of horns and the smell of street food that lingered like a friendly ghost. I took a deep breath, inhaling the mix of exhaust and fried dough, letting it fill my lungs and drown out the remnants of stale conversation still echoing in my mind.

"Let's go," I declared, more to myself than to Connor. "Let's take that road trip."

"Now?" He raised an eyebrow, a smirk dancing on his lips as if I had just suggested we swim with sharks. "You want to leave right this second? You do realize it's nearly midnight, and I don't think my car can handle the weight of your spontaneous enthusiasm."

"Your car can handle anything," I replied, shoving him lightly. "Besides, I'd rather be careening down the highway than drowning in that same old routine."

He sighed dramatically, yet the glint in his eyes told me I had ignited something. "Alright, let's find your 'freedom.' But you owe me a strong coffee for the impending sleep deprivation."

With that, we wandered toward the diner, its neon sign flickering like a tired eyelid. The inviting glow promised warmth and the essential caffeine needed for our impromptu adventure. As we stepped inside, the bell above the door jingled, announcing our arrival in a way that felt both mundane and magical. The air was thick with the aroma of coffee brewing and bacon sizzling, a combination that felt like home, yet tantalized with the promise of something more.

We slid into a booth by the window, the faux leather cracked and worn, echoing stories of late-night meals and whispered dreams. I perused the menu, my excitement bubbling like the soda in my glass. "Alright, what's our fuel for this trip?"

"Triple espresso," he replied, glancing over the menu with a serious expression, "and a side of the diner special. We'll need all the energy we can muster."

"Good choice, Captain Responsible." I teased, biting my lip to suppress my laughter. "And how do you plan on packing for this spontaneous journey? I mean, we can't just run off without some essentials, right?"

He leaned back, considering. "Essentials? Well, I'll need my phone charger, a hoodie that smells like adventure, and... your delightful company, of course."

"Flattery will get you everywhere," I shot back, rolling my eyes playfully. "I think I can manage a few things too—my trusty water bottle, a playlist that will be the soundtrack to our rebellion, and a large bag of gummy bears for emergency sugar rushes."

"Can't forget the gummy bears," he agreed, chuckling as our orders arrived. The coffee was dark and rich, the perfect antidote to our growing excitement.

We sat in companionable silence, sipping our drinks and sketching out vague plans. My mind raced with images of open roads, forgotten towns, and late-night adventures where our laughter could fill the voids left by uncertainty.

"Have you ever done something this reckless before?" Connor asked, his tone half-serious, half-joking.

"Reckless? Well, there was that time I tried to eat an entire pizza by myself during a movie marathon," I quipped, feigning deep thought. "But if we're talking about real recklessness, then no. This feels like the most daring thing I've done in ages."

"Then we're officially reckless adventurers," he declared, raising his coffee cup in mock salute. "To us, the bold explorers of the unknown!"

I clinked my cup against his, and for a moment, everything felt possible. The world outside the diner seemed to blur, and I allowed myself to dream of possibilities that had long felt out of reach.

After finishing our meal and giddy with caffeine, we strolled outside, the cool air brushing against our faces like a refreshing reminder of our new path. As we headed toward his car, I noticed a small, bright shop across the street—a thrift store, its windows crowded with a colorful array of vintage clothes and quirky trinkets.

"Let's check that out," I said, pointing. "You never know what treasures we might find."

"Only if you promise not to spend all our travel funds on a neon lava lamp," he shot back with a grin. "Though, I have to admit, that would be quite the conversation starter."

Inside, the shop was a treasure trove of memories and oddities. I ran my fingers along the racks of clothes, savoring the textures and colors. A sequined jacket caught my eye, glinting in the low light. I pulled it out, holding it up to Connor, who feigned shock.

"Do I look like a disco ball?" I asked, spinning dramatically.

"More like a very stylish disco ball," he replied, stifling a laugh. "If we're going to hit the road, we might as well do it in style."

After a few more minutes of exploring and more than a couple of questionable fashion choices, I found an old Polaroid camera hidden among the dusty shelves. It was like finding a piece of my childhood—something raw and real, full of potential for capturing moments.

"I'll take this!" I declared, clutching it to my chest like a prize.

Connor grinned, his eyes sparkling with encouragement. "That's the spirit! Now we can document all our reckless escapades."

We stepped back into the cool night air, my heart fluttering with excitement as I imagined the snapshots we would create. The stars above were twinkling, each one a reminder of the countless stories waiting to unfold, but just as we began to head toward the car, I spotted a shadowy figure lingering near the alleyway beside the store.

The hair on my arms prickled. Something about the figure felt off, like a dark cloud obscuring our radiant adventure. I turned to Connor, my voice dropping to a whisper. "Do you see that?"

He squinted in the dim light, his expression shifting from carefree to cautious. "Yeah, let's keep moving."

But before we could take another step, the figure stepped into the light—a woman, wild-haired and wearing a tattered jacket, her eyes wide and frantic.

"Help! Please!" she cried, her voice cutting through the night.

My heart raced as she stumbled toward us, desperation etched on her face. This wasn't how our night was supposed to go. Our road trip was meant to be filled with laughter and freedom, not this chaos. But as

I looked into her eyes, I realized that sometimes, the unexpected twists were the ones that truly defined our journey.

"Please, you have to help me!"

Chapter 17: New Beginnings

The morning sun streamed through my bedroom window, casting a golden hue across the scattered remnants of my past life—crumpled receipts, a half-drunk mug of coffee, and a vibrant poster of a long-lost band that had once inspired my dreams. I stretched languidly, the soft cotton sheets tangled around my legs like affectionate vines, and for the first time in ages, I allowed myself to breathe deeply. Today was different. I could almost hear the city humming beneath me, a symphony of hope and possibility, each note vibrating with the potential of a fresh start.

As I prepared for the day, I relished the mundane rituals—the sound of water bubbling in the kettle, the aroma of toasting bread mingling with the crisp morning air, and the raucous laughter of children playing outside, unaware of the complexities of adulthood that loomed like shadows over their innocence. I grinned at my reflection in the mirror, a stubborn curl falling rebelliously over my forehead. "Today is yours," I whispered, feeling a flicker of confidence ignite within me.

I stepped outside, the chill of early autumn wrapping around me like a snug scarf. The streets were alive, each corner thrumming with life. I walked to my favorite café, a quaint little spot with mismatched furniture and the kind of barista who remembered my name. The scent of freshly ground coffee danced through the air, teasing my senses as I entered. "The usual?" asked Nora, her eyes bright with mischief.

"Make it a double. I need the courage," I replied, laughing as I leaned against the counter.

Nora raised an eyebrow, a playful smirk curling at the corners of her mouth. "Courage for what? Another risky life choice? I'm beginning to think you thrive on chaos."

"Maybe I do," I shrugged, savoring the rich, warm brew she slid toward me. I took a sip, feeling the familiar jolt of caffeine swirl through me, nudging my spirits higher. "Or maybe I'm just trying to find my way in a world that feels like it's spinning out of control."

She nodded, her expression softening. "You'll find it, you know. Just keep your heart open."

With a wave, I headed to the small park nearby, a hidden gem lined with trees that whispered secrets in the breeze. I settled on a weathered bench, the wood cool beneath me, and opened my notebook, the pages blank and inviting. Words began to spill out, tracing the contours of my thoughts—the fears, the dreams, and the maddening uncertainty that had once anchored me. I scribbled about new beginnings, the thrill of the unknown, and the tantalizing thought of starting over.

It was in this moment, lost between ink and imagination, that my phone buzzed. Connor's name lit up the screen, a warm reminder of our late-night conversations and the laughter that felt like sunlight breaking through clouds. "So, what's the plan?" he asked, his voice smooth and steady.

I laughed, the sound bubbling up unexpectedly. "I have no idea."

"Excellent," he replied, a hint of mischief lacing his tone. "That means the world is your oyster, right? Or maybe your bagel with extra cream cheese."

"Only if it's from that deli on Fifth," I teased, glancing at a couple nearby who were sharing a pastry, their laughter infectious. "But really, Connor, I've been thinking—maybe it's time for me to explore something entirely new. Open my own place or, I don't know, take a leap into the unknown."

There was a brief silence, the kind that felt charged with anticipation. "That sounds... liberating. Do you have a plan for that leap?"

I could hear the smile in his voice, the encouragement wrapping around me like a warm blanket. "Not a solid one, but I've got some ideas simmering. I might even look into the local art scene—maybe I could host workshops or something."

"You'd be great at that. You have this knack for bringing people together," he replied, and I could almost picture his encouraging nod. "What kind of workshops? Paint and sip? Maybe a crash course in existential dread?"

"Very funny. But really, something about creativity and expression. Maybe teach people how to let loose and embrace the chaos." I found myself leaning into the idea, the words flowing like warm honey. "I could call it 'Creating Calm Amidst the Chaos.'"

"Now that sounds like a hit," he said, laughter in his voice. "And I can already picture the crowd—artsy types, frazzled souls looking for inspiration. You could charge them a ridiculous amount, and I'll help you count the cash."

"Ha! You think I'd share that with you?" I feigned indignation, but my heart soared at the thought of not just surviving but thriving. "Maybe I'll have to find a sidekick with a cute smile and an excellent sense of humor."

"Good luck finding one. Those are rare," he shot back, the teasing lilt in his tone igniting a spark of affection I hadn't anticipated.

As we continued to talk, my mind whirred with ideas, possibilities blooming like wildflowers in spring. Each suggestion, each shared laugh, propelled me further into this vibrant new world I was tentatively stepping into. There was a thrill in the uncertainty, a promise of freedom that felt intoxicating.

As I hung up the phone, I looked up at the brilliant blue sky, the clouds drifting lazily, embodying the carefree spirit I longed to embrace. Today wasn't just a day; it was the beginning of everything. With my heart racing and my notebook filled with dreams, I stood up, ready to chase them down one step at a time.

I wandered through the park, the leaves crunching beneath my feet like confetti celebrating my newfound resolve. The air was crisp, hinting at the approaching chill of winter, but today felt imbued with a warmth that was all my own. I could feel the pulse of the city around me, a heartbeat filled with opportunity and promise, the vibrant energy coursing through every street, café, and corner.

With Connor's encouraging words still dancing in my mind, I made my way toward a community center that had always intrigued me. The old brick building stood proudly, its windows glinting in the sunlight like gems. I could picture it brimming with life—classes in art, cooking, and self-discovery. My heart raced at the thought of transforming this space into my sanctuary, a hub for creativity and connection.

As I approached, I spotted a small sign announcing an open house that afternoon. My curiosity piqued, I decided to venture inside. The moment I crossed the threshold, a wave of nostalgia washed over me, the scent of paint and wood mingling with the warm undertones of cinnamon from a nearby bakery. The large room was filled with folding chairs, some already occupied by enthusiastic faces, each one buzzing with anticipation.

"Welcome! We're glad you're here!" A woman with vibrant purple hair and an infectious smile greeted me, extending her hand as though we were long-lost friends. "I'm Mia, the center's coordinator. Are you interested in one of our classes?"

"I might be," I replied, the warmth of her enthusiasm catching me off guard. "I'm actually thinking about hosting my own workshops here. Something focused on creativity and finding calm amidst the chaos."

"Fantastic idea!" she exclaimed, her eyes lighting up. "We've been looking for fresh programs to offer. Come on in, the more, the merrier!"

As I settled into a chair, I couldn't help but overhear snippets of conversation from a group of artists discussing their latest projects, each word dripping with passion. The discussions felt like a warm embrace, pulling me into their world. I found myself leaning closer, eager to soak up every detail.

"Do you ever wonder if art is just a way to distract ourselves from the chaos?" one artist pondered aloud, her voice thoughtful.

"Maybe it's more than that," another replied, their tone light yet contemplative. "Perhaps it's a way to make sense of the chaos. A little slice of order in the madness."

Their words sparked something deep within me. Here, in this building filled with creativity and raw emotion, I realized that this was the perfect space for my vision to flourish. As the discussions unfolded, I felt my own ideas coalesce, the anticipation of bringing my workshops to life becoming a tangible reality.

Later, I approached Mia, my pulse racing with excitement. "I'd love to collaborate with you. Maybe start with a trial workshop to see how it goes?"

"Let's do it!" she said, her enthusiasm palpable. "How about we schedule something for next month? I can help you with promotions and set everything up."

As we discussed potential dates and themes, I could hardly contain my glee. The world felt alive with possibility, and for the first time in what felt like ages, I could see a future shimmering on the horizon.

After the open house, I decided to treat myself to a slice of cake at that bakery I'd been smelling all afternoon. The café was cozy, its walls lined with cheerful artwork that seemed to echo the laughter of patrons indulging in sweet delights. I slid into a corner table, cradling a steaming mug of tea and my slice of lemon cake, the tartness perfectly offsetting the sweetness.

"Excited about something?" a voice broke my reverie, and I looked up to see a tall guy with tousled brown hair and a smirk that could charm the stars down from the sky. He leaned against the counter, a napkin in hand, as if he'd been caught red-handed admiring the dessert display.

"Just plotting my takeover of the art world, one workshop at a time," I replied, raising an eyebrow, the wry humor slipping easily from my lips.

"Bold move," he said, grinning. "I'm Sam, by the way. I like to think of myself as a connoisseur of cake and chaos. Mind if I join you? Your ambitions sound far more interesting than my average afternoon."

I gestured for him to sit, curiosity piqued. "What do you usually do?"

"Oh, you know, the usual—trying to find meaning in life while sampling every cake I can get my hands on," he quipped, sliding into the chair opposite mine. "But seriously, I'm a freelance graphic designer. I do a lot of branding for artists and local businesses."

"Sounds exciting. Any wild tales of chaos in the art world?" I leaned in, intrigued.

"Just last week, I accidentally mixed up a client's branding colors with those of a donut shop," he chuckled. "Let's just say that the campaign for a serious art exhibit ended up looking like a sugary sweet advertisement for sprinkles."

Laughter erupted between us, and the vibrant energy of our conversation began to fill the small space. It felt effortless, each quip building upon the last, the playful banter weaving us closer together like the threads of a tapestry. As we exchanged stories of our creative misadventures, I found myself wishing that this moment could stretch on forever, that perhaps this sweet slice of chance could become a new beginning for more than just my career.

But as the sun began to set, casting long shadows across the café, my phone buzzed again, this time with a message that froze my laughter in my throat. The words, terse and urgent, sent a chill racing down my spine: We need to talk. It's about your past.

The warmth of the moment evaporated, replaced by a cold grip of anxiety. I glanced up at Sam, whose easy smile faltered as he sensed the shift in my demeanor. The room suddenly felt smaller, the air heavier.

My thoughts spiraled into a chaotic whirlwind, the sweetness of the cake turning bitter on my tongue. I realized that while I was ready to embrace new beginnings, shadows from my past were not yet ready to let me go.

Chapter 18: A Taste of Freedom

I navigated the city streets like a wanderer rediscovering a long-lost love. The air was thick with the scent of roasted coffee beans mingling with the sweet, tantalizing aroma of fresh pastries wafting from a nearby bakery. I felt alive in a way I hadn't in years. Each step felt lighter, each corner I turned an invitation to possibility. The sun poured over me, bright and unyielding, chasing away the shadows of my former life—one I had clung to far too tightly for comfort.

Connor ambled beside me, a silent anchor, his presence as steady as the rhythm of the city. I caught glimpses of his profile as we strolled past storefronts, his brow furrowed in thought. I wondered if he was contemplating the same future I was, imagining a world where our dreams intertwined like the thick vines climbing the wrought iron balconies above us. I could feel his energy, a vibrant hum that seemed to sync perfectly with my newfound freedom.

We stopped at a food truck parked by the corner of the park, a bright red beacon of creativity against the backdrop of mundane lunchtime fare. "What do you think?" Connor asked, tilting his head towards the menu scrawled on a chalkboard in playful, colorful lettering.

"I think," I began, tapping my chin thoughtfully, "that their pulled pork tacos could use a splash of something unexpected—maybe a pineapple salsa? Or what if we added a drizzle of chipotle aioli?"

Connor raised an eyebrow, a smirk dancing on his lips. "Look at you, getting all chef-y on me. What's next, starting a blog called 'Tacos and Dreams'?"

"Don't tempt me," I said, feigning seriousness. "I'll be the taco queen of the internet, and you'll be my loyal sous-chef, documenting all my culinary misadventures."

He laughed, the sound warm and infectious. "As long as I don't have to wear a silly apron with ruffles, I'm in."

The laughter hung in the air like the scent of grilling meat, grounding me. It was in moments like this, amidst the playfulness, that I could almost touch my dreams. With each bite of the taco—sweet, tangy, smoky—I felt a pulse of inspiration, a reminder of the vibrant flavors that had once danced in my kitchen.

As the sun dipped lower in the sky, we wandered deeper into the heart of the city, our conversation shifting from tacos to the business I envisioned. "Imagine a place that feels like home," I said, my hands gesturing wildly as I spoke. "A little eatery where every dish tells a story—family recipes and local ingredients, maybe even a rotating menu inspired by the seasons. I want it to feel alive."

Connor listened, a soft smile playing on his lips as I painted my dreams with the fervor of an artist before a blank canvas. "You're going to need a plan, you know. Dreaming is one thing; executing is another."

"I know," I admitted, the weight of reality settling slightly on my shoulders. "I've been doing my research, looking into what it would take. I want it to be more than just a restaurant; I want it to be an experience."

His eyes sparkled with encouragement. "You've got the passion, and I've seen you turn a plate of nothing into something magnificent. It's like you sprinkle magic into your dishes."

"I think I just have a knack for knowing what flavors work together," I replied, a hint of modesty creeping into my tone. "But it's also about connecting with people, you know? Creating a space where they feel welcome, like they belong."

As we strolled along the riverbank, the twilight sky shimmered like melted gold, reflecting on the water's surface. The light seemed to dance, and I felt a surge of courage rising within me. "What if I host pop-up dinners? Just to test the waters, see if people like what I create?"

Connor's brows furrowed in concentration. "That could work. It's low-risk and gives you a chance to experiment. You could gather a few friends, maybe some locals, and see how they respond."

"Exactly! I can start small," I said, excitement bubbling in my chest. "I could use my apartment. It's cozy, and I can set the mood with candles and soft music. It'll be like a dinner party, but with a focus on the food."

His eyes widened, a glimmer of pride shining through. "Now that sounds like a night to remember. Plus, who wouldn't want to eat a home-cooked meal in a cozy apartment with the promise of something special?"

"Right?" I felt a thrill race through me. This was it—the spark I had been searching for, igniting my passion and transforming it into action. "And I could use it as a way to gather feedback. What dishes do they love? What would they change? It's a learning experience."

I could see the wheels turning in Connor's mind, and I loved that he was in this with me, not just as an observer but as an active participant. "You're a natural, you know that? It's like you were born to cook. Just be prepared for the inevitable mishaps. Remember that time you tried to flambé dessert and nearly set my kitchen on fire?"

"Hey, that was a learning experience!" I retorted, laughing as I recalled the charred remnants of what was supposed to be a show-stopping dessert. "I'll have a fire extinguisher ready this time."

Our laughter echoed along the river, weaving itself into the fabric of the moment, and I felt a warmth spread through me, wrapping me in hope. As we continued walking, I realized that this moment was more than just an idea bubbling to the surface; it was a promise I made to myself. I would dive headfirst into this world of culinary dreams, and with Connor by my side, I felt ready to face whatever came next.

The sun dipped beneath the horizon, painting the sky in shades of pink and orange, as we finally settled on a park bench, our legs swinging lightly above the ground. Connor, his hands casually tucked behind his head, gazed up at the sky as if searching for answers in the clouds drifting by. I took the moment to appreciate how easy it was to be around him—his presence was like the comfortable old couch you never wanted to part with.

"What do you think we should call this little pop-up of yours?" he mused, turning his head slightly to catch my eye.

I chewed on my lower lip, the gears in my mind whirring with possibilities. "How about 'Tasteful Escapes'? No? Too pretentious?"

"Maybe just a tad," he replied, chuckling. "What about something that hints at adventure, like 'Wanderlust Bites'?"

"That's not bad!" I felt a grin spreading across my face. "But what if we went for something a little more…personal? Like 'A Taste of Home'?"

His brow furrowed slightly. "I like it, but are you ready to open up like that? What if people expect something sentimental?"

"Everything I cook has a piece of my heart in it," I said, my voice steady. "That's what I want—each plate to tell a story, to evoke a memory."

"Okay, 'A Taste of Home' it is," he agreed, nodding thoughtfully. "Just be prepared for some tough critics. People have high expectations of home-cooked meals."

"I can handle that. If I can survive Chef Marco's fiery tirades, I can survive anything."

Connor chuckled, the sound brightening the evening air. "Fair point. But we might want to keep the fire extinguisher handy anyway."

We settled into a comfortable silence, watching the golden light wane into twilight. The park around us was bustling with life—families picnicking, couples laughing, and kids racing after each other, their joyous squeals mingling with the distant sound of a street performer strumming a guitar. It was a vivid reminder that the world was brimming with opportunities, and my dreams didn't have to remain buried under layers of hesitation.

"Alright," I said, breaking the silence, "I'm going to need your help with the logistics. What's our first step?"

"Well," Connor started, stretching his arms like a cat waking from a nap, "you need to secure a location. Maybe scout out a community kitchen where you can set up for the pop-up?"

"That's a solid idea. I've seen a few spots around the city. And I should probably create a menu."

"Look at you, diving right in!" He feigned surprise, eyebrows shooting up. "I thought you might procrastinate a bit, let the fear set in. You know, wallow in self-doubt like a true artist."

"Shut up," I laughed, swatting his arm playfully. "I'm trying to be proactive here! Besides, it's easier to envision this whole thing when I have a menu to work with."

He grinned back, the warmth of his smile washing over me. "Well, how about we make this a planning date? I'll bring the pizza, and you bring the genius."

"Deal," I said, a flutter of excitement igniting within me.

The next few days blurred into a flurry of activity, each moment infused with a heady mix of anticipation and anxiety. I spent hours jotting down ideas for the menu, each dish a tiny reflection of my heart and soul. Flavors intertwined with memories: the spicy enchiladas my grandmother used to make, the vibrant salad bursting with fresh herbs from my childhood garden, and a decadent chocolate torte that had seen many a celebration.

On the day of our planning session, Connor arrived with a box of pizza that smelled divine, the cheesy aroma teasing my senses as I ushered him into my modest apartment. My walls were adorned with mismatched plates and art from local artists, each piece adding to the cozy chaos that made me feel at home.

"Do you think this is enough cheese?" Connor asked, holding a slice in the air like a trophy.

"If we're judging by your standards, probably not," I replied, grabbing a slice and sinking my teeth into the gooey goodness. "This is perfect."

We settled on the couch, half-eaten pizza strewn across the coffee table like a tribute to our culinary endeavors. With my notebook perched on my lap, I sketched out the menu, debating over the order of dishes like an artist choosing colors for a masterpiece.

"This is solid," Connor said, scanning the scribbled words. "But you might want to add a few vegetarian options. You know, to cater to the masses."

"I was thinking about that," I replied, tapping my pen against my chin. "How about a roasted beet salad with goat cheese and candied pecans?"

He nodded thoughtfully. "Very nice. It feels fancy without being pretentious. What's next on the list?"

"Dessert," I said with a mischievous grin, flipping the page. "We can't forget the pièce de résistance. I'm thinking mini chocolate tarts. They always make a splash."

Connor raised an eyebrow. "Mini? Are you sure you want to limit people? You might want to consider giant chocolate tarts, just to ensure they're completely satisfied."

"Is this a tactic to sabotage my dessert menu? Because it's working," I said, smirking.

"Not at all. I'm merely looking out for your future customers, you know? Happy diners are the best kind of diners."

Our laughter filled the room as we navigated through the menu, throwing ideas back and forth like an impromptu game of catch. With each passing hour, I could feel the excitement building, igniting the dreams I had almost buried under layers of fear and indecision.

As we wrapped up the night, I leaned back against the couch, exhausted but exhilarated. "I can't believe how much we accomplished tonight. I feel like I'm finally on the right path."

"I knew you would get there," Connor replied, a soft sincerity threading through his words. "You have an incredible talent, and you just needed to believe in yourself a little more."

Before I could respond, the doorbell rang, breaking the warm moment. My heart raced—who could it be?

I opened the door to find a figure shrouded in shadow, holding a bouquet of flowers that seemed to glow against the dim light of the hallway. The sudden appearance of an unexpected guest sent a jolt of uncertainty through me. "Can I help you?" I asked, my voice barely a whisper as my mind raced with possibilities.

The figure stepped forward, and as the light illuminated their face, a chill swept through me. It was someone I hadn't seen in years—a face I had thought was long behind me, a ghost from my past I had not anticipated.

"Surprise," they said, a smirk playing on their lips, sending my heart into a frenzied beat. "I'm back."

Chapter 19: Stirring Up Trouble

The aroma of fresh-brewed coffee swirled around me like a warm embrace as I sat across from Connor in the tiny café, its walls lined with mismatched vintage posters and flickering fairy lights. He wore that familiar grin, the kind that made my heart do an involuntary little flip, even amidst the chaos swirling around us. The chatter of the early afternoon crowd enveloped us, punctuated by the soft clinking of cups and the occasional laugh, but my focus was entirely on him, the way his tousled hair caught the light and how the sunlight danced across his freckled skin.

"I've been thinking," I said, tucking a strand of hair behind my ear, my fingers lingering on the soft cotton of my shirt—a shirt that felt like a badge of honor, a silent proclamation that I was moving forward, leaving behind the dark shadows of Tony's kitchen. "What if I host a pop-up dinner? A one-night event to showcase my style and ideas, something fresh and different?"

Connor leaned back in his chair, his eyes narrowing thoughtfully. "You mean, like your own restaurant for an evening?"

"Exactly! A taste of my culinary vision, with a twist," I said, the excitement bubbling within me. "I could combine my experience with the classics and infuse them with some new flavors. Plus, I want to create a vibe, something intimate where people feel more than just guests. They should feel like they're part of something special."

"That sounds amazing," he replied, his enthusiasm brightening the already cheerful atmosphere around us. "But you know that putting together a dinner like that requires a lot of planning and a location. Have you thought about where you might host it?"

A shadow flitted across my mind—a fleeting thought of Tony's restaurant, the very place that had birthed my culinary dreams but also suffocated them. "Not yet," I admitted, and the lingering hurt of his betrayal washed over me. It would have been too easy to fall into the trap of seeking approval from him again, a dangerous cycle I was determined to break. "But I can't let his negativity keep me from moving forward. I have to be brave."

"Bravery looks good on you," Connor said, and his smile was a lifebuoy thrown my way in choppy waters. "But what if we took it a step further? What if you gathered some local chefs, made it a collaboration? You could turn this into an event that showcases the whole community, not just you."

The idea hit me like a bolt of lightning. I imagined a gathering of eclectic flavors, each chef contributing their unique touch, transforming an ordinary night into an unforgettable experience. "That's brilliant!" I exclaimed, my pulse racing at the possibilities. "We could feature a different course from each chef, a sort of culinary story told through dishes. It would be a celebration of the local talent—"

"Not to mention, the food scene," he added, and I could see the gears turning in his mind as he envisioned the whole thing unfolding. "And it gives you a chance to network with people who could help you find a more permanent venue down the line."

"Networking," I echoed, the word tasting sweet on my tongue. "I like the sound of that."

We spent the next hour crafting plans, sketching out ideas on napkins, brainstorming potential chefs and themes. Each suggestion felt like a stepping stone, a way to reclaim my identity after Tony's harsh dismissal. With each passing moment, the walls around my aspirations cracked open, letting in a rush of light and possibility.

But as the afternoon sunlight waned and the café began to empty, a nagging thought crept into my mind, twisting the edges of my excitement. What if no one showed up? What if I poured my heart and soul into this event only to have it fall flat? Wouldn't that just prove Tony right?

"Hey," Connor interrupted my spiraling thoughts, his hand reaching across the table to squeeze mine gently. "What's going on in that beautifully chaotic head of yours?"

"It's just... what if it's not enough? What if I'm not enough?" I murmured, the vulnerability in my voice betraying the bravado I'd been trying to muster. "What if they all think I'm just the girl who walked away from her chance?"

"Then you show them what you're made of," he replied firmly, a spark igniting in his eyes. "You're not defined by Tony or what happened there. You're an artist, and this is your canvas. You get to paint it however you want."

His words wrapped around me like a safety net, coaxing me out of the shadows of self-doubt. "You really think so?"

"I know so," he said, and his unwavering faith in me ignited a flicker of hope within. "And who cares what anyone else thinks? This is about you reclaiming your narrative, showing the world your flavors, your style. You've got this."

My heart swelled, a mixture of gratitude and affection, a warmth that surged deeper than I expected. "You're right. I'm going to do this, and it's going to be amazing. I want to create something memorable, something that tells my story."

Just as I began to embrace the possibilities, the bell above the café door chimed, drawing our attention. A figure entered, and I immediately recognized the shape and swagger—the unmistakable silhouette of Tony. My stomach twisted, a knot of anxiety tightening within me.

He spotted us, his expression morphing into a blend of surprise and something darker. I could almost feel the daggers he was throwing our way, the weight of judgment thickening the air between us. My heart raced, a mix of defiance and dread, as I wondered what would happen next. Would he confront me? Would he lay bare his bitterness for the world to see?

"Speak of the devil," Connor murmured, glancing at me with a mixture of amusement and concern.

I forced a smile, a fragile facade of confidence. "Well, well, looks like I might not be rid of him just yet."

The door swung open, and Tony's presence felt like a thunderclap in the intimate café, reverberating through the cozy space where Connor and I had been planning my culinary comeback. He stepped inside, the late afternoon sun casting an angular shadow behind him, emphasizing the bitterness etched into his features. I could see the slight twitch of his lips, the way his gaze swept over us like a storm cloud, ready to unleash its fury.

"Fancy seeing you here," he said, his voice a low growl that rumbled through the cheerful chatter around us. He sauntered over, exuding an air of self-satisfied arrogance, as if he had walked in on a private joke meant to mock him.

"Hey, Tony," I replied, my voice steadier than I felt, a practiced smile plastered on my face. "Just enjoying a coffee and brainstorming some ideas."

He chuckled, but there was no humor in it, only a sharp edge that cut through the lighthearted ambiance. "Brainstorming, huh? That's a nice way to say you're floundering." His eyes darted to Connor, and a flicker of disdain crossed his features. "Didn't know you needed a babysitter."

I felt the heat rise in my cheeks, a rush of indignation sparking within me. "I'm just exploring options, Tony. Something you clearly wouldn't understand." I wanted to add more, to unleash the frustration that had simmered beneath my skin ever since I left his kitchen, but Connor's steady presence calmed me, reminding me of my goal.

"Options, right." He leaned on the table, too close for comfort. "You think a few fancy dishes are going to make up for the chaos you left behind? You're running from your responsibilities."

I could hear the crowd's whispers around us, their curiosity piqued by the tension rising like steam from the coffee cups. It felt invasive, a spotlight on my private moment of courage. But I wouldn't let him take this from me. "I'm not running away; I'm moving toward something better. Something that actually aligns with my vision."

His laughter was a harsh bark. "Vision? You think you can just waltz back into this industry and turn heads? You're not ready for the heat, my dear." The mockery in his voice stung, and I clenched my fists under the table, but Connor's hand slid over mine, grounding me.

"Maybe you're just afraid she'll outshine you," Connor interjected, his tone firm and unwavering, like a shield between us. "Sounds like you're projecting, Tony."

Tony's gaze flickered to Connor, then back to me, his expression morphing into a mask of annoyance. "You're barking up the wrong tree, kid. You have no idea what this business demands."

"Then maybe you should consider sharing your knowledge instead of hoarding it like a greedy little dragon," Connor shot back, his voice laced with challenge.

I barely contained a smile, a flicker of pride igniting within me. I didn't need Tony's approval; I had found a champion in Connor, someone who believed in my ability to rise from the ashes of that kitchen.

"Look, Tony," I said, forcing a calmness into my voice, "I'm done with this conversation. You don't get to dictate my future."

His laughter held an edge, cold and unyielding. "We'll see about that. The industry has a way of sorting out the weak from the strong. Just remember, the last time you cooked, you left the stove burning."

I flinched, his words igniting old insecurities, but I wouldn't let him see my doubt. "I've learned from my mistakes. I'm ready to embrace the challenge."

"Challenge?" he scoffed, his gaze piercing through me. "You think a pop-up dinner is going to change anything? You're just a blip on the radar, sweetheart."

As he turned to leave, Connor leaned closer to me. "Don't let him get under your skin. He's a bitter man because he knows you're better than him."

"Better? I'm not better; I'm just... different." I swallowed hard, trying to shake off the feeling of inadequacy that threatened to seep back in.

"Different is good," he said, determination lacing his voice. "You're going to show everyone that your version of cooking is something they've never experienced before."

"Do you really think I can pull this off?" I asked, a hint of vulnerability breaking through my bravado.

"I know you can," he replied, sincerity shining in his eyes. "And if you need help with anything, I'm all in."

The warmth of his support wrapped around me, banishing Tony's negativity into the corners of the café. I was more than ready to turn the page on my story, to write a new chapter full of my flavor and flair. As the sunlight began to dip below the horizon, painting the world in soft hues of orange and pink, I felt a spark of hope ignite within me.

"Alright then," I said, excitement bubbling in my chest. "Let's make this dinner happen. We'll call it 'A Taste of Rebirth' or something equally pretentious."

"Perfect," Connor laughed, his enthusiasm infectious. "And I'll help with the logistics—venue scouting, invitations, everything."

The mere thought of moving forward filled me with a rush of energy, but just as we began brainstorming again, my phone buzzed, interrupting our flow. I glanced down, and my heart plummeted. A message from Tony, the tight grip of dread wrapping around my chest.

"I hope you're ready for the fallout. This isn't over."

I showed it to Connor, the uncertainty reflected in my eyes. "What does that even mean?"

His expression turned serious, the lightness of our earlier moment slipping away. "It sounds like a threat. He might not be done trying to drag you back down."

I could feel the weight of his words settle around me, a fog of anxiety creeping into the vibrant atmosphere. "I thought I was moving on, but it feels like he's still trying to pull me back into his world."

"Then we'll just have to show him you're not going back," Connor said firmly. "This is your time, and you won't let anyone dim your light."

I nodded, but the uncertainty gnawed at me, a tight knot of fear intertwined with my determination. Just then, the door opened again, and a new figure entered, shaking off the chill of the evening air. I turned, my breath hitching as I recognized the unmistakable silhouette. It was Mia, my old sous chef from Tony's restaurant, and she had an unreadable expression on her face.

"Hey," she said, her voice quiet, almost hesitant, as she approached our table. The moment felt electric, charged with a thousand unsaid words.

"Mia!" I exclaimed, torn between excitement and the nagging feeling that something was amiss.

"Can we talk?" she asked, glancing nervously at Tony's retreating figure before focusing on me.

"What's going on?" I asked, my heart racing.

She took a deep breath, her eyes darting between Connor and me. "I think you might need to know about what Tony's been saying... and what he's planning next."

The air in the café shifted, thickening with anticipation and dread, as I braced myself for the impending storm.

Chapter 20: Shadows of the Past

The rustle of leaves overhead accompanied the soft chatter of couples nestled on nearby benches, their laughter mingling with the crisp air, while dogs chased after scattered fallen foliage. I had come to treasure this park, a tiny oasis amid the relentless pace of Manhattan, where the weight of expectation felt a little lighter, if only for a moment. I closed my eyes, taking in the mingling scents of pumpkin spice and cinnamon wafting from a nearby café, wishing I could bottle that warmth and carry it with me.

"Hey, you," a voice cut through my reverie, playfully accusatory. I opened my eyes to find Lena, my friend and the only person who could breach my defenses with effortless ease. Her wild curls danced around her shoulders like flames, and her hazel eyes sparkled with mischief. "I thought I'd find you sulking here."

"Not sulking," I protested, feigning indignation. "Just contemplating life and the vastness of the universe."

"Which is code for 'avoiding responsibility,'" she quipped, plopping down beside me with the grace of someone entirely too confident in her own charm. She produced a cup of steaming coffee, the kind that could wake the dead, and offered it like a peace offering. "Want some?"

I took a sip, grateful for the warmth spreading through me, and suddenly the shadows felt a little less heavy. "Thanks. I could use a pick-me-up. Or maybe just a reason to stay awake while I ponder the future of my very existence."

"Oh please," Lena rolled her eyes. "You're a hotshot chef in a city that practically begs for your talent. Your existence is far from mundane."

The words hung in the air, vibrant yet slightly suffocating, like the last vestiges of summer lingering in a cool breeze. I wanted to believe her, to let that hope ignite a fire in my chest, but I felt like a pretender, a kid playing dress-up in someone else's life. It was hard to shake the nagging feeling that one wrong move could expose me for what I truly was—a girl with a dream wrapped around a past that never seemed to let go.

"Have you thought about Tony?" Lena asked, sipping her coffee as if it were the elixir of life itself.

"Not today," I lied, my heart sinking slightly at the mere mention of his name. Tony, my former mentor and the man who had once championed my culinary ambitions, had turned bitter and cynical in the wake of my decision to leave his kitchen. The way he had looked at me, that final day—disappointment etched on his face—had been a look I'd worn myself far too often. "Well, maybe a little."

"I get it," she replied, her voice softer now. "But you know he'll come around eventually. Maybe it's just too soon."

"Maybe," I murmured, staring at the bare branches above me, their skeletal outlines against the gray sky. My thoughts drifted back to the frantic moments leading up to my departure from his restaurant, the joy that had once bubbled in my chest turned to panic as I'd realized I was stepping away from a dream that had slowly started to feel like a cage.

"Listen," Lena interrupted my spiral of self-doubt, her tone firm. "You need to embrace this new chapter, not just for yourself but for the countless people out there who'll benefit from your talent. Think about it. What if your next venture is something that could change everything?"

"Like opening my own place?" The idea had danced in my mind like a playful flame, but the reality felt daunting. "And what if it fails? What if I end up as a cautionary tale?"

She waved her hand dismissively. "You won't. You're too good for that. Besides, failure is just a pit stop on the way to success. It's not the end; it's a twist in the plot. Just like every good story, right?"

I chuckled softly, feeling the weight of her words. "Are you always this wise, or is it the caffeine talking?"

"Definitely caffeine." She winked. "But also, I've seen you in action. You're passionate about food, and that passion will draw people in. You can't bottle that magic, but you can serve it on a plate."

A smile crept onto my lips as I imagined the dishes I could create, each one a reflection of my journey, layered with flavors and memories, echoing the heartbeat of the city that had embraced me. My mind swirled with possibilities, like a vibrant painting coming to life. What if I could combine my roots with my future? What if the new beginning was a chance to rewrite the narrative?

"Okay, let's say I entertain the idea," I said, leaning into the warmth of that thought. "Where would I even start?"

"Research. Network. Try out a few pop-up dinners or food events. Get your name out there," she replied, her enthusiasm contagious. "I can help. We'll make a plan, and I'll be your sous-chef or whatever you need me to be."

"Lena, you don't even cook!" I laughed, picturing her struggling with a whisk.

"True, but I'm a great taste-tester! And I've always got your back." Her tone turned serious, the humor fading. "Just promise me you won't let the shadows of the past pull you under. You're not that girl anymore."

"Yeah, well..." I began, but the weight of my father's voice seeped back into my thoughts, a distant echo reminding me of his disapproval. "Sometimes, I feel like those shadows are all I've got."

"Not if you fight for the light."

With those words, the lingering ghosts felt just a little less suffocating, and the world around me seemed to brighten, even if only slightly. I looked up at the expanse of sky peeking through the trees, the faint glow of sunlight piercing the gray. "Alright, I'll consider it. But only if you promise to keep being annoying about it."

Lena laughed, her voice ringing out like a bell in the stillness of the park. "Deal."

The sun dipped lower, casting a warm glow across the park, and with it came the scent of evening—a mix of fresh grass, damp earth, and a hint of cinnamon from the vendor across the street. I took a deep breath, letting it fill my lungs, hoping to clear out the last remnants of doubt and despair. Lena's laughter echoed in my mind as I pictured her in a flour-dusted apron, probably attempting to juggle her culinary dreams while being the most uncoordinated sous-chef in history.

"Okay, I'm in," I finally declared, turning to her with a newfound resolve. "I'll start planning something. A pop-up. Maybe I'll call it 'A Taste of My Journey.' It sounds pretentious, but you know what I mean."

"More like a taste of your tenacity," she shot back, her eyes gleaming with enthusiasm. "And you've got the perfect backdrop for your story. Let's make it happen."

Just then, a flash of movement caught my eye. A small girl, no older than six, darted past us, her bright red jacket a burst of color against the autumn landscape. In her hands, she clutched a cardboard box that looked suspiciously like it was meant for something else—maybe a shoe box or an old takeout container. She stopped in front of a couple sitting on a bench, her face scrunched in concentration as she opened the box to reveal a small assortment of glittering stones.

"Look! Pretty rocks!" she exclaimed, her voice ringing with delight. The couple exchanged amused glances before one of them reached out, handing her a quarter in exchange for a shiny pebble. I felt a pang of nostalgia; it was the kind of moment that reminded me of simpler joys, of being unburdened by life's complexities.

"See? It's all about the simple things," Lena said, nodding in the direction of the little girl. "That could be you, making people smile over food."

A soft chuckle escaped my lips, and I couldn't help but feel a rush of determination. "Fine, I'll work on a menu tonight. But I need your help with marketing. If I'm going to sell food, I need people to know it exists first."

"Consider it done!" Lena beamed, her enthusiasm infectious. "We'll take over the world one dish at a time."

As we dove into brainstorming, the evening air grew cooler, the sun's last rays slipping behind the skyline like a shy child hiding from the spotlight. We traded ideas—everything from seasonal soups that spoke of comfort to adventurous desserts that would evoke childhood dreams. I felt a spark ignite in my chest, something I hadn't felt in a while. It was the exhilarating feeling of purpose, of creation, of leaning into the chaos instead of shying away from it.

Just as we began to hash out the details, my phone buzzed in my pocket, pulling me momentarily out of our food-induced reverie. I glanced at the screen, my stomach twisting when I saw the name. It was my father.

"Is that who I think it is?" Lena asked, her voice low, her tone shifting from buoyant to cautious.

"Yeah." I hesitated, staring at the screen as if it were a live grenade. "He never calls."

"Answer it. This could be a breakthrough!"

"Or a disaster," I shot back, the words laced with a mix of anxiety and dread.

"Or it could be the perfect opportunity to confront whatever's been holding you back!" she countered, her excitement spilling over into impatience. "You've been avoiding this for too long. If you're really going to step into this new chapter, you need to do it with all the baggage unpacked."

She had a point. My heart raced as I tapped the green button, the connection crackling in my ear. "Hello?" I said, trying to keep my voice steady.

"Jessica," he said, his tone curt and serious, as always. "We need to talk."

"I gathered that," I replied, crossing my arms defensively. "You don't usually call just to check in."

"I know how you feel about me," he began, his words thick with the weight of unspoken truths. "But there are things you need to understand. Things that—"

"I don't want to hear another lecture about my choices, Dad," I interrupted, the familiar irritation bubbling to the surface. "I'm not that scared little girl anymore."

His silence stretched, filled with the unspoken tension of years of distance. Finally, he sighed, and the sound was heavy, like the prelude to a storm. "It's not about that. I'm trying to help you. You don't have to do this alone."

"Help? Is that what you call it? Because last I checked, your idea of help came with a side of judgment."

"Jessica, I—"

"Do you even know what I've been up to?" I cut him off again, my heart pounding. "Do you care at all about what I want? Or is this about you? Because if it is, then I'm not interested."

"Stop being so dramatic. I'm not trying to—"

"Dramatic?" I scoffed, my voice rising. "You have no idea what drama is. I've spent my life fighting to escape yours!"

"Maybe you should have stayed closer to home. This city is changing you."

I could feel Lena's supportive gaze on me, but it did little to dampen the storm brewing inside. "You think I'm changing? Maybe I'm just finally becoming who I'm meant to be—who I've always wanted to be. And you should want that for me!"

"I want you to be happy," he replied, his voice softening. "I really do. But happiness isn't just about chasing dreams. You need to be practical."

"Practical?" I laughed, the bitterness in my tone slicing through the air. "Practical is what's kept me shackled to your expectations. What I need is to break free from that."

"Jessica—"

"Goodbye, Dad." I hung up, the finality of my decision echoing in my mind like the toll of a bell.

Lena's hand found mine, squeezing tightly. "That was intense."

"Understatement of the century," I muttered, my heart still racing, caught between the exhilaration of standing my ground and the weight of unresolved tension.

"Are you okay?" she asked, her brow furrowing with concern.

"I don't know," I admitted, feeling the tremors of uncertainty creeping back in. "I thought I was ready to leave the past behind, but it's clear I'm still tangled in it."

Lena opened her mouth, probably to offer more platitudes about overcoming adversity or something equally infuriatingly optimistic, but before she could speak, a sudden movement in the corner of my eye caught my attention.

A figure loomed at the edge of the park, partially obscured by the growing shadows. I squinted, recognizing the tall silhouette. It couldn't be.

"Jessica," the figure called out, and the voice sent a chill down my spine.

"Dad?" I whispered, my heart dropping into the pit of my stomach.

The world around me faded as I turned to face him, and for the first time, I wondered if perhaps the shadows weren't just lingering—they were watching, waiting for me to make my move.

Chapter 21: The Price of Dreams

The afternoon sun hung low in the sky, casting long shadows that danced across the grass like fleeting memories. I watched a couple nearby, their laughter bubbling over like a fizzy drink, blissfully unaware of the weight that sat heavy on my chest. Connor shifted beside me, his gaze fixed on the children chasing each other through the golden beams of light, their innocent joy almost unbearable in its contrast to the turmoil swirling within me.

"I know it sounds daunting," I murmured, fingers tracing the cool wood of the bench beneath me. "But it feels like I've been waiting for this moment forever. Like I can't not try."

He sighed, a sound that felt like the soft whisper of a tide retreating, leaving behind a mixed bag of shells and stones. "And what if it doesn't work out? What if you lose everything you've built?"

There was a certain vulnerability in his tone, a subtle shift that hinted at fears buried beneath his usually confident demeanor. I turned to him, the corners of my mouth lifting slightly as I recalled the way he'd once tossed a paper airplane at my head during a late-night brainstorming session, insisting that the most creative ideas always flew under the radar.

"Do you remember that night?" I asked, a wry smile breaking through the anxiety that had coiled around my heart. "When you decided to try and convince me that a cardboard box could be a better headquarters for our project than an actual office?"

His lips quirked at the memory. "I stand by that. The box was spacious. And let's not forget the best brainstorming happened under its roof."

The nostalgia washed over me, a fleeting comfort that reminded me of why I was here with him, sharing this moment. Connor had always been the one to transform even the bleakest of situations into a canvas for possibility, painting our dreams with broad strokes of humor and whimsy. Yet, the laughter faded as reality set back in.

"Okay, but really—what's the plan?" I asked, tilting my head to meet his eyes. "You say you'll help, but I can't ask you to carry the weight of this alone."

He leaned back, the slight creak of the bench echoing the tension in the air. "I'm not asking you to shoulder it all. But we need to think strategically. Do you know anyone in the industry? Someone who might believe in your vision?"

The question hung between us like a question mark over an unfinished thought. "Not exactly," I replied, feeling the weight of truth press down on my shoulders. "I've mostly been on the outside looking in, watching the successful ones from a distance, admiring their sleek portfolios while I've... well, I've been figuring things out as I go."

"And that's okay," he said, earnestness radiating from him like warmth from a fireplace. "You're talented, and you've got passion. Those are your strongest assets. But we need more than that if we're going to make this happen."

"Passion doesn't pay the bills," I muttered, a bitter taste creeping into my words. The idea of standing in front of investors, laying bare my dreams and aspirations, filled me with dread. I could already imagine their skeptical expressions, the polite nods that would signal my failure before I'd even had a chance to begin.

"True, but it can inspire others. Look, let's start by brainstorming a list of potential investors. We can leverage connections, maybe even set up some meetings. If we craft your pitch just right, you'll turn those skeptical nods into enthusiastic agreements."

I nodded, though doubt crept in like an unwelcome guest. What if my ideas weren't enough? What if I stumbled over my words? Would I freeze like a deer in headlights, heart racing, palms sweaty, as I tried to convince strangers that I was worth the risk?

"Okay," I said, forcing optimism into my tone. "Let's make that list. But... what if I fail?"

"Then we get back up," he replied, determination flooding his voice. "Failure is just another word for experience. Think of it as research."

"Research?" I chuckled, the sound a mix of disbelief and reluctant amusement. "You make it sound so easy."

"Because it can be," he insisted, his blue eyes steady and reassuring. "And when you're knee-deep in the chaos, you'll have stories to tell. We'll find the humor in it. After all, life's too short to take everything seriously."

I couldn't help but grin at his infectious optimism. "You make it sound like an adventure."

"Because it is," he replied, nudging me playfully. "Just imagine it—sailing into uncharted waters, dodging storms, but always coming back to tell the tale."

"Right," I said, a little breathless from his enthusiasm. "And if I sink?"

Connor's expression softened, and the warmth of his gaze wrapped around me like a snug blanket. "Then you swim. And if you need a lifeboat, I'll be right there with you."

I inhaled deeply, the scent of grass and the sweet hint of impending autumn filling my lungs, bolstering my courage. Maybe, just maybe, we could navigate these murky waters together. It wouldn't be easy, and the path ahead was uncertain, but with Connor by my side, the possibility of failure didn't seem quite as daunting.

The sun dipped lower, casting a warm glow that wrapped around us like a comforting shawl. As the park began to empty, the laughter of children faded into the distance, replaced by the rustling leaves whispering secrets of autumn. Connor's words lingered in my mind, each syllable a knot tightening around my resolve. I could feel the

BREAKING THE MOLD

electric pulse of uncertainty racing through my veins, yet something deeper stirred—a flicker of hope.

"Let's make a game plan," I suggested, trying to sound more composed than I felt. "If we're going to do this, I want to approach it like a real project. Start with the basics: vision, goals, maybe even a timeline?"

Connor nodded, the corners of his mouth lifting into a half-smile. "Good idea. So, what's your vision? Paint me a picture."

I took a deep breath, conjuring images in my mind. "I want to create a community space—a haven for artists and dreamers. Somewhere they can share their work, collaborate, and find inspiration. Think cozy corners with big windows, local art on the walls, and maybe a small café where people can sip coffee and talk about their projects."

His brow furrowed as he considered my words. "That sounds... beautiful. But how do you plan to make it happen? You mentioned funding. Are you thinking crowdfunding, or do you have other ideas?"

"Crowdfunding feels like diving into a pool of sharks without knowing how to swim," I admitted, shaking my head. "But maybe I could host workshops and events to generate some income while building a following?"

Connor's eyes lit up, and I could see the gears turning in his mind. "That could work! You could teach classes on anything—painting, writing, photography—whatever you love. Plus, it would draw people in and create a sense of community."

"Exactly!" I said, excitement bubbling within me. "I could also partner with local businesses for sponsorship. We could showcase their products at events, and in return, they could help promote the space."

"Now you're thinking like an entrepreneur," he said, a proud grin spreading across his face. "But let's not forget the investors. You'll need to impress them."

I winced at the thought. "Right. That's the part that terrifies me. How do I even begin to pitch this to someone who might not see the vision?"

"You start with passion," Connor replied, leaning closer. "You tell them why it matters to you. The connection to your community. The need for creative spaces in a world that often feels... sterile. And you don't have to be perfect—just authentic."

A wave of determination surged through me, and I could feel my earlier fears begin to recede, like the tide pulling back from the shore. "You're right. I can't just focus on the numbers. I need to weave in the heart of the project. What it means for people, how it could change lives."

"Exactly. And I'll be right there with you, helping craft the narrative." He reached out, his hand brushing against mine, and the warmth sent a spark of courage shooting through me. "We'll get through this together."

The connection between us shimmered, and for a moment, the world around us faded away. I could almost believe that everything was going to be okay. But then, like an unwelcome cloud overshadowing the sun, doubt crept back in. "What if it's not enough? What if I fail miserably?"

"We won't know until we try," Connor replied, his voice steady, but I could hear a hint of uncertainty there too. "And even if you do fail, it's not the end of the world. You'll learn. You'll grow. You'll adapt."

As the last rays of sunlight slipped behind the horizon, painting the sky in hues of orange and purple, I felt a surge of determination. "Let's do it," I said, my voice firm. "Let's make this dream a reality."

"Then let's start drafting your pitch," he said, standing up and offering me his hand. "But first, coffee. A good idea deserves caffeine."

I took his hand, allowing him to pull me up, and together we began walking toward the coffee shop, the cool evening air invigorating.

Laughter floated around us, and I could almost taste the possibilities hanging in the air.

As we reached the café, a buzz of activity enveloped us. The smell of freshly brewed coffee wafted through the air, mingling with the sweet aroma of pastries. It felt like stepping into a cozy embrace. I glanced around, feeling the excitement bubbling within me, ready to take on the world.

Inside, the walls were adorned with local art, each piece telling a story. My mind raced with ideas for how I could transform this place into something even more magical, a canvas for creativity. I could imagine hosting open mic nights or collaborative art exhibits, a fusion of talents converging in a vibrant space.

"Two coffees, please!" Connor called to the barista, his energy infectious. He turned to me, his expression thoughtful. "Do you have a specific message you want to convey in your pitch?"

"Something that speaks to the importance of creativity in our lives," I replied, my heart racing at the thought of weaving my vision into words. "It's not just about art; it's about connection, community, and healing."

"Perfect," he said, handing me my coffee. "Now let's find a spot to brainstorm. The right atmosphere is key."

We settled at a small table by the window, sunlight spilling across the surface like liquid gold. I took a sip of my coffee, the warmth spreading through me, igniting my senses. This was where I belonged, amidst the energy of people sharing ideas and creating connections.

As we began brainstorming, the ideas flowed effortlessly, each thought building on the last. We sketched out plans for workshops, events, and ways to foster collaboration among artists. Laughter punctuated our conversation, the atmosphere charged with enthusiasm.

But then, as I jotted down a particularly ambitious idea, my phone buzzed on the table, breaking the moment. I glanced down to see a message from an unknown number.

"Are you still planning on pursuing your dream?" it read, the tone ominous and chilling.

I felt the hairs on the back of my neck prickling, and I exchanged a wary glance with Connor. "Who is that?" he asked, concern shadowing his features.

"I don't know," I replied, my stomach knotting. "But it doesn't feel friendly."

My fingers trembled as I typed a response, my heart racing. "Who is this?"

The reply came almost immediately: "You have no idea what you're getting yourself into."

Connor leaned closer, the warmth between us replaced by a creeping sense of foreboding. "What do you want to do?" he asked, his voice low and serious.

I swallowed hard, a lump forming in my throat. "I don't know. But I can't let this stop me."

The adrenaline surged through me, a mix of fear and defiance, and I met Connor's gaze, feeling the weight of his unwavering support. Whatever lay ahead, I was determined to face it head-on, even if it meant navigating through shadows I hadn't anticipated.

Chapter 22: Cracks in the Foundation

The elevator ride down was a silence I could almost taste, thick and uncomfortable. Each floor we descended felt like a countdown, the numbers blinking mockingly above me as I replayed every moment of the meeting. I stared at the polished steel doors, willing them to part with a burst of confetti and cheers, but instead, the ding was a hollow reminder of reality. Outside, the city buzzed like an over-caffeinated beehive, oblivious to my internal struggle.

As the doors opened, the bright light of the lobby hit me like a slap, and I stepped into the chaos of midday Manhattan. It was a sensory overload, the sounds of honking taxis, street vendors shouting about pretzels, and the distant thrum of music from a nearby café wrapping around me like a chaotic blanket. Connor's voice broke through the din, steady and grounding. "You did great in there, really. They're just old-school suits trying to rattle you."

I forced a smile, appreciating his attempt to bolster my spirits. "Thanks, but I'm not sure they were even listening. It felt like they were deciding my fate before I even finished speaking."

He shrugged, his dark curls bouncing with the movement. "That's their loss. You've got something special. Just remember, you're not the only one who can back out of a deal."

I shot him a playful glare. "Don't you dare suggest I ghost them. I'm in this for the long haul."

"Wouldn't dream of it," he said, feigning innocence. "Just checking. You know, for future reference."

We wandered down Fifth Avenue, the crisp autumn air tinged with the scent of roasted chestnuts from a nearby cart. I was acutely aware of every step I took. The confidence I'd mustered in that conference room felt like a fading echo. I needed to prove to them—and myself—that I could weather the storm this time. My dream wasn't just a whimsical notion; it was a fiery ember that needed nurturing.

"Want to grab a drink?" Connor suggested, glancing at me sideways. His expression was a mixture of concern and the kind of mischief that suggested he was already plotting a way to cheer me up.

"Are you asking me out or just being a good friend?" I raised an eyebrow, matching his playful energy.

"Why can't it be both?" he shot back, grinning.

"Fine. A drink sounds perfect, but you're paying," I replied, nudging him playfully with my shoulder as we strolled toward a quaint little bar tucked between two towering glass buildings. The neon sign flickered with a retro charm, beckoning us into its warm embrace.

Inside, the dimly lit space wrapped around us like a cozy blanket. Wooden beams lined the ceiling, and the walls were adorned with eclectic art that spoke of stories untold. The bartender, a woman with vibrant purple hair and a smile that seemed to light up the room, greeted us as we slid onto the bar stools.

"What can I get you two?" she asked, her voice bright amidst the low hum of conversations.

"Two of your strongest drinks," Connor said, flashing a charming grin.

I laughed, shaking my head. "Just one for me, thanks. I don't need to be knocked out again."

"Suit yourself," he teased, leaning back in his seat, his gaze playful as it danced across the bar. "But let's be real. After today, you deserve a little liquid courage."

The bartender returned with our drinks—a vibrant crimson concoction for me and a frothy beer for him. I raised my glass, the cool glass against my palm feeling reassuring. "To new beginnings," I said, my voice firm despite the unease knotting in my stomach.

"To new beginnings," Connor echoed, clinking his glass against mine with a wink.

We sipped our drinks, and I let the warmth of the alcohol seep into me, easing the tension that had tightened around my chest since the meeting. As the minutes passed, laughter bubbled up between us, the worries of the day fading like the last rays of sunset outside. I had always found solace in these moments with Connor, our banter a gentle reminder that not everything needed to be weighed down by seriousness.

"Okay, real talk," he said, suddenly serious, setting his drink down with a thud. "What's the plan if they don't bite? I know you've got something up your sleeve."

I swirled the remnants of my drink, contemplating the boldness of my next words. "If they don't see the potential, then I'll find someone who does. I've been thinking about crowdfunding."

Connor raised an eyebrow, intrigued. "Really? You'd go that route?"

"Why not? It's not like I'm asking for a handout. It's more about rallying people behind the idea," I said, the excitement coursing through me like a jolt of caffeine. "If I can show them the community aspect, how people want this place to exist... It could work."

"Or you could end up with a bunch of disappointed backers," he countered, a hint of concern lining his features.

"True," I admitted, biting my lip, "but I'm not afraid of a little disappointment. I've faced worse, and I'm still standing, right?"

He nodded, his eyes softening. "You are. And that's what makes you unstoppable. But promise me you won't ignore the risks."

I smirked, the tension between us turning lighter, teasing. "Risk? That's just part of the fun, isn't it?"

"You're a madwoman," he chuckled, shaking his head in disbelief.

"Only when it comes to my dreams," I replied, my heart swelling with a renewed sense of purpose. We lingered at the bar, laughter and ideas weaving around us like the twinkling lights of the city outside, a reminder that even amidst uncertainty, hope could still flourish.

The laughter and camaraderie of the bar began to ease the weight pressing on my chest, yet doubt still lurked in the corners of my mind.

Connor and I had settled into a rhythm, our conversation punctuated with sips of drink and easy laughter, but the specter of that meeting hovered just beyond our bubble. It wasn't until I spotted a familiar face near the entrance that the warmth of our shared moment began to chill.

"Isn't that..." I trailed off, my gaze locking onto a woman whose confident stride and unmistakable aura turned heads like a magnet. Sarah Collins, the celebrity chef whose star had risen faster than a soufflé, entered the bar with a flourish, her entourage trailing behind like a comet's tail. The last time we had crossed paths, I'd been the one in the limelight—just a year ago, during a chaotic food festival where she had swooped in to steal my thunder.

"Do you want to say hi?" Connor asked, eyeing me with a mixture of amusement and concern.

"Say hi?" I echoed, feeling the weight of my insecurity twist in my stomach. "Or say 'why are you still relevant?'"

He rolled his eyes, encouraging me with a slight nudge. "You're not her competition, remember? You're trying to carve out your own path."

I watched as Sarah laughed, her voice ringing out like chimes, and felt an uninvited twinge of envy. She had the kind of effortless charm that made everything seem easy, while I was fumbling through uncertainty like a child learning to walk. "What if she's here for a meeting too? Or worse—what if she's about to pitch her next big thing?" I felt a wave of defensiveness wash over me.

"Then you'll just have to show her what you've got," Connor said, leaning closer. "Come on, let's go introduce ourselves. Besides, wouldn't it be fun to shake up her universe a little?"

Before I could protest, he was standing and tugging me toward her. My feet moved almost of their own accord, and soon we were standing beside Sarah, who was surrounded by admirers. She spotted us, her gaze shifting from recognition to surprise, and then a broad smile spread across her face.

BREAKING THE MOLD

"Wow, look who it is!" she exclaimed, her voice lilting with genuine excitement. "What a pleasant surprise! How have you been?"

"I've been... busy," I replied, forcing a smile. Connor glanced at me, and I could almost hear him muttering, "You're doing great," from behind his charming facade.

"Busy's good! I'm in the middle of launching a new restaurant, actually," she said, her eyes sparkling. "It's all about sustainability and local farms—something you'd probably appreciate, right?"

"Oh, definitely!" I said, too eagerly, mentally kicking myself. "I mean, that's a great approach. What's the vibe?"

She launched into a passionate description of her new venture, and I found myself half-listening, half-analyzing my own path in comparison. Each word she spoke seemed to add another layer to her already impressive resume. I was sinking in a sea of self-doubt, each wave crashing harder than the last.

Connor, sensing my discomfort, shifted the conversation. "So, what's your secret, Sarah? Any tips for someone looking to make a comeback?" His smile was disarming, and it redirected the focus away from me.

"Oh, Connor, darling," she laughed, a musical sound that filled the room, "there's no secret! Just hard work and a little luck. Right, sweetie?" She leaned in, giving me a conspiratorial wink.

"Yeah, well, I've got a plan," I blurted, emboldened by her unexpected warmth. "A crowdfunding campaign. Aiming to launch a bistro that focuses on community, creativity, and comfort. You know, something with heart."

Sarah's eyes widened in genuine interest. "That sounds incredible! I love the idea of community involvement. What's the theme?"

"Um, it's more of a 'home-style' approach—comfort foods from various cultures," I said, feeling a flush creep up my cheeks as I began to elaborate. "I want to create a space where people feel connected, like a gathering place where every dish tells a story."

She nodded, her expression softening. "That's beautiful. I can see the passion behind it. You'll get there."

A part of me wanted to believe her words, but the anxiety that had shadowed my steps since that meeting lingered. As the conversation flowed, I tried to lean into the moment, but my mind raced ahead, conjuring worst-case scenarios—what if my idea fell flat, or worse, what if I had to face Sarah again in a more competitive light?

As our drinks dwindled, Sarah's attention drifted, and soon her entourage whisked her away for more networking. I was left with Connor, who studied me with an expression that balanced concern and encouragement. "You handled that well," he said, leaning back on the bar.

"Did I? I felt like a floundering fish," I admitted, crossing my arms defensively.

"You've got a lot to offer. You just need to trust it." He paused, his eyes glinting with mischief. "Besides, I'm convinced you could outshine her any day."

"Thanks for the vote of confidence, but I'm pretty sure that's just your optimism talking," I shot back, a hint of a smile breaking through my doubt.

He laughed, a sound that lifted the heaviness just a little. "Okay, but seriously—let's make a plan for your pitch. You need to get those investors eating out of your hands, not throwing shade."

Just then, my phone buzzed in my pocket. I pulled it out, my heart quickening as I read the notification. My stomach dropped, a sudden pit forming as I realized it was from one of the investors from that morning.

"Let me guess, they want to pass?" Connor's tone turned serious, the playful light in his eyes dimming.

"Not quite," I whispered, my pulse racing. The email was concise, but it carried weight. They wanted to meet again to discuss further details, to explore "possible avenues for collaboration."

"Is that good or bad?" Connor asked, leaning in.

"It could be..." My voice trailed off as I read the last line, feeling a sharp pang of apprehension. "They're going to bring in a consultant to 'evaluate my vision further.'"

Connor's brows knitted together. "What does that mean?"

"More scrutiny," I replied, my voice barely above a whisper. "They're going to pick apart everything I've built."

Just as I turned to face him, the bar door swung open, and in strode a figure that made my heart drop even further—one of the investors from earlier, flanked by an unfamiliar woman whose confident stride echoed Sarah's.

"Just when I thought the day couldn't get any worse," I muttered under my breath.

"What now?" Connor asked, his voice low.

I straightened, every instinct screaming to retreat, but the weight of the moment held me in place. This was my shot, and I couldn't let it slip away. Just as I was about to gather my courage, the woman turned, catching my eye with an intensity that sent a chill down my spine. I could feel her evaluating me, as if she already knew everything about my dreams and fears.

"Is this a good time?" she asked, her smile deceptively warm.

And in that instant, I knew things were about to get complicated, as my future hung precariously in the balance, ready to tilt one way or the other.

Chapter 23: In the Heat of the Kitchen

The kitchen pulsed with life, each sizzling note of garlic a reminder of the culinary symphony I was orchestrating. I could see Connor out of the corner of my eye, focused yet carefree, a rogue charm in his demeanor that drew me in like the aroma of basil. His dark curls bounced as he moved around the counter, and for a moment, the chaos of the malfunctioning stove faded into a hum of laughter and kitchen banter.

"Did you ever think cooking would be so romantic?" he teased, eyes sparkling with mischief as he sliced through a ripe tomato, its juices bursting forth like a clumsy secret. "I mean, who knew you could almost taste the tension?"

"Trust me, if I could taste the tension, it would be the most expensive dish on the menu," I shot back, my voice playful but tinged with an edge of desperation. The critic was due to arrive in less than an hour, and the thought of serving subpar food sent shivers down my spine.

Just then, the stove gave a pathetic sputter, as if mocking me. "This isn't happening," I muttered, throwing my hands in the air. I didn't have the luxury of defeat; I had put everything on the line for this night. Every penny I had saved, every dream I had chased was tied to the success of this meal.

"Okay, okay," Connor said, stepping closer, the warmth of his presence both a comfort and a distraction. "Think of it this way—great chefs are like great artists. It's all about adapting, right? We'll turn this setback into something spectacular."

"You make it sound so simple," I said, eyeing the flames that flickered teasingly, like they were conspiring against me. "I'm not sure I can whip up magic with a half-functioning stove."

"Let's reframe this," he said, a grin spreading across his face as he grabbed a handful of herbs and tossed them into the air like confetti.

"We're the heroes of our own cooking drama. Let's improvise, let's be fearless!"

His enthusiasm ignited a spark in me. I had always loved the unexpected twists of cooking, the way a mistake could lead to a revelation. "Alright, chef. What do you suggest?"

"Let's start by using the grill outside. We can sear the meat there and bring out those smoky flavors. You handle the sauce—make it rich and bold. I'll take care of the sides."

With the urgency of a fire drill, we raced to gather our supplies, hearts pounding as we flung open the kitchen door and stepped into the cool evening air. The grill awaited us, its metallic surface glistening under the dim patio lights, a little beacon of hope in our culinary crisis.

As I fired up the grill, Connor moved gracefully, arranging vegetables like they were his best friends, coaxing their vibrant colors into a playful medley. "You know, I never thought I'd end up in a kitchen like this," he said, flipping a zucchini with the flair of a seasoned performer. "I've always imagined I'd be scaling mountains or saving the world, not sautéing."

"Cooking can be an adventure," I said, realizing just how true that was. "Each ingredient has a story, a journey. This—" I gestured to the vegetables sizzling and caramelizing on the grill "—this is our little expedition. We're explorers of flavor!"

"Explorer and chef extraordinaire," he countered, mock bowing as he presented the plate of grilled veggies like a trophy. "Shall we add 'daring hero' to our resumes?"

"Only if we make it out of here with at least one dish worthy of a five-star review," I joked, though my stomach twisted in knots at the thought.

With a renewed sense of purpose, we worked like a well-oiled machine, laughter bubbling between us as we assembled the plates. Each dish was crafted with the kind of care reserved for a masterpiece. I tossed the sauce together, the aroma of garlic mingling with the sweetness of roasted red peppers, the flavors dancing as I tasted it—a perfect blend of spicy and savory.

"Now that's what I call a bold move," Connor said, watching me with an impressed nod. "You've turned panic into perfection."

"Only because you're here to keep me sane," I admitted, catching his gaze. There was something in the way his eyes shone that felt electric, a current of unspoken connection threading between us like the very ingredients we were combining.

Just then, the doorbell rang, shattering the moment. I froze, spatula in hand, a wild mix of dread and excitement washing over me. The critic had arrived.

"Showtime," Connor said, the challenge twinkling in his eyes. He was right. This was our moment, a chance to let the food shine, to share a piece of my heart with someone who could help us soar or dash our hopes in a single review.

As I wiped my hands on my apron, Connor turned to me, seriousness in his voice. "We've got this, okay? Just remember—no matter what happens, we've already won by creating something amazing together."

"Right. We're heroes," I said, taking a deep breath as I opened the door, ready to face whatever awaited us.

I could feel the weight of the world pressing against my chest as I turned the knob on the grill. The heat leapt to life, a flickering flame that mirrored the tumult in my stomach. Connor was a whirlwind of energy beside me, tossing the vegetables with the confidence of a man who truly believed in the magic of the moment.

"Don't worry," he said, a teasing lilt in his voice as he glanced over. "This is just a little obstacle, like a plot twist in a rom-com. We'll make it work and laugh about it later."

I chuckled, appreciating his ability to lighten the mood, even as anxiety coiled tighter around my insides. "Right, because nothing says romance like burnt meat and a malfunctioning stove."

His grin widened. "Maybe not in your typical love story, but in ours? I think it adds character."

With the grill sizzling, I focused on my sauce, mixing a splash of red wine with the rich, roasted pepper base. The flavors mingled like old friends, creating a harmony that soothed my nerves. "You do know how to make a girl feel better about kitchen disasters," I said, tossing in a pinch of salt. "I'll give you that."

"Just wait until you see my secret weapon," he replied, reaching into his pocket and pulling out a small bottle. "A drop of this truffle oil, and your sauce will go from 'eh' to 'oh my God, what is this sorcery?'"

I raised an eyebrow. "Truffle oil? Are you sure we're not aiming for a Michelin star tonight?"

"Only the finest for our critic," he said, mockingly serious. "But really, it's all about elevating the flavors."

As he drizzled the oil into the sauce, the kitchen was filled with an intoxicating aroma, like an embrace from the earth itself. For a fleeting moment, I felt the tension fade. But that bliss was quickly overshadowed by the reality of our situation. The critic was in the neighborhood, and every tick of the clock sent another wave of urgency through me.

The doorbell rang again, this time followed by the unmistakable sound of footsteps. "Get ready!" I shouted, feeling my heart race.

"Showtime!" Connor echoed, and we hurriedly plated our masterpiece—a vibrant array of grilled vegetables, succulent meat, and a glossy drizzle of sauce that glimmered under the kitchen lights.

I opened the door, bracing myself as I faced the critic. She stood there, framed by the fading daylight, a notebook clutched in her hand like a weapon. The sharp lines of her tailored suit contrasted starkly with the warm, rustic charm of our kitchen.

"Evening," she said, her voice a blend of authority and curiosity.

"Welcome! We're thrilled to have you," I managed, my voice steadier than I felt.

As I led her inside, I could see Connor in my periphery, working his charm as he arranged the first course. "Tonight, we've prepared a selection of dishes inspired by local flavors," he explained, his tone inviting as if he were wooing a date rather than a critic.

"I can't wait to see what you've conjured up," she replied, her eyes narrowing as she scrutinized the plates.

My heart raced as I watched her take her first bite. Time seemed to stretch, each second heavy with the weight of expectation. I barely dared to breathe.

Her expression transformed; for a moment, surprise flickered across her features before she masked it with professionalism. "This is..." she began, pausing to gather her thoughts, "unexpectedly delightful."

"Just unexpectedly delightful?" Connor shot back, raising an eyebrow in a mock challenge.

She smiled slightly, a glimmer of appreciation breaking through her stern demeanor. "Don't get cocky, chef. I've only just begun."

With each subsequent course, the rhythm of the evening began to flow. As the critic tasted, Connor and I exchanged glances filled with shared triumph. The connection between us deepened, not just in our culinary journey but in the unspoken understanding of what this moment meant for both of us.

But just as I felt the tide of nerves start to ebb, a muffled shout erupted from outside. "Hey! You in there!"

My stomach dropped. "What is that?" I whispered, anxiety creeping back in like a dark cloud.

"I think it's just the neighbor," Connor replied, his brow furrowing.

The shouting escalated, growing louder and more frantic. I glanced at the critic, whose eyes narrowed with skepticism, clearly distracted from the meal before her. "Shouldn't someone check on that?"

Before I could respond, Connor moved toward the door. "I'll go," he said, offering a reassuring smile. "You keep the critic happy."

I nodded, my mind racing. The last thing I needed was for the evening to devolve into chaos. I forced a smile and turned back to our guest, who was tapping her pen against her notebook, her interest waning.

As Connor stepped outside, the door swung shut behind him, muffling the shouts. I focused on the plate in front of the critic, forcing myself to sound upbeat. "So, how's the flavor profile working for you?"

Her eyes were still on the door, a faint line of worry forming between her brows. "It's... interesting. But I would really prefer to—"

Before she could finish, the door burst open, and Connor's face was a canvas of alarm. "We've got a situation," he said, breathless.

"What?" I shot back, dread pooling in my stomach.

"There's a guy out there—he's demanding to speak with you!"

I felt my breath hitch, the world closing in. "What do you mean?" I asked, my heart racing.

"Let's just say it's not the kind of visit you want during a tasting," Connor said, his tone grave.

The critic straightened, her expression sharp. "Is this going to affect the review?"

"Depends on how you define 'affect,'" I muttered under my breath, my mind racing with possibilities.

"Let me handle it," Connor said, but I could see the uncertainty etched on his face.

"Wait!" I called out as he started toward the door. "What if it's someone from my past? I can't just leave you alone with her."

He paused, a flicker of realization flashing in his eyes. "You think it's about that?"

"I don't know!" I shot back, frustration boiling beneath the surface.

But the moment hung thick in the air, charged with tension and a hint of impending chaos. Just as I took a step forward, the door swung wide open, revealing a figure standing at the threshold—a face I hadn't seen in years, yet one that was seared into my memory.

"Surprise!" he shouted, a wicked grin splitting his face, completely oblivious to the storm brewing inside me.

Chapter 24: The Taste of Failure

The tasting didn't go as planned. The critic, a woman with severe glasses and a reputation for being hard to please, had kept her comments short. Too short. As she left, I could feel the sting of her disappointment in the air, like a bitter aftertaste lingering long after the meal was done.

I sat on the floor of the kitchen that night, my back against the stainless steel fridge, feeling the weight of my failure pressing down on me. Connor sat beside me in silence, offering no empty reassurances, no false hope. He knew better than anyone that sometimes, words didn't fix things.

But the silence didn't feel comforting this time. It felt like a chasm, opening wider with every passing moment.

"I'm not sure I can do this," I whispered, the words tasting like defeat.

Connor didn't respond immediately. He reached for my hand, squeezing it gently. "You can. But you have to want it bad enough."

The flickering fluorescent lights above cast a harsh glow on our faces, turning the kitchen into a stage where we were both performers, desperately trying to save a sinking show. I could still see the plates from the tasting scattered across the table like remnants of a war that I'd lost. Each dish had been a labor of love, yet they'd been met with a discerning gaze and thinly veiled criticism that cut deeper than any knife I had in my drawer.

"Bad enough? You think I don't want this?" My voice cracked, revealing the raw edges of my frustration. "I've given everything. I've sacrificed nights and weekends, meals with friends, my sanity, and yet..."

I let the sentence hang in the air, letting the unspoken truth weave its way around us. Connor, ever the unwavering support, remained calm. "You know it's not just about how much you want it. It's about how well you can adapt and evolve. Every chef has a moment like this."

But I wasn't every chef. I was me—the girl who had spent summers watching my grandmother create magic in the kitchen, her hands moving with the grace of a dancer as she conjured up dishes that didn't just fill bellies but also filled hearts with nostalgia. I was the girl who had turned a dilapidated food truck into a thriving little oasis where the flavors of my heritage mixed with modern culinary twists. And now? Now I was simply a failure, sitting on the floor of my own kitchen, drowning in self-doubt.

"Maybe I'm just not cut out for this," I murmured, staring down at my hands, the nails chipped and caked with remnants of flour. The reflection of my dreams glinted off the edges of the metal appliances, mocking me.

"Hey." Connor turned to me, his expression fierce. "Look at me." I hesitated, but his voice was like an anchor, drawing me back to the surface. I met his gaze, those warm brown eyes filled with an intensity that somehow sparked a flicker of hope within me. "You're not a failure. You're learning. This is just a stepping stone."

"A stepping stone that feels more like a brick wall," I shot back, frustration boiling inside me. "What am I supposed to do? Keep baking and hoping that the next critic will like my soufflé?"

He chuckled, the sound low and rich. "Well, it helps if you're not throwing your soufflés at the wall in frustration."

I couldn't help but laugh, the sound a little watery and unsure. "Very funny. Maybe I should take up stand-up comedy instead."

Connor's smile faded slightly, but his eyes sparkled. "You know you're better than this. You just need to find your voice again. Remember that time you cooked for that farmer's market competition?"

How could I forget? The way the sun had poured over the bustling square, casting golden rays on a hundred makeshift stalls, the aroma of fresh produce and baked goods swirling in the air like an intoxicating potion. I had set up my little booth, my heart racing as people lined up to sample my dishes. I could still picture the delighted faces, the way they'd closed their eyes with each bite as if trying to hold onto the moment forever. I had won that competition, not just because of the food, but because I had shared a piece of my story, my culture, with everyone who tasted it.

"I thought that was it," I said softly. "The moment I'd found my groove. But now..."

"Now you're just going through a rough patch," he interjected, his tone firm but gentle. "Like the pastry you overcooked last week. It happens. The key is to adjust the heat, right?"

"Only if I had a pastry chef for a best friend," I retorted, a smirk threatening to break through my melancholic mask.

"Well, you do. And I have a few culinary tricks up my sleeve." His grin returned, and suddenly the tension between us shifted. "We'll come up with something new. Together."

"You're right," I said, straightening up against the fridge. "I need to find my passion again, but I can't do it alone."

"Then let's make a pact." He leaned closer, his voice dropping conspiratorially. "We'll create something together. We'll experiment, make mistakes, and when you're ready, we'll face the critic again. And this time, you'll knock her socks off."

I could feel a spark igniting within me, a small flicker of the fire that had once burned bright. "You really think so?"

"Absolutely. But you have to promise me one thing."

"Name it."

"Promise you won't throw any soufflés this time. I'm not sure I can handle being the sous chef in that kind of kitchen."

With a newfound resolve, I laughed and pushed his shoulder playfully. "Fine, no throwing soufflés. Just an epic comeback."

"Now that's the spirit," he said, bumping his shoulder against mine. "Let's bake our way out of this."

And as we sat there, the darkness of failure receding like a tide, I felt something shift. With Connor at my side, I could taste the beginnings of something sweet rising from the ashes of my disappointment.

The heaviness of defeat lingered like the scent of burnt sugar, clinging stubbornly to my clothes and hair. I wanted to shake it off, to scrub it away with the soapy suds of a thousand late-night experiments, but there it was, an unwelcome guest in my kitchen and my heart. Connor's presence was a comfort, but even the warmth of his hand couldn't banish the chill of disappointment that wrapped around me like a too-tight apron.

"Okay, Mr. Positive," I said, taking a deep breath. "What's the first step in this culinary comeback?"

"Well," he leaned back, crossing his arms, the slight tilt of his head indicating he was entering his serious brainstorming mode. "We could start by focusing on the basics. What's your signature dish? The one that always gets rave reviews?"

I paused, searching my memory for the flavor that ignited my passion. "My grandmother's bolognese. It's not just a sauce; it's a symphony of flavors, like a hug on a plate."

"That's it then!" he exclaimed, eyes sparkling with enthusiasm. "Let's take that hug and make it a full-on bear hug! We can give it a twist that'll make it unforgettable. Something the critic will never forget."

"Bear hug, huh?" I chuckled, a smile cracking through my earlier gloom. "What are you thinking? Bolognese with a side of bear claws?"

"Exactly!" he replied, grinning like a child who had just discovered the world's best candy. "No, seriously. Let's add a modern twist—maybe some smoked paprika or a hint of cinnamon. Something unexpected."

I mulled it over, the idea of blending my grandmother's traditional flavors with something audacious tugging at the corners of my mind.

"You might be onto something there. A blend of the old and the new. It's like putting my heart on a plate."

"Exactly," he said, nudging my shoulder playfully. "Plus, I bet your bolognese is like a culinary love letter. So let's make sure the critic feels the heat of your passion when she takes a bite."

With newfound energy, I scrambled to my feet, brushing off the flour-dusted floor like it was a badge of honor. "You're right! It's time to start experimenting. Are you ready to get messy?"

"Messy? I was born ready," Connor replied with mock seriousness, grabbing a kitchen towel like it was a superhero cape. "Lead the way, culinary queen."

As I gathered ingredients, I felt the initial flicker of excitement bloom within me, fighting back the shadows of self-doubt. The kitchen transformed as I moved, pots clanging and pans sizzling, each sound echoing like a battle cry. Connor flitted around, fetching herbs and spices, his enthusiasm infectious.

"Do we have fresh basil?" I called over my shoulder, my mind racing with the layers of flavor I envisioned.

"Right here! And rosemary!" He brandished the herbs triumphantly like a knight showcasing his sword.

I couldn't help but laugh. "What are you, the herb knight?"

"Absolutely," he replied, striking a dramatic pose. "Protector of the parsley, savior of the sage!"

With each playful exchange, I found myself weaving through the fog of uncertainty, anchored by the comforting rhythms of chopping, simmering, and tasting. The scent of garlic sautéing in olive oil filled the air, mingling with the heady aroma of the tomatoes that simmered like a sweet summer memory, coaxing out the warmth of nostalgia.

"Okay, what about the critic?" I asked, my brow furrowing as I stirred the sauce. "She's not going to just let me waltz in with my bolognese, is she? I'll have to impress her—again."

Connor leaned against the counter, arms crossed, a contemplative look on his face. "That's the thing. You're not the only one who gets to decide what impresses her. You're the chef. Cook from the heart, and let your dish tell your story."

I nodded, letting his words sink in. It wasn't about her expectations; it was about mine. I would reclaim my narrative, painting my culinary tale with the brush of authenticity.

As the sauce thickened, I felt a spark of inspiration igniting. "What if we included some roasted vegetables? Maybe caramelized onions to deepen the flavor profile?"

"Brilliant! You're a genius!" Connor exclaimed, his enthusiasm bringing a flush to my cheeks. "Let's throw in some roasted red peppers for color. We want her to not only taste it but see it as a masterpiece."

With every new ingredient, the atmosphere in the kitchen shifted. I felt like I was not just cooking but crafting something monumental—an artistic endeavor.

Just as I was about to taste the simmering concoction, the doorbell rang, jolting me from my reverie.

"Expecting someone?" Connor asked, eyebrows raised.

"Not at all," I replied, wiping my hands on my apron. "Could it be the critics' assistant, come to deliver the verdict on my culinary skills?"

"Or a door-to-door salesperson with a fondness for 'Are you prepared for the apocalypse?' pamphlets?" Connor quipped, moving to open the door.

As he swung it open, I heard a gasp. My heart raced as I moved closer, catching a glimpse of a figure standing just beyond the threshold. A woman in a strikingly bright red dress, her hair pinned up elegantly, radiated a confidence that instantly put me on edge.

"Can I help you?" Connor asked, his voice surprisingly steady in the face of the woman's intensity.

"I'm here to speak with the chef," she said, her tone all business. "I'm a food blogger, and I've heard some... intriguing things about this kitchen."

The realization hit me like a thunderbolt. The critic had a reputation, yes, but this woman was another force entirely. She was known for tearing dishes apart with words sharper than any chef's knife.

"Uh, I'm just in the middle of—"

"No need to apologize," she interrupted smoothly, her eyes scanning the kitchen, taking in the simmering pot, the flour on the counter, the fragrant herbs. "I'll only take a moment."

A moment? I glanced at Connor, and I could see the shock mirrored in his eyes. The very air around us shifted, the warmth of the kitchen turning cold and prickly as I realized that today was going to be about so much more than just a dish—it was a test, and I was holding the ingredients to my fate in my hands.

With a deep breath, I stepped forward, my heart racing as I prepared to face this unexpected challenge. "Well, then, let's see if I can whip up something worthy of your taste."

The woman's smile was enigmatic, and I couldn't shake the feeling that this would be my moment of reckoning.

Chapter 25: Rising from the Ashes

The air was thick with the aroma of sautéed garlic and fresh herbs, weaving through the cramped, sun-drenched kitchen as I stood over the stove, stirring a bubbling pot of marinara sauce. Each swirl felt like a tiny act of rebellion against the shadows of doubt that had crept into my mind after the disaster. I let the heat of the sauce coax me back to life, savoring the vibrant notes of basil and oregano mingling with the sharpness of crushed tomatoes. It was my therapy, a healing balm for the wounds left by my last venture's failure.

As the sauce simmered, I turned my attention to the modest stack of prepped ingredients laid out like a culinary army, ready to fight for my attention. I had started small, with a humble offering of hand-rolled gnocchi and a selection of seasonal vegetables sourced from the local farmers' market. There was something poetic about those vegetables, their colors a riotous display of life: deep greens, radiant yellows, and the occasional blush of crimson red. They were a reminder that even the smallest seeds could grow into something extraordinary, given enough care and patience.

I wiped my brow with the back of my hand, feeling the warmth of the sun pouring through the window. It was the perfect backdrop for the latest pop-up I had arranged, and I was determined to make it memorable. With every diced onion and minced garlic clove, I visualized the faces of the guests who would soon fill the room, hungry not just for food but for an experience that resonated with authenticity.

"Let's hope this isn't another disaster," I muttered to myself, the thought sending a quick jolt of anxiety through my chest. It was impossible to shake the memory of the tasting event that had fallen flat. That evening had started with such promise: glitzy invitations, an enticing menu, and a venue that sparkled with potential. But as the hours passed, I had watched my dreams dim, flickering like a dying candle. People had trickled in, sure, but not in the numbers I had imagined. They sampled the food with polite smiles, their eyes darting elsewhere, as if they were waiting for something more exciting to come along.

I had left that night feeling as hollow as an empty shell, the echoes of laughter from the corner of the room haunting me. It felt like a cruel joke—my aspirations paraded in front of me, only to be scoffed at by the very audience I had hoped to captivate. But this time was different. I was ready to claw my way back up.

As I meticulously rolled the gnocchi, my mind flitted to the vendors I had reached out to over the past few weeks. There was Marco, the eccentric taco truck owner with a penchant for spicy fusion, and Janine, a pastry chef whose desserts could make the most hardened critic swoon. They were all in this together, a collective of dreamers desperate to create something meaningful. I couldn't help but smile at the thought of us—culinary misfits collaborating to serve up something fresh, unexpected, and undeniably delicious.

I was almost finished with the sauce when a sharp knock shattered the tranquility of my culinary oasis. My heart jumped, but I masked it with a frown, wondering if I had forgotten an appointment. I wiped my hands on my apron and made my way to the door, hoping it wasn't some persistent delivery person or worse, an angry neighbor upset with the aromas wafting from my kitchen.

When I opened the door, I was met with a gust of cool air and a figure silhouetted against the afternoon light. It was Leo, my former sous-chef and the very embodiment of culinary chaos wrapped in a bearded enigma. His arrival was always both a blessing and a curse—a whirlwind of unpredictable energy that could either elevate my creations or send them spiraling into oblivion.

"Surprise! I brought snacks!" he declared, his arms laden with bags from a local bakery, their fragrant offerings spilling out like a bounty from some mythical kitchen. I couldn't help but laugh, the tension in my shoulders easing.

"Leo, if those are from that dreadful place downtown, I'm going to toss them out the window," I teased, stepping aside to let him in.

"Harsh but fair," he replied with a wink, plopping down a particularly suspect-looking pastry onto my counter. "But you're going to want to try these," he said, fishing out a few delicate macarons that glistened like jewels.

He placed them in front of me, and I caught the scent of almond and raspberry. My stomach growled in appreciation, and I picked one up, savoring the delicate crunch of the shell and the burst of flavor that followed. "Okay, I'll give you this one. These are decent."

"Just decent? I'll take it as a win," he chuckled, his laughter a melody that filled the kitchen with warmth. "I couldn't resist when I heard about your pop-up. Figured you could use a little backup."

"More like a little chaos," I retorted, my heart swelling at the unexpected support. "But I'll take any help I can get."

"Consider me your culinary knight in shining armor," he quipped, dramatically placing a hand over his heart. I rolled my eyes, unable to suppress a grin. With Leo around, it felt like the weight of the world had been lifted, even if just for a moment.

As we bantered back and forth, the kitchen transformed into a symphony of laughter and sizzling pans. It was a dance of creativity and camaraderie, the kind of partnership that felt both comforting and invigorating. I realized that with every joke, every playful jab, I was piecing together not just a meal, but a sense of hope. There was something intoxicating about our collective effort, a reminder that I was not alone in this venture. We were crafting a story together, and I was ready to rise from the ashes once more.

The afternoon light poured in through the window, casting golden streaks across the kitchen as Leo and I continued our culinary choreography. With every chop of the knife and stir of the pot, the air crackled with possibility. The laughter from earlier had faded into a comfortable hum, a subtle reminder of the friendship we'd forged through our shared chaos.

"Alright, chef extraordinaire," Leo said, nudging me aside to claim the stovetop. "You know what this sauce needs? A little zing. Something to make it pop!" He grabbed a small jar of chili flakes from my spice rack, shaking it enthusiastically.

"Zing? Are we still talking about the sauce?" I shot back, raising an eyebrow. "Or have we crossed over into the realm of the bizarre?"

"Both!" he laughed, his eyes gleaming with mischief. "A little heat never hurt anyone. Besides, you want people to remember this dish, don't you? 'That's the sauce that lit my taste buds on fire!'"

I smirked, a playful challenge sparking in my eyes. "Alright, Mr. Firestarter, just don't burn down my kitchen. I like it too much to see it go up in flames."

With an exaggerated flourish, he tossed a generous sprinkle of chili flakes into the bubbling sauce, his face transforming into a mask of exaggerated concentration. "And now we wait. The magic happens," he proclaimed, leaning back against the counter, arms crossed.

As we watched the sauce meld into a crimson masterpiece, I felt a flutter of excitement. This was more than just food; it was a labor of love, an offering to the community that had almost overlooked me. I imagined the crowd that would gather tonight, faces illuminated by candlelight, laughter mingling with the clinking of glasses. For a fleeting moment, I was lost in the vision of how it would feel to see people enjoying something I had created with my own hands, a sensory celebration of resilience.

"Do you remember that time we had to cater that wedding for your cousin?" Leo suddenly asked, breaking my reverie. "The one where the groom's mother declared war on the appetizer table?"

"War is a strong word," I replied, suppressing a laugh. "She was simply... passionate about the shrimp cocktail."

"Passionate? She nearly had a meltdown when we ran out of cocktail sauce!" He grinned, and I could see the memory dancing in his eyes. "You handled it like a pro, though. You whipped up a new batch in record time while wearing that apron that said 'Kiss the Cook'—like an edible superhero."

I chuckled, remembering the chaos of that day—the kitchen in disarray, my cousin's panicked face as guests grew restless, and how I had managed to salvage the evening by improvising with pantry staples. It was a moment of clarity, a realization that culinary disasters could be transformed into triumphs with just a little ingenuity and determination. "I think I still have that apron," I said, grinning. "Somewhere buried beneath layers of flour and regret."

"Regret?" he teased, raising an eyebrow. "That sounds dramatic. Is that how you see your life now? A sad tale of a talented chef buried in flour?"

"Flour is merely a part of the journey, my friend. It's what you do with it that counts," I replied, the weight of my earlier struggles creeping back in. But I shoved it aside, unwilling to let it ruin our moment. "Now, let's focus on this sauce. I need it to be extraordinary tonight."

Leo nodded, an encouraging glint in his eye. "You've got this. Just channel your inner culinary goddess."

As the hours passed, we diced, sautéed, and assembled our menu, laughter flowing as freely as the olive oil we drizzled over our dishes. The kitchen transformed into a haven of creativity, a safe space filled with the rhythmic sounds of chopping and sizzling that drowned out the doubts lurking in my mind.

With the sun setting, we plated the first batch of gnocchi, arranging them delicately like a work of art on a canvas. The soft pillows of dough nestled against the vibrant sauce, garnished with fresh basil and a sprinkle of Parmesan, radiating warmth and comfort. I took a step back, admiring our handiwork, the weight of anticipation settling in my stomach.

"Do you think it's too late to change the name of this dish to 'Gnocchi with a Side of Redemption'?" I quipped, my heart racing at the thought of the impending evening.

"Maybe not too late," Leo mused, his expression mock-serious. "But I'd stick with the classic 'gnocchi' for tonight. Save the drama for your next pop-up. We want them to come back for more, not leave wondering what on earth just happened."

With the clock ticking down, we set up the dining space, stringing twinkling lights across the room to create an inviting atmosphere. The soft glow enveloped the tables, which were adorned with mismatched plates and colorful cloth napkins, lending an air of casual elegance. I wanted every detail to invite warmth and familiarity, a cozy gathering that felt less like a formal event and more like a communal celebration.

As the first guests trickled in, my heart raced with a mix of excitement and apprehension. The room filled with laughter and chatter, a cacophony of voices blending into a delightful hum. I moved through the crowd, greeting familiar faces and newcomers alike, my heart swelling at the sight of them.

"Your reputation precedes you," a woman said, her eyes sparkling as she accepted a plate piled high with gnocchi. "I've heard nothing but good things about your food!"

"Let's hope I can live up to the hype," I replied, trying to maintain my composure as my cheeks warmed under her gaze.

The evening unfolded beautifully. Plates were cleaned, compliments flowed, and laughter bounced off the walls like musical notes. I felt a rush of satisfaction as I watched people savoring the dishes, their smiles a balm to my earlier anxieties. For the first time in weeks, I allowed myself to enjoy the moment, to celebrate the small victories that had brought me here.

Just as I was about to pour myself a celebratory glass of wine, a commotion erupted at the entrance. I turned to see a tall figure silhouetted in the doorway, the room dimming around them. My heart skipped as I recognized the familiar silhouette of Nathan, the food critic whose words could make or break a chef's career. He stepped forward, scanning the room with an inscrutable expression, and my stomach dropped.

"Why is he here?" I whispered to Leo, my voice barely audible over the murmur of the crowd.

"Looks like we're about to find out," he replied, eyes wide with a mix of excitement and dread.

Before I could brace myself for the impending confrontation, Nathan approached, a glimmer of curiosity flickering in his eyes. "I've heard whispers about tonight's menu," he said, his voice smooth like butter, "and I couldn't resist the urge to see for myself what all the fuss is about."

My heart raced, a mix of hope and anxiety swirling within me. This was it—the moment that could change everything.

Chapter 26: The Sweetest Victory

The first time I saw a line outside one of my pop-ups, I thought it was a mistake. The sun draped golden rays over the bustling street, illuminating the laughter and chatter of a Saturday market. I peeked out from behind the counter, my heart a wild drum in my chest, expecting the crowd to disperse at any moment. But they stayed. They waited for my food. My food. The aroma of sizzling garlic and fresh basil hung in the air, weaving itself around the delighted faces of strangers, yet I was still skeptical.

"Is this real life?" I muttered, half to myself, half to Connor, who stood beside me, his arms crossed with a playful smugness that made him look far too self-satisfied for my nerves.

"Told you," he said, a wide grin plastered on his face, the kind that lit up his whole being. "They come for the flavor, and you've got it."

Connor was a whirlwind of energy, effortlessly charming in a way that made him the unofficial mascot of my little venture. His curly hair bounced as he gestured animatedly, pointing to the throng of eager customers eyeing my makeshift menu. Each item was a love letter to my childhood, infused with the nostalgia of family gatherings and summer barbecues. The words "Pesto Caprese Sandwich" and "Grilled Peach Salad" rolled off my tongue like poetry, but seeing them in the hands of strangers made the whole dream feel unreal.

As I settled into the rhythm of serving, a heady mix of excitement and anxiety surged through me. I flipped open the old, battered notebook where I jotted down my recipes, hoping that my grandmother's meticulous notes would guide me through the chaos. Each sandwich felt like an homage to her, my culinary compass as I navigated the tangled web of flavors and textures. The market around me buzzed with life, colors popping everywhere; the vibrant red of tomatoes mingling with the earthy greens of fresh herbs, just like my memories of those sun-drenched kitchens back home.

"Two Caprese, one Peach," I shouted to Connor, who was working the register with a contagious enthusiasm that somehow made every order feel like an event. He was a master of banter, weaving in clever quips and friendly jabs that had customers laughing, creating a cozy bubble around our little stall.

"Did you ever think you'd be this popular?" he teased, handing over a bag to a smiling customer, who walked away with a satisfied nod. "Next, you'll be too famous for us little people."

I rolled my eyes but couldn't help but grin. "Let's not get ahead of ourselves. I'm still just a girl selling sandwiches."

Yet, the line grew longer, a ribbon of anticipation stretching toward the far end of the market. Each face mirrored a mix of curiosity and desire, a collection of stories waiting to be woven into the fabric of my day. I focused on the rhythm of my hands as they moved with practiced ease—slicing bread, layering fresh mozzarella, and drizzling homemade balsamic reduction like an artist adding the finishing touch to a masterpiece. The moment felt electric, the adrenaline coursing through me, reminding me why I had started this journey in the first place.

Then, as if the universe wanted to remind me that every success has its hurdles, disaster struck. A loud crash resonated through the air, and I turned just in time to see a fellow vendor drop a large pot of something soupy, the contents splattering across the pavement like a messy Jackson Pollock. It sent a ripple of chaos through the crowd, the atmosphere shifting from laughter to tension in seconds.

"Stay calm, folks!" Connor shouted, his voice cutting through the murmur. He moved to help, but my instincts kicked in. "No! Stay here!" I yelled, moving to the front of our stall as the tension hung thick like the humidity in the air. "Everyone, stay right here! We're still serving! Delicious food right here!"

I could hear the waver in my voice, the tension creeping in, but the determination surged through me. I locked eyes with a woman in the front of the line, her eyebrows raised in concern. "Are you okay?" she asked, her voice soft yet probing.

"Of course! Just a little market excitement," I said, forcing a smile, hoping it looked more convincing than it felt. "How about a Peach Salad? I promise it's a sweet distraction!"

To my surprise, she chuckled, the warmth of her laughter cutting through my anxiety. "I'll take two! One for me and one for my partner, who is somewhere in that mess."

I nodded, realizing that laughter was my ally here, a way to connect and ease the tension. I turned back to the counter, focusing on the bright colors of the ingredients in front of me, their vibrancy stark against the backdrop of the chaos just a few feet away. Each slice, each drizzle of oil, became a meditation as I fought to maintain my balance in the storm.

Moments later, just as I was settling back into the groove, the chaos shifted again. A little girl, no older than six, tugged at her mother's sleeve, pointing at the vibrant display of fresh ingredients. "Can I have that one?" she asked, her eyes wide with delight.

Her mother smiled, and before I knew it, my heart melted at the sight. "Absolutely, sweetheart! That's our special today, and it's all yours."

As I crafted the sandwich, I engaged in playful banter with her, crafting a tiny world of whimsical ingredients and imaginary flavors, hoping to spark her excitement. The world around us faded as we shared that moment, laughter bubbling between us, and for a brief second, I wasn't just serving food—I was building connections, memories even, one sandwich at a time.

The day stretched on, filled with laughter, the smell of basil wafting through the air, and the satisfaction of serving a community hungry for something real. Each order placed was a testament to my hard work, a small victory stacking up against the mountain of doubt that had once overshadowed my dream.

The energy was infectious. As the minutes stretched on, each customer's delighted reaction fed into my confidence, creating an electric loop of joy that filled the air. I ladled generous portions of tangy balsamic vinaigrette over the fresh salads, its sweetness mingling with the earthy notes of the ripe peaches. The steady rhythm of my hands slicing through ingredients became my mantra, a soothing repetition amid the whirlwind of the market. Connor kept the spirits high, weaving through the crowd like a master conductor, ensuring everyone felt welcomed and entertained.

"Did you know?" he said, leaning closer to me as he accepted another order. "You could start charging a 'happiness fee.' This place is practically a therapy session with all the smiles you're serving up!"

"Let's not get ahead of ourselves," I replied, playfully rolling my eyes while adjusting my apron. "It's just sandwiches, not therapy. I'm not ready for the Yelp reviews to include 'food with a side of emotional support.'"

His laughter echoed, an uplifting sound that brightened the space around us. But in the midst of our banter, my thoughts drifted to the reality of it all. The dreams I had harbored for so long were slowly transforming into something tangible. I had spent countless nights researching and experimenting, my kitchen the laboratory where flavors collided, and here I was, witnessing the fruits of my labor unfold before my eyes.

As the line of customers dwindled, a familiar face broke through the throng. Anna, my college roommate, with her signature wild curls and the same insatiable curiosity that had led her to take a semester abroad in Italy for the sole purpose of mastering pasta. She wove through the crowd, her eyes wide with excitement. "Oh my God, is this what you've been up to? You didn't tell me you were becoming a sandwich wizard!"

"More like a sandwich witch," I retorted, a laugh escaping me. "I've conjured up some magic with these recipes, but I still have my moments of being a complete disaster."

"Disaster? Honey, this line says otherwise," she said, glancing around at the few lingering customers, clearly still savoring their meals. "Can I get a grilled peach salad? I need to know if your cooking has evolved beyond boiling water."

"Just you wait," I said, grabbing fresh ingredients from the counter and tossing them into a bowl with practiced ease. "You're in for a treat. I won't just impress you; I'll blow your culinary socks off."

Her playful smirk turned into genuine anticipation as she accepted the bowl, and for a moment, we were whisked away from the busy stall, bound by shared memories of late-night study sessions and culinary disasters. I had always admired her passion for food, and now here we were, two dreamers in a bustling market, worlds apart from the mundane grind of everyday life.

"Are you still working that soul-sucking office job?" I asked, glancing sideways at her as she took a bite.

Anna sighed dramatically, the kind that drew laughter from those around us. "Oh, you mean the one where I pretend to care about quarterly reports? Yes, it's as thrilling as it sounds. But I do it for the paycheck, you know? Gotta fund the dream somehow."

I nodded, knowing all too well the sacrifices we made for our passions. "Well, at least you're getting your daily dose of creativity through me now."

"I could use a side of your magic in my life," she said, her expression turning serious. "Have you ever thought about taking this beyond the pop-ups? Maybe opening a café or something?"

The idea slipped through the air between us like a delicious aroma, tempting yet daunting. My heart raced at the thought, but a cold wave of doubt crashed over me. "That's a big leap, Anna. What if it flops? What if it all crumbles?"

"Or what if it soars?" she countered, her voice firm. "You're talented, and you've got something special here. You owe it to yourself to see how far you can take it."

Before I could respond, a sudden commotion from the end of the line pulled my attention away. A man in a sharp suit was waving his arms, clearly agitated, his voice cutting through the cheerful hum of the market like a knife. "Excuse me! Excuse me!" he called, his tone sharp enough to slice through the warmth.

I felt a knot form in my stomach. Did I do something wrong? Were my ingredients unapproved? As he approached, his eyes narrowed at me like a hawk zeroing in on its prey.

"What's your name?" he demanded, glancing at the sign that bore my modest brand name.

"Uh, I'm—"

"Doesn't matter," he interrupted, shaking his head. "Do you realize you're operating without a vendor's license?"

I blinked, shock washing over me. "What? No, I—"

"Look, I understand you're just trying to hustle," he continued, his voice dripping with condescension. "But you can't just set up shop wherever you feel like it. There are rules, and I'm here to enforce them."

My heart raced, the taste of fear mixing with the earlier sweetness of victory. "I was under the impression that as part of the market, I was covered—"

"Not my problem. You need to pack up," he said, his eyes scanning my setup with disdain.

Connor, who had been fetching more ingredients, reappeared beside me, confusion washing over his face. "What's going on?"

"Just a little misunderstanding," I said, trying to maintain my composure. But as I looked back at the man, my heart sank deeper. The crowd around us began to murmur, sensing the tension, and suddenly I felt as if I were on a stage, my performance unraveling in front of an audience that had once been captivated.

"Pack up?" I echoed, panic clawing at my throat. "But the customers are still waiting! I've just started to—"

"Not my concern," he snapped, the coldness in his eyes suggesting he relished this moment of power.

The laughter and chatter that had enveloped me moments ago faded into an eerie silence, the laughter now replaced by whispers of judgment and doubt. My dreams hung in the balance, threatened by a man in a suit who seemed to derive pleasure from my predicament.

"Excuse me!" Connor stepped forward, his voice rising. "You don't have to do this. She's just getting started."

But the man shrugged, his indifference as sharp as the lines of his suit. "I have a job to do. It's nothing personal."

"Nothing personal?" I repeated, incredulous. "It feels pretty damn personal when you're ruining someone's chance at success!"

Just then, a voice broke through the tension, deep and resonant. "Is there a problem here?"

I turned to see a woman in a bright yellow sundress, her presence both commanding and comforting. She exuded warmth, an aura of authority that shifted the energy in the air. The man in the suit stiffened, his bravado faltering slightly as he faced her.

"Not your business, ma'am," he shot back, but there was a tremor in his tone.

"I think it is," she replied, stepping closer to us, a protective force. "I own this market, and I'd like to hear what you think you're doing."

My breath caught in my throat. The market owner. My heart raced, hope mingling with the fear that had previously engulfed me. Just when I thought my dreams were slipping away, the tides shifted, and the winds of fate might finally be in my favor.

Chapter 27: A Seat at the Table

It was a typical Tuesday morning, and the sun filtered through the café window, creating patterns on the table that reminded me of the intricate latticework in my grandmother's garden. The sweet scent of vanilla wafted from the kitchen, and my heart raced with anticipation. I was meeting Connor, the culinary genius whose presence lit up the room like a perfectly flamed crème brûlée, but today felt different. The clinking of coffee cups and the low murmur of conversations faded as I braced myself for what was to come.

As he strode in, a gust of cool air followed him, rustling the papers scattered on my table. Connor, with his tousled hair and that half-smile that could melt glaciers, was a vision in his charcoal chef's jacket. I couldn't help but admire the way he moved, each step radiating confidence, his eyes sparkling with unspoken jokes that danced just beyond reach.

"Sorry I'm late," he said, sliding into the chair opposite mine. "I had a slight disaster with a soufflé that demanded immediate attention. I swear they're plotting against me."

I couldn't suppress a laugh. "I thought only pastries were dramatic. Next, you'll tell me the croissants are conspiring to overthrow the macarons."

Connor grinned, and for a moment, the tension that had started to build between us melted away like butter on a hot skillet. We chatted easily, slipping into our comfortable rhythm, discussing everything from the upcoming food festival to our mutual love for spicy tacos. But beneath the playful banter lingered an unspoken weight, a sense of something simmering just out of sight. The buzz of my burgeoning success had turned into a cacophony, drowning out our once effortless connection.

As I sipped my latte, I couldn't help but notice the way Connor's gaze drifted toward the window. It seemed he was caught in a web of his own thoughts, tangled between the dreams we had shared and the reality that now stretched between us like a chasm. The accolades and invitations were pouring in, and while I was thrilled, I also felt a creeping dread that this newfound success was reshaping our lives in ways I hadn't anticipated.

"Are you excited about the gala next week?" he asked, breaking my reverie.

"Absolutely! But I'm also terrified. There's going to be so much pressure to impress the critics." I leaned in, my voice lowering. "What if I bomb? What if I trip over my own feet on the way to the podium? What if—"

"Hey," he interjected gently, placing his hand over mine. "You're going to knock it out of the park. Just remember why you started. You love food, and that passion will shine through."

His touch sent a shiver down my spine, igniting something that I had tried to quell in the whirlwind of my rising career. The moment lingered like the last notes of a favorite song, and I desperately wished I could bottle it up, but as quickly as it came, it slipped away. We withdrew back to the edges of our conversation, tiptoeing around the undeniable connection that felt both exhilarating and suffocating.

The week raced by in a blur of meetings and tastings, each moment filled with the electric hum of creativity and opportunity. I had never imagined my vision would attract such attention, yet here I was, juggling collaborations like a circus performer, each invitation weighing heavier than the last. They were accolades, yes, but they also felt like chains, binding me to a version of myself that was evolving faster than I could keep up.

The night of the gala arrived, and the venue was a spectacle in itself—glittering chandeliers dripped with crystals, casting prismatic rainbows across the polished marble floor. The air was thick with anticipation and the rich aroma of gourmet dishes being whisked past on silver trays. I stood backstage, my heart thudding like a drum, surrounded by the hum of voices and the shuffling of feet.

"Breathe," I muttered to myself, clutching the edge of the curtain. "You've got this."

As I stepped out onto the stage, the spotlight illuminated the sea of faces, some familiar, others not. I could see Connor in the audience, his expression a mix of pride and concern, and for a moment, everything faded away. The audience held their breath, and in that pause, I found my center. I spoke from the heart, sharing the story of my journey—the struggles, the triumphs, and the sheer joy of creating something beautiful through food.

Applause erupted as I finished, a wave of sound crashing over me, and I felt a rush of euphoria. But as I stepped off the stage, reality crashed back in. The whirlwind of conversations and congratulations swirled around me, and despite the applause, a shadow crept into my heart. I had poured everything into this moment, yet I couldn't shake the feeling that with every new opportunity, I was losing something precious—something that had once felt like home.

In the midst of the celebration, I spotted Connor near the bar, his expression contemplative. I approached him, feeling the weight of the world on my shoulders.

"Did I do okay?" I asked, searching his eyes for reassurance.

"You were brilliant," he said, his voice low and steady. "But I can see the storm brewing behind your smile."

I opened my mouth to respond, but the words tangled in my throat. I didn't want to admit that beneath the success was a growing distance, a chasm threatening to swallow the bond we had forged. Instead, I opted for levity. "Just chalk it up to an excessive amount of caffeine and a touch of drama."

He chuckled, but his gaze remained serious. "You can't keep pretending everything is fine."

As the evening wore on, the laughter and joy around us felt increasingly distant, a facade that couldn't mask the fissures developing between us. I had climbed to the top, but at what cost?

As the night progressed, the gala morphed into a dizzying whirlwind of laughter, clinking glasses, and the occasional startled squeak as a waiter narrowly avoided a collision with a velvet curtain. I felt like I was floating on a cloud of success, yet beneath that cloud, thunder rumbled ominously. The applause had faded, but the weight of expectations pressed on my chest like a heavy soufflé, about to collapse.

"Let's get some air," Connor said, his hand gently squeezing my elbow as he led me toward a quieter terrace, adorned with twinkling fairy lights strung across the wrought iron railing. The cool evening breeze tousled my hair, bringing with it the fragrant notes of blooming jasmine, which momentarily soothed the tension building inside me.

"Why does this place feel so much like a set from a rom-com?" I mused, glancing around. "You know, where the protagonists have a heart-to-heart about life choices while some dramatic music plays in the background?"

He chuckled, leaning against the railing, his eyes reflecting the soft glow of the lights. "As long as I don't have to jump into a fountain to prove my love, I'm good. I'm still drying out from last week's soufflé debacle."

We both laughed, the sound mingling with the night air, but the moment felt fragile, like a delicate glass sculpture waiting for someone to breathe too hard. I shifted my weight, struggling with the words I wanted to say but couldn't quite shape into sound. The opportunity to share my passion with the world had arrived, yet it felt as if I were losing the very person who had inspired that passion in the first place.

"Connor, I..." I started, but he turned to me, his expression earnest, cutting through the laughter like a knife through butter.

"Are you okay?" he asked, a hint of concern flickering in his gaze. "I know it's a lot, but I want you to be happy. I can see the stress, and you don't have to carry it alone."

"It's just—" I hesitated, my heart racing as I searched for the right words. "I love what I'm doing, but it's becoming overwhelming. The more I succeed, the less time I have to focus on...well, us."

"Us?" he echoed, his brow furrowing slightly. "What do you mean by that?"

"Exactly that," I said, frustration creeping into my voice. "We used to dream about our future over taco nights and spontaneous kitchen experiments. Now it's all about deadlines and appearances, and I feel like I'm losing touch with everything that mattered."

Connor took a deep breath, his expression softening. "You're not losing touch. You're growing, and that's a beautiful thing. But you can't forget to nurture the roots of what got you here. You can still have both."

I bit my lip, torn between gratitude for his support and the rising panic that swirled around us like the fragrant smoke from a distant barbecue. "I want both, but it feels like I'm being pulled apart. There are moments I look at you, and I'm reminded of everything I love, but the chaos feels all-consuming."

"Chaos can be managed," he said, his voice steady. "Just like a recipe. You gather your ingredients and adjust as you go. You're the chef in this kitchen of life. You just have to find the right balance."

A part of me wanted to cling to his words, but another part whispered that the balance we once had was slipping away, like sugar dissolving into boiling water. I could almost feel the divide widening, an invisible gap that threatened to swallow the dreams we had once shared.

Before I could respond, the sound of laughter erupted from inside, and my phone buzzed in my pocket. I pulled it out to see a flood of notifications from my team about upcoming events and culinary collaborations. Each message felt like a reminder of how much was at stake, how many people relied on me, pulling me further away from the simplicity of just being together.

"Sorry, it's work," I muttered, swiping through the messages, frustration gnawing at me. "I should probably head back inside."

"Is that what you really want?" he asked, his voice low, almost a whisper. "To just dive back into that whirlwind?"

I paused, my finger hovering over the screen. Did I want to return to the madness, or did I want to stay here, breathing in the cool night air with the man I cared about? A part of me longed for the chaos, the opportunity to shine, while another part ached for connection, for shared moments of laughter over burnt toast.

"I..." I began, but before I could find the words, a flash of movement caught my eye. I turned to see a figure darting toward us, a woman with wild curls and an exuberance that seemed to vibrate through the air like a maraca.

"Leila!" she called, her voice cutting through the moment like a chef's knife through a delicate tomato. "You're not going to believe who just walked in! Chef Daniel Rossi! He's looking for collaborators for his new pop-up restaurant, and I told him about you!"

I blinked, the name hitting me like a jolt of caffeine. Chef Daniel Rossi was a culinary sensation, the kind of chef whose mere presence could catapult careers into the stratosphere. Suddenly, the weight of everything shifted, and the chaos I had been trying to escape surged back like an ocean wave.

"Wait, he's here?" I asked, my heart racing with a mix of excitement and anxiety. "And he's looking for collaborators?"

"Yes! You have to go talk to him!" She practically bounced on her heels, enthusiasm bubbling over. "This could be your big break!"

My gaze darted back to Connor, who stood watching me with an unreadable expression. The excitement in the air crackled, the moment both an opportunity and a threat. I could feel the pressure building, a crescendo of ambition and longing.

"I should go," I said, uncertainty lacing my voice. "This is a huge opportunity."

"But what about us?" Connor asked, his voice rising slightly above the crowd.

I hesitated, caught in the crosshairs of my aspirations and the quiet chaos of my heart. The night held a promise, but the decision weighed heavily, and as I turned toward the door, the tension twisted tighter.

"Leila, wait!" he called, desperation threading through his tone.

But as I stepped inside, the roar of the gala engulfed me, and I could only hope I wasn't stepping into something I couldn't escape. The flickering lights danced around me, each heartbeat a countdown to the moment I might lose everything I had fought to build—and everything I held dear.

Chapter 28: Crumbling Foundations

The weight of the past few months settled onto my shoulders like a heavy cloak, wrapping around me in an unwelcome embrace. I often found myself standing at the edge of my kitchen, staring into the depths of a coffee pot that could rival a black hole in its relentless draw. It felt easier to gaze into the abyss than to face the glaring reality of my life. My days had morphed into a frenzied blur of meetings and deadlines, punctuated by a cacophony of ringing phones and the incessant chatter of colleagues whose faces had begun to blend into a monochrome of familiarity.

The work was supposed to feel exhilarating, a climb up a steep mountain where every step promised a breathtaking view. But instead, I was trapped in a never-ending loop of client calls and project updates, each request echoing in my mind like a bad pop song that refused to fade away. I could almost hear the relentless tick of the clock on the wall, counting down the moments until my next obligation, and each tick whispered a reminder of the things I was losing—my laughter, my spontaneity, my evenings spent wrapped in the comfort of Connor's arms.

At first, Connor's support felt like a buoy, lifting me above the waves of my rising responsibilities. His gentle encouragement flowed through our conversations like a warm stream, a soothing balm for my frayed nerves. But lately, the buoy had transformed into an anchor, pulling me down into the depths of a sea that felt colder with every passing day. When I glanced at him, his eyes held an unmistakable concern that only deepened the sense of isolation swelling within me. We used to share everything—our dreams, our worries, even our silly little inside jokes that no one else understood. Now, those conversations were punctuated by awkward silences and the occasional forced smile.

The distance felt like a chasm, and each passing day, I feared that the bridge we'd built was collapsing under the weight of unspoken words and unshed tears. Our once vibrant banter had dwindled to functional exchanges about grocery lists and the weather. I missed the lightness, the way we'd laugh at the silliest things—the time we tried to bake cookies only to end up with a kitchen disaster that resembled something from a horror movie, or the spontaneous trips to nowhere that led us to quaint little diners that served the best pancakes. Now, we were reduced to discussions about schedules and chores, and I couldn't help but wonder if the love we'd shared was crumbling just like the foundation beneath my feet.

One evening, I found myself slumped on the couch, the flickering light from the TV casting a dull glow in the dim room. Connor was in the kitchen, his silhouette framed against the light as he rummaged through our cluttered cabinets. I watched him move, each gesture filled with a quiet grace that made my heart ache. He hummed a tune that was achingly familiar, a melody that had once danced between us, intertwining our hearts with each note. I opened my mouth to speak, to bridge the growing chasm, but the words caught in my throat like a stubborn pebble.

"Hey, do you want to order in?" he called out, his voice cutting through the silence, rich and inviting.

"Sure," I replied, trying to match the enthusiasm I felt slipping away. "What do you feel like?"

His answer was muffled, drowned by the rattle of dishes. I could almost hear the gears in his mind turning as he contemplated options, his brow furrowing in that adorably serious way. "How about Thai?"

"Perfect," I said, forcing a smile as I scrolled through my phone, searching for our usual place. But as I tapped the screen, the weight of the moment pressed down on me, and I realized that I didn't want to just order dinner. I wanted to order back the spark we'd lost.

"Can we talk?" I finally ventured, my heart racing at the prospect of laying bare my thoughts.

Connor turned, his expression shifting from casual to cautious. "About what?"

"Us." The word hung in the air, charged with an electricity that crackled between us. I watched him swallow hard, his Adam's apple bobbing as he processed my request.

"Okay," he said slowly, placing the dishes down with a gentleness that belied the tension swirling around us. He sat beside me, his presence warm yet somehow distant, like the first hints of a sunset that promised darkness to come.

"I feel like we're drifting," I admitted, my voice trembling slightly as I navigated the minefield of our emotions. "And I don't want that. I don't want to lose you."

Connor's gaze met mine, and I could see the turmoil swirling in his deep brown eyes. "I know," he said, his voice low and sincere. "But it's hard. I see you working so much, and I'm proud of you, but I miss... I miss us."

His honesty hit me like a slap, and the sting cut deeper than I expected. I bit my lip, holding back a flood of emotions that threatened to spill over. "I don't know how to balance it all," I confessed, feeling more vulnerable than I had in ages. "It's like I'm constantly chasing something, and I don't even know what it is anymore."

"You don't have to chase anything. You've already caught so much," he said, a hint of frustration creeping into his tone. "You're amazing at what you do, but if you're not careful, you'll lose the things that matter most to you."

The truth of his words sank in, and I felt the foundations of my world shake, not from fear, but from a profound realization. It was time to rebuild, to refocus, to ensure that what mattered most wasn't lost in the chaos of ambition. I took a deep breath, feeling the air fill my lungs, and made a silent vow to confront the cracks in our relationship before they became a chasm too wide to cross.

The air in the room grew thick with unspoken words, and for a moment, I wished I could take a mental snapshot of Connor's expression, etching it into my mind. His brow was furrowed, not in annoyance, but in concern that only deepened my resolve. "I want to find a way back to us," I said, my voice firm despite the tremor beneath it.

Connor's mouth curved into a small, tentative smile, the kind that always made my heart skip a beat, even now. "We can definitely do that. But you need to promise me something."

"What's that?"

"Promise me you won't let this work consume you. You're a force of nature, but I don't want to be just a bystander in your life." His eyes sparkled with a hint of mischief, attempting to lighten the mood, but the underlying tension still shimmered between us.

"I can't help it if my job is trying to outpace me," I said, rolling my eyes in a way that hopefully conveyed my lightheartedness. "I mean, who knew being a project manager came with the side effects of existential dread?"

"Ah, the classic combo. If only they had a warning label." Connor chuckled softly, but the laughter felt a little strained, like a too-tight rubber band ready to snap.

"Okay, maybe I'll try to carve out more 'us' time," I offered, half-sincere, half-hoping to ease the tension. "How about a date night this weekend? I'll even let you pick the restaurant."

"Wow, high stakes! I better choose wisely then," he replied, his playful tone returning for just a moment. I could see the flicker of excitement in his eyes, a tiny flame fighting against the darkness of our uncertainty.

"Don't screw it up, okay? We might have to go to that weird burger joint again if you do," I teased, nudging him gently.

Connor feigned shock. "You take that back! The Flaming Bun has a cult following for a reason!"

I laughed, the sound rich and full, and for a moment, it felt like we were back in our comfortable groove, two misfits bantering over ridiculous food choices. But as the laughter faded, the reality of our situation loomed over us like an ominous cloud.

As the week unfolded, I tried to implement my promise. I carved out time to reconnect with Connor amidst the chaos, sneaking in coffee dates between work calls and squeezing in walks through the neighborhood, where the trees were beginning to don their fall colors. Each conversation felt like a delicate dance, a step forward and a pause, as we navigated the delicate terrain of our shifting relationship.

One afternoon, while sipping a pumpkin-spiced latte (my guilty seasonal pleasure), I found myself lost in thought, scrolling through social media. I stumbled upon a post about an upcoming community fundraiser, featuring a talent show where local artists could showcase their skills. The notion sparked a wild idea in my mind, something I hadn't entertained in ages.

"What if we entered?" I blurted out, nearly spilling my drink as I turned to Connor, who was busy scrolling through his own phone.

"Entered what?" He looked up, confusion swirling in his brown eyes.

"The talent show! We could do it together! You could juggle or something, and I could... I don't know, tap dance?" I offered, my excitement bubbling over.

He raised an eyebrow, clearly entertained. "You know I can't juggle. I can barely catch a ball without looking like I'm trying to swat a fly."

"Exactly! It'll be hilarious. We could use a little laughter, right?"

Connor leaned back, considering it. "And what would your act be? I can't have you tapping your way into a heart attack on stage."

"I'd simply tap my way to the best performance ever!" I replied, gesturing dramatically.

His laughter echoed, and for a moment, it felt like old times again. "You're ridiculous," he said, shaking his head. "But fine, let's do it. If nothing else, we'll have a good story to tell."

As we dove into our plans, the reality of our routine faded into the background, replaced by a shared mission. We spent evenings rehearsing, transforming our small living room into an impromptu stage. I practiced my best (read: terrible) tap dance moves, while Connor found himself volunteering for impromptu juggling lessons from YouTube, our laughter ringing off the walls like music.

Yet, amidst our playful antics, the cracks in our foundation remained. It was clear we were trying to patch things up, but each time we laughed, I sensed an underlying urgency—the ticking clock of our unresolved issues loomed larger, like an ominous shadow.

Then came the day of the talent show. The air was charged with excitement as we entered the community center, a buzz of energy filling the room. Tables were adorned with homemade decorations, and a colorful banner hung above the stage, announcing the event. I could feel my heart racing, a mixture of anticipation and dread swirling within me.

"Ready to rock the stage?" Connor asked, his playful grin masking his own nerves.

"Only if you promise not to drop any props," I shot back, elbowing him playfully as we made our way backstage.

As we stood in the wings, waiting for our turn, I caught sight of the crowd. Friends, neighbors, and strangers filled the seats, their faces illuminated by the warm glow of the overhead lights. Anxiety clawed at me as I realized just how many eyes would be on us.

"Okay, deep breaths," Connor murmured, his hand finding mine. The warmth of his touch sent a wave of calm through me, grounding me in the moment. "No matter what happens, we've got this."

"Yeah, but if we flop, you're going to have to juggle all of our embarrassment," I teased, my heart still racing.

Just as I thought I'd found my rhythm, the emcee called our names, and the crowd erupted in applause as we stepped onto the stage. The spotlight hit us like a freight train, bright and blinding. For a moment, the world narrowed down to just the two of us standing there, the air thick with unspoken feelings and the weight of expectations.

With a deep breath, I launched into my routine, tapping my feet with determination, trying to drown out the self-doubt that threatened to creep in. Connor joined in, attempting his juggling, a comical mix of focus and frustration. The audience erupted into laughter, but it wasn't the laughter of mockery; it was genuine, infectious, and somehow that buoyed us.

In that moment, surrounded by the warmth of shared joy, I thought we might just be on the path to mending our crumbling foundations. Until, with a sudden flick of the wrist, Connor's juggling ball slipped from his hand, and in a slow-motion catastrophe, it flew straight into the audience, hitting a woman right in the face.

The gasp that rippled through the crowd turned my heart into lead, and before I could react, Connor's expression shifted from playful to horror. The moment hung suspended, an electric tension filling the air, as all eyes turned toward the unfortunate recipient of our unintentional comedy.

"Uh-oh," I murmured, feeling the heat rush to my cheeks, bracing myself for what was sure to follow.

Chapter 29: Breaking Point

The aroma of simmering garlic and rich tomato sauce filled the air, blending with the sweet scent of caramelized onions as the vibrant energy of the festival buzzed around me. Each stall was a universe of flavors, and I had crafted mine with meticulous care—a charming corner showcasing the culinary spirit of my childhood. Yet, beneath the festive façade, a tempest swirled within me, churning like the chaos of a summer storm on Lake Michigan.

"Where's the basil?" I shouted, the sound barely cutting through the thrumming music that wafted from the nearby stage. My assistant, Jenna, darted past me, her dark curls bouncing as she juggled multiple tasks. She was a whirlwind of energy, and yet, even she couldn't keep up with my mounting demands. "I need it now! The sauce is supposed to sing, not whimper!"

"Calm down, Amelia!" she shot back, her voice tinged with exasperation. "I'm getting it!"

In that moment, I could have sworn I saw the edges of my carefully constructed sanity fray like a worn-out dishcloth. My heart raced, thrumming a wild beat that matched the cacophony of laughter and chatter surrounding me. The festival was supposed to be my moment, my triumph, a culmination of late nights and relentless dedication. Instead, it felt like a performance on a stage set to collapse, the spotlight glaring down as I played my part, desperately trying to maintain composure.

As the sun dipped lower, casting an orange hue across the vibrant booths, I turned to Connor, who stood a few feet away, arms crossed and an unsettling calm in his eyes. His presence was always a balm to my anxiety, but today, it only added to my frustration. "You're just standing there! Help me with the setup!" I barked, my voice sharper than intended.

His brow furrowed, confusion flickering across his face before it settled into a mask of resignation. "I'm trying to, Amelia. But you're making it really hard to help when you keep snapping at everyone."

I felt the sting of his words, like a cold splash of water that brought me momentarily back to reality. This was not the first time I had lashed out, but it was the first time I had noticed the toll it was taking on him. The laughter around us faded into the background, replaced by the pulse of my heartbeat as I watched him take a step back, as if I had pushed him away with the force of my frustration.

"I'm sorry," I said, the words slipping out too late, drowned in the ocean of chaos swirling around us. The apology hung heavy in the air, weighed down by unspoken emotions and the bitter taste of regret. But Connor turned, his face a mask of hurt that cut deeper than I expected. He nodded, the gesture small yet monumental, and walked away, leaving me staring at his retreating figure, feeling like the villain in my own story.

The festival continued to pulse with life, but my world was crumbling, piece by piece, like an overcooked soufflé. I wanted to chase after him, to pull him back into my whirlwind of panic and promise, but my feet felt anchored to the ground, as if the earth beneath me had transformed into quicksand. I glanced around at the laughter and celebration, at the delicious creations being served, and all I could feel was the weight of my own failures pressing down on me.

Time blurred as I lost myself in the rhythm of the event, my hands moving almost mechanically to plate the dishes I had worked so hard to perfect. Each ingredient felt heavy, laden with expectations that gnawed at my insides. The crowd laughed, cheered, and clinked glasses, while I stood at the center, a silent witness to my own unraveling. It was a cruel irony—the very festival that was meant to showcase my culinary journey now felt like an indictment of my capabilities.

Jenna returned, basil in hand, but the moment was lost. "You're going to burn the sauce if you keep this up," she warned, her tone softer now, as if she understood the storm raging within me. I nodded, but it was like nodding at a tempest; the acknowledgment didn't quell the fury.

The evening wore on, and as twilight enveloped the festival, I could feel the energy shifting. People swarmed to my stall, eager to taste the creations I had dreamed of sharing. But each smile directed my way felt like a dagger; they didn't see the cracks in my façade, the insecurity that twisted my stomach into knots. I pushed through the interactions, serving plates with a practiced smile, but inside, I was screaming for someone to notice, to see the chaos beneath the surface.

Then it happened—a young couple approached, beaming, their enthusiasm infectious. "We've heard amazing things about your food! Can we try everything?" The man's voice was rich with excitement, his eyes sparkling with anticipation. I could feel my pulse quicken, a flicker of hope igniting amidst the turmoil.

"Of course! You won't be disappointed," I replied, my voice a shade more confident, as I ladled sauce over pasta, the familiar act bringing a momentary sense of control back into my hands. I could almost hear my mother's voice in my head, reminding me that cooking was meant to be an expression of love, a celebration of flavors. I wanted to wrap these strangers in warmth, to share not just food, but the essence of who I was.

But as the couple savored their first bites, their expressions shifting from delight to confusion, I felt that familiar dread creep back in. "This isn't... what we expected," the woman said, her voice hesitant. "It tastes... off."

And just like that, the flicker of hope extinguished, leaving behind a cold void that mirrored the emptiness in my chest.

The woman's words hung in the air like a rancid aroma, permeating the festive atmosphere and igniting a heat of embarrassment that rose to my cheeks. I forced a smile, but it felt like wearing a mask made of glass, ready to shatter at the slightest pressure. "Oh, really?" I said, attempting to sound casual while my heart raced. "Maybe it just needs a little... extra love."

Her partner raised an eyebrow, his fork hovering mid-air, his enthusiasm rapidly deflating like an overbaked soufflé. "Love is great and all, but we were hoping for something a bit more flavorful."

Each word hit me like a slap, echoing the familiar refrain of inadequacy I had fought so hard to silence. "Let me fix that for you," I blurted, scrambling to the pots simmering on the stove behind me, the sizzling sauce now feeling like molten lava threatening to consume my confidence.

With frantic precision, I adjusted the heat, throwing in fresh herbs and a generous splash of red wine. The aroma danced through the air, tantalizing my senses, but I couldn't help but feel like a magician performing a trick for a skeptical audience. As I stirred, the couple stood in awkward silence, the tension thickening like the sauce I was working with. I could practically feel the weight of their judgment, and all I wanted was to retreat into the comforting embrace of my kitchen, where I ruled as queen and the only expectations were the ones I set for myself.

"Here, try this," I said, my voice tinged with forced cheer as I presented a fresh plate, decorated with a flourish that I hoped conveyed more confidence than I felt. The couple exchanged glances before tentatively diving in. The first bites were drawn out, the seconds stretching into an eternity as I awaited their verdict with bated breath.

"What do you think?" I asked, my voice a whisper, both hopeful and trembling on the edge of despair.

The woman chewed thoughtfully, her brow furrowing as if she were deciphering some ancient text. "It's... better. Definitely better. But I think it still needs something—maybe a little salt?"

Salt. Of course, the most basic of seasonings, something I had overlooked in the chaos. My stomach twisted at the thought of my failure echoing in her innocent suggestion. "You're absolutely right!

One moment!" I rushed to grab the salt, trying to hide my burning humiliation behind a façade of professionalism.

As I sprinkled it onto the plate, I felt my heart heavy with every grain, each one representing a tiny sliver of my shattered confidence. The couple nibbled cautiously, and I noticed the slight shift in their expressions—a flicker of interest. "Now that's more like it!" The man grinned, his eyes sparkling with renewed excitement.

Before I could bask in that moment of triumph, however, the chaos around me surged again. A commotion broke out at the neighboring stall, where a chef was frantically waving his arms, trying to salvage a tower of soufflés that had decided to take a collective nosedive. Laughter erupted, the kind that comes from camaraderie rather than cruelty, and the sound sent a ripple of anxiety through me.

"Is this festival really going to be my moment or my downfall?" I muttered to myself, barely aware of how close I was to spiraling back into panic.

"Hey, you good?" Connor's voice pierced through my chaotic thoughts, and I looked up to see him standing just a few feet away, arms crossed, his expression a mix of concern and determination. The sight of him both comforted and unnerved me. It was like a familiar song played at the wrong tempo—intensely nostalgic yet painfully disruptive.

"Fine," I replied, a little too quickly, plastering on a smile that felt more like a grimace. "Just serving up my culinary masterpieces."

"Your masterpieces look great," he said, an eyebrow raised, but the sincerity in his voice caught me off guard. "You always have this way of making magic happen."

Magic? I scoffed inwardly, wishing I could believe him. Instead, I was just a juggler trying to keep too many flaming torches in the air while walking a tightrope strung over a pit of despair. "Thanks, but I think I might need a bit of help," I admitted, and my throat tightened as I acknowledged the truth lurking beneath my bravado.

"I'm here for you," he said, stepping closer. "I know you're stressed, but you can't do this alone."

His words, simple yet powerful, crashed into me like a wave. I wanted to drown in his support, yet my stubborn pride clawed at me. I opened my mouth, ready to let my defenses spill forth, but instead, I merely nodded. "Right. Let's get this food out, and we'll see what happens."

As the night wore on, the rhythm of the festival seemed to settle. People came and went, their laughter blending with the clinking of glasses and sizzling pans. But as the crowd thickened, so did my sense of dread, like a shadow lurking just outside the flickering light. I moved through the chaos with newfound purpose, but Connor remained close, his presence a steadying force.

"Good job!" Jenna called out from across the stall, and I glanced over just in time to see her balancing a tray piled high with colorful cupcakes. My heart swelled at her enthusiasm, but then I noticed the crowd surging closer, eager for a taste of what she had created.

"Hey, maybe I should set up a cupcake station next year!" I joked, trying to lighten the mood. "You know, the sweet to balance out my savory genius."

"Why not?" Jenna laughed, flipping her hair as if it were an integral part of her culinary skill set. "I could make you a master of desserts!"

"Maybe we should combine forces and become a culinary powerhouse," I teased, though a part of me wondered if that could ever happen.

But as the crowd continued to grow, excitement began to shift into something darker. Suddenly, I felt the pressure building once again, a sense of impending doom creeping in like the storm clouds that had earlier threatened to ruin our perfect day. I looked around, searching for something, anything, to ground me.

Then it happened. A loud crash resonated from the back of the festival, the sound of glass shattering, quickly followed by a chorus of startled gasps. My heart dropped as I spun toward the noise, fear coursing through my veins. People began to scatter, their laughter morphing into panicked whispers.

"Amelia!" Connor shouted, but my gaze was fixed on the chaos unfolding before me.

Panic surged like a tidal wave as I noticed a figure stumbling through the crowd, their clothes stained with red. My heart stopped, and everything else faded into a blur as I realized what was happening.

Milton Keynes UK
Ingram Content Group UK Ltd.
UKHW041822201024
449814UK00001B/65